OPEN
AND
SHUT

OPEN
AND
SHUT

DAVID
ROSENFELT

Published by Warner Books

An AOL Time Warner Company

Warner Books, Inc., 1271 Avenue of the Americas, New York, NY 10020

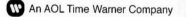 An AOL Time Warner Company

Printed in the United States of America

ISBN: 0-89296-748-X

To Debbie,
who makes everything possible,
and worthwhile,
and fun

And to Heidi, Ross, and Brandy,
who have given me the gift of pride

OPEN
AND
SHUT

• • • • •

THE LINCOLN TUNNEL IS A SCARY

place. Especially now, at the end of the workday. I'm one link in an endless chain of drivers, all moving our cars through an atmosphere of one hundred percent pure carbon monoxide. Tunnel workers patrol walkways along the walls; I assume they are there to make sure no car achieves a speed above three miles an hour. Their lungs must have a life expectancy of an hour and a half. Surrounding us all are thousands of tons of dirt and water, just waiting for a crack to come crashing through.

I usually avoid this tunnel. It is one of three main passageways between New York City and Northern Jersey, where I live. I prefer the George Washington Bridge, where oxygen is plentiful and it doesn't feel like I'm driving through an enormous MRI machine.

The fact is, I don't come into New York that often, and when I do it's rarely during the absurdly misnamed "rush" hour. But I needed to go to the NYU law library to do some research for an appellate case I'm handling, and I was stuck in court all day, so here I am.

I have two choices. I can ponder my impending death by suffocation under all this mud and water, knowing my loved ones will forever wonder whether my final resting place was in New York or New Jersey. Or I can think about the case, and what my strategy will be if the Court of Appeals turns us down. I go with the case, but it's a close call.

My client is death row inmate Willie Miller, a twenty-eight-year-old African-American convicted of murdering a young woman named Denise McGregor in the alley behind the Teaneck, New Jersey, bar where he worked. It's a case my father, Nelson Carpenter, prosecuted seven years ago, when he was the State District Attorney. Ironically, it's also my father's fault that I'm on the case now.

I think back almost two years to the day I was at home watching the Giants play the Redskins on television. It was a frigid, windy, December Sunday, the kind of day that passing would be difficult, so each team would try to run the ball down each other's throats. My father had come over to watch the game with me. He was never a big football fan, and my fanaticism about the Giants was clearly learned elsewhere. But he had been joining me to watch the games with increasing regularity since my mother died a year before. I don't think it's that he was liking football any more; I just think he was liking loneliness even less.

It must have been halftime that he brought it up, since if it were during the game I never would have heard him. "Do you remember the Willie Miller case?" he asked.

Of course I did. My father had sought and received the death penalty; this was not something I was likely to forget.

"Sure. What about it?"

He told me that some information had recently come to his attention. He wouldn't tell me how, or even what the specific information was, but he said that he had learned that a juror lied in voir dire, a significant lie that could result in a new trial if revealed to the court.

He was grappling with what to do with the information, since revealing the specifics would amount to breaking a privilege. Yet as an officer of the court he felt uncomfortable with concealing it, since Willie Miller was entitled to have the truth come out.

"How would you feel about representing him on an appeal?"

"Me?" I'm sure my mouth was stuffed with potato chips, so it probably came out "Mnnpphh?"

"Yes. You could have an investigator look into it, find out the facts without me having to tell you, and then go to the appeals court."

The case, as I remembered it, was open-and-shut. Willie Miller, even when seen through my skeptical defense attorney's eyes, was a murderer. I was not about to get involved in an appeal based on a technicality. What if it succeeded? I'd have to go through a trial I was bound to lose.

"No thanks."

"It would be important to me."

There it was, the sentence from which there was no defense. In my family, when you asked a favor of someone, it was acceptable to refuse. But once the person said that it was important to them, it crossed a line and became an absolute imperative. We did not use those words frivolously, and they carried an awesome weight.

"Then I'll do it."

"You've got no chance, you know."

I laughed. "Then why the hell is it so important to you that I enter the swamp?" That is how we referred to legal cases that dragged on forever with little or no chance of ultimate victory.

"Because the man is on death row."

The Giants kicked off to start the second half, the Redskins drove the length of the field for a touchdown, and I was on a case that might well leave me forever stuck in the Lincoln Tunnel.

But, no! Suddenly, without warning, a burst of speed by the cars ahead lets me gun the accelerator to almost five miles an hour. At this rate, there's a chance I might make it home in time to leave for court tomorrow morning.

THERE IS NOTHING LIKE A GOLDEN RE-

triever. I know, I know, it's a big planet with a lot of wonderful things, but golden retrievers are the absolute best. Mine is named Tara. She is seven years old and the most perfect companion anyone could ever have. She is also funny and playful and smart. The only problem she has ever caused is that I spend so much time with her in the mornings that I am almost invariably late for work.

This morning is a case in point. I take Tara for an hour walk, throw a ball with her in the park, then come home and feed her. I've got to be in court by nine-thirty, so I wind up taking an eight-second shower and mostly get dressed in the car on the way. I'd love to take her with me, and she often comes to my office, but the bailiffs take a dim view of canines in court. What they don't realize is that she's smarter than half the lawyers that practice there.

Having said my goodbyes and given her a biscuit, I stop at a newsstand on the way to court, even though I'm in grave danger of being late. The decision to stop is essentially an involuntary one; I have long ago certified stopping at this particular newsstand as a permanent superstition. I would rather face the wrath of a judge by being late than irritate the newsstand god.

The name of this particular superstition is Eastside News, so named I'm sure because it's just a few blocks from Paterson Eastside High School. Not only does it have every conceivable magazine in the entire world, but there is a sign proclaiming it to be "Paterson's Only Out-of-Town Newspaper Stand." I can easily understand why there is no competition for this honor; in all the years I have been stopping here, I've yet to see anyone buy a *Des Moines Register*.

The proprietor of Eastside News is Cal Morris, a forty-five-year-old African-American. After all this time I consider Cal a friend, though my knowledge of him consists of his occupation and the fact that he hates the Knicks and Rangers. I also once overheard him talking about his football exploits at Eastside High, though that would have been about ten years before I was there. In any event, we never talk about these things. Cal seems like a nice enough guy, but his role in my life is strictly to satisfy my superstitions.

As I said, I'm late, so I quickly initiate the rest of the ritual. Cal is ringing up another customer, but he sees me out of the corner of his eye.

"How they hangin' today, Cal?"

"Low, Andy, mighty low."

"Gotta hoist 'em up," is my practiced response.

"I try, but they keep gettin' lower."

We both laugh, though neither of us have thought this is funny for a few years. I buy a *Bergen Record,* which is what serves for the local paper now. I remember when there was a *Paterson Evening News* and a *Paterson Morning Call,* but both have long ago ceased to exist. The *Record* doesn't have the feel of a local paper, but it covers the national news pretty well. Besides, I'll be in court all day and won't have time to read it. I just feel silly stopping at the newsstand and not buying a paper.

The Passaic County Courthouse is a venerable old building, and to say it is the most impressive in downtown Paterson is to shower it with faint praise. My father once told me that the stature of the building and the courtrooms it contains can work against defendants, particularly those charged with relatively minor offenses. A juror looks at the majesty of the place and says, "This must be an important crime if it's tried here. Let's throw the book at the bastard." These days the person usually representing the bastard is me, Andy Carpenter, attorney at law.

Today my client is Carmen Hernández, a twenty-three-year-old Puerto Rican immigrant accused of breaking into a jewelry store. There wasn't exactly a pitched battle in the legal community to land Carmen as a client. I got the assignment because his mother is Sofía Hernández, who owns a fruit stand next door to my office. What I know about Sofía is that she works sixteen hours a day, has a smile on her face every morning, and gets summer fruit before anyone else. I also know she asked for my help, and money wasn't an issue because she doesn't have any. What I don't know is whether her son is a crook. But that's what we're here to determine.

This is the third and last day of the trial. The Assistant DA, Norman Trell, has done his usual competent job of presenting his competent case to this competent jury, and soon they will be sent in to competently deliberate and find Carmen guilty. The only thing standing in the way of all this competence is my summation.

I take a quick glance at the large door in the back of the room, though I know it won't be opening for three minutes. I then take another look at Carmen, wearing a suit as if it is the first time in his life he has ever worn one. It probably is; that suit was hanging in my closet until the trial started. Carmen is six foot four and I'm five foot eleven; he looks like he spent the last six hours in a dryer.

I stand and begin my summation, walking toward the jury, though I know I'm about to be interrupted. Their faces are bored, their eyes glazed, twelve poor slobs who couldn't get a doctor's excuse or a valid note from their boss to get them off jury duty. To these concerned citizens, the only positive aspect to this upcoming speech is that it is the last one they will have to hear.

"Ladies and gentlemen, you've had to listen to a lot of talking these past few days, and I'm smart enough to know not to chew your ears off much longer."

Two of the jurors smile, which shows how little humor they've been exposed to lately. The other ten think I'm bull-shitting them.

"There are only two things for me to talk about, and then I'll shut up. The first is circumstantial evidence. Carmen Hernández stands accused on this kind of evidence. No one saw him break into that store. No one saw him take any jew-els. No one saw him leave the store. Instead we have guess-work, and seem-to-be's, and probably's. The prosecutor, Mr. Trell, says, 'Gee, with these circumstances, it sure seems to me that Mr. Hernández did it.'"

I look over at Trell, but he does not return the stare. He neither likes nor trusts defense lawyers, and as far as he's con-cerned, I'm the worst of the lot. I extend the stare, mainly be-cause it will be fifteen seconds until the door opens.

"Well, ladies and gentlemen, that's not good enough." An-other pause for dramatic effect, as I wait impatiently. Open, door.

And open it does. Laurie Collins enters from the back. I turn, but then again so does everyone else. When Laurie Collins enters a room, you turn to see her. It's as simple as that. She is a beautiful, sexy woman, and I would say this even if I weren't sleeping with her. I would say it even if she weren't able to kick the shit out of me.

Laurie, as instructed, is dressed in a conservative pants suit. She is five foot ten, with blond hair and a perfectly propor-tioned body. That figure comes across despite the otherwise nonrevealing attire, but then again Laurie's body would look great if she were wearing a Winnebago.

Laurie seems excited about something, and she makes a motion to get my attention, a singularly unnecessary act. I nod and turn to Judge Kasten.

"Your Honor, if I could have a moment."

Moments aren't something Judge Kasten is inclined to dis-pense, and he stares at me with an intensity designed to make me withdraw the request. When I don't do so, he finally says, "What is the problem, Mr. Carpenter?"

"I'm not really sure, Your Honor, but Ms. Collins certainly would not be interrupting were this not important."

If there is such a thing as a stern sigh, Kasten pulls it off. "Make it brief."

I walk over to Laurie, whose facial expression still shows excitement. Her words do not, though she speaks softly enough that I'm the only one able to hear them.

"Hi, Andy," she says. "What's new in the legal world?"

Now, you may not think this is big news, but I look stunned, as if she had dropped a bombshell.

"Not a hell of a lot," I say. "Still hot out there?"

She nods enthusiastically. "Yeah, close to eighty, although they're predicting a thunderstorm. By the way, you do realize your father is going to be upset by this, don't you?"

My father is not only the retired State District Attorney, he is also a legend in the legal profession. As the next few minutes are about to demonstrate, the legend gene obviously skipped a generation.

"You think I'm afraid of my father?" I ask her, incredulous at the possibility.

"Petrified," she says.

"Then I'll tell him this was your idea."

I make a triumphant fist and look skyward, as if thanking God for this good fortune. I may be laying it on a little thick, but these aren't the brightest jurors in the world.

Barely able to contain my excitement, I turn and walk to Carmen at the defense table. Since he can only speak about four words of English, I don't bother making sense when I whisper in his ear.

"All the while I'd be thinkin', I could be another Lincoln, if I only had a brain."

I break out in a big grin and hug him. He figures something good must have happened, so he breaks out in just as big a grin and hugs me back. We are one happy lawyer-client team. Among the people who aren't quite as happy is Judge Kasten.

"Perhaps you would like to enlighten us as to what is going on, Mr. Carpenter?"

Smile painted on my face, I turn and walk toward the bench. "Sorry, Your Honor, but I thought my client should be the first to hear the good news."

"And just what good news is that?" he asks.

"Well, I'm not sure why we had to learn about it this way . . ." I take the smile off long enough to stare a silent reprimand at Prosecutor Trell. ". . . but I've just heard a report that another man has confessed to the crime my client is being tried for. The media has the story. He is under arrest and is being held at this very moment."

There is an uproar in the courtroom, or at least as much uproar as this scraggly group can manage. My eyes are on the jury, now fully awake and talking excitedly among themselves. "Can this be true?" they're thinking. "Does this mean we can go home?"

Carmen shakes hands and hugs everyone in sight; for a moment I think he's going to accidentally strangle the bailiff. My eyes are on the prosecution table, where one of Trell's assistants gets up and rushes out of the room, already drawing his cell phone out of his pocket as he goes. I watch him until I turn to the sound of an increasingly annoying noise. It's Kasten's gavel, and he's pounding it as hard as he can.

Eventually, order is restored, if for no other reason than to quiet that stupid gavel. Kasten turns to Trell, who is still looking befuddled.

"Mr. Trell, what is your information on this?"

Trell doesn't know what attitude to take, since he doesn't know if it's true. He plays it down the middle. "I'm having it checked right now, Your Honor." He turns toward the doors in the back of the court as if to show Kasten where the answer will come from.

On cue, the assistant opens those doors and comes back in the room, holstering his cell phone as he does. He quickly goes to Trell and whispers in his ear. The jig, I am aware, is about to be up.

Trell nods vigorously, then turns back to Kasten. I think he so relishes what he's about to say that he's actually salivating. He uses his deepest voice. "Your Honor, I am told there is no truth whatsoever to this report." Roosevelt spoke with less drama when he announced the attack on Pearl Harbor.

No sooner does Trell finish speaking than Kasten's head, as well as every other head in the courtroom, swivels toward me.

I shrug, as if I'm an innocent bystander. "I'm as surprised as you, Judge. The media in this town is getting out of hand."

He, of course, is not buying it. "This is bizarre behavior even by your standards."

Obviously he doesn't know my standards, but now is not the time to educate him. I shrug so hard my shoulders hurt. "Your Honor, surely you don't think—"

He interrupts me, which is just as well, since I wasn't quite sure how to finish the sentence. "Finish your summation, and then I'll want to see both counsel in chambers. The jury will disregard this entire incident."

I walk toward the jury, shaking my head in amazement at this turn of events. Let's see if they disregard this . . .

"The second thing I wanted to talk to you about is reasonable doubt. If any of you believed, even for a few moments, that someone else had confessed to the crime my client stands charged with, then you must have a reasonable doubt as to his guilt."

A cannon goes off in Trell's chair, sending him soaring to his feet. "Objection! Objection!"

He yells so loud that I have to yell over him to the jury, while I'm pointing to Carmen. "You cannot be absolutely positive about this man's guilt and at the same time be ready to believe that someone else did it!"

"Objection! Objection!" That Trell is quite a conversationalist. Meanwhile, Jean Valjean never pounded rocks as hard as Kasten is pounding the gavel.

"Bailiff, remove the jury."

As I watch the jury file out, I know that Kasten is going to come down on me, even contempt is a possibility. I also know that I'm my father's son, and Kasten has too much respect and friendship for Nelson Carpenter to destroy his first and only born.

Besides, Carmen Hernández is going to be a free man within the hour, which makes this a very good day.

• • • • •

MY CHILDHOOD IS FILLED WITH GREAT MEMO-

ries, in fact, great ones are the only memories I have. I talked
to a shrink about it, and we pretty much agreed that unpleasant things must have happened when I was growing up, but
that I had just repressed them. I asked him how long I could
go on repressing them, and he said maybe forever. That
worked for me, so I left therapy before I could blow it and get
in touch with my true feelings.

That was eight years ago. So far, so good.

But if one memory stands out over all others, it's my father
and I going to Yankees games. We lived in Paterson, which is
where I still have my office. The drive from our house to Yankee Stadium was eight miles on Route 4 to the George Washington Bridge, then the Cross Bronx to the Major Deegan to the
stadium. Without traffic it's about twenty-five minutes, which
means that in real life it takes about an hour and a half. But I
never minded, because I knew at the end I was going to walk
through the tunnel and out to our seats, and I would see the
most beautiful sight in the world. The Yankee Stadium infield.

The green of that infield was and is unlike any color ever
produced anywhere else. You could buy a box of half a million Crayolas and never begin to match that color. Set against
it is the understated tan of the dirt part of the infield, which

becomes a deep, powerful brown when watered by the groundskeepers. Their job, the job of maintaining the Yankees' home field, is a heavy but rewarding burden that they shoulder flawlessly.

Today I'm going to get to see that infield, as my father and I have tickets to the game. As always, I pick him up at his house and head for the stadium. The drive there is just as glorious, just as filled with anticipation, as it was in my youth. The only difference is that I'm the one behind the wheel, which can't be right, since when we go to the games I'm eight years old again.

But we'll get there, we'll park in our special place, which gets us out after the game faster than anyone else, my father will become my "Dad," and everything will be right with the world.

Today the Yankees are playing the Red Sox. I used to hate the Red Sox, just like I hated the Orioles, and the Indians, and the White Sox, and anybody else not in pinstripes. But I don't hate anymore, I'm too arrogant for that. To hate is to grant a level of importance that those teams don't deserve. We dismiss our opponents, we don't hate them. They are not worthy of that.

Our seats are field level boxes, third row behind third base. If there is a more perfect six feet of real estate, I have no idea where it is. I am sucking on a snow cone and wondering why food sold at the seats by vendors tastes better than the same items bought anywhere else, when my father nudges me and points to the scoreboard. He doesn't have to say a word; it's the fourth inning, time to start betting.

I don't know when this started, but I think it was in my early teens. My father and I bet on everything in the fourth inning. We keep track of the bets; at one point, I think I owed him a million dollars. It was a big burden for a high school sophomore, but I won it back and then some. Today he owes me forty-one thousand, three hundred and fifty-five dollars. I'm on a roll.

Trot Nixon steps up to the plate to face Roger Clemens. It's my father's turn to choose the bets because he's behind. His mind calculates the infinite possibilities as if he is planning a legal argument.

"I'll bet you five hundred dollars the first pitch is a strike," he says with confidence.

"You're on," I say unnecessarily, since every bet is on. Clemens throws a slider a foot outside. Good start for me, but I don't get cocky. The fourth can be a very long inning.

"Six hundred says he gets a base hit. You give me three to one."

I just nod this time, he knows he's on. Nixon pops up to center, Williams calls off Knoblauch and handles it easily. I make a fist in triumph. "Yesssss."

While we're waiting for Garciaparra to come up, my father says, "I was hoping Nicole would join us."

Not now, Dad. You're supposed to leave the real world out in the parking lot.

"Nicole and I are separated, Dad. You sometimes seem to forget that." He also forgets that I go back to being eight years old when I'm here. How could I have an estranged wife?

"An old man can't hope?"

"An old man should concentrate on the game, because I'm cleaning the old man's clock." I'm trying to refocus him, but I'm having a tough time.

He looks at his program, so I think maybe he's getting back to baseball. Unfortunately, he isn't.

"Judge Kasten told me about your stunt in the courtroom."

Uh, oh. I'm caught, but not backing down. "You mean the stunt that got my client acquitted?"

"I mean the one that could have gotten you disbarred."

"It was worth the risk," I parry.

"In the future, you might want to substitute solid preparation for risk taking," he thrusts. "By the way, how are you doing on the Miller appeal?"

"The ruling could come down anytime," I say. "I'm hopeful." Dad is worried about something as trivial as a death sentence in the fourth inning?

"You need to understand that even on a retrial, it's a case you can't win," he says. "I covered all the bases."

"Speaking of bases, Garciaparra is up." This seems to work, and our legal careers are moved to the back seat. More fake money is about to be put on the table.

"Garciaparra will foul off the first pitch. Eight hundred bucks. Nine to two." He seems pretty confident, so I just as confidently tell him that he's on.

Clemens winds up and Garciaparra lines one down the right field line. I'm on my feet. It's curving . . . it's curving . . . fair!

"Fair ball! Fair ball! Fair ball!" I scream. I hate cheering for something against the Yankees, and everybody around us is staring at me with disdain, but my competitive juices are flowing. I turn to my father in triumph, and he has bowed his head appropriately in defeat.

"Can't even watch?" I crow. But it's more than that. In a brief, terrible instant, I realize that in fact he can't watch, can't speak, can't even sit up. He falls over and his head hits the railing in front of us, and then he slumps to the ground, his body grotesquely wedged between the seats.

And then I start screaming, screaming louder than anyone has ever screamed in Yankee Stadium. Screaming louder than anyone has ever screamed in any stadium.

But my dad can't hear me, and I'll never be eight years old again.

• • • • •

THE CROWD AT THE FUNERAL SEEMS LARGER THAN the crowd at the stadium, except everyone here finds themselves compelled to talk to me, to convince me they knew my father, and to let me know how sorry they are. It's supposed to make me feel better. It doesn't come close.

The cemetery itself covers miles and miles of gently rolling hills, which would be beautiful and uplifting if they were not dotted by endless rows of headstones. Can there really be this many people buried here? Have their loved ones all felt the same kind of pain I am feeling?

I tell someone I want to deliver the eulogy, but I dread the prospect of it. Laurie tells me I don't have to, that no one will think less of me if I don't. She's right, but I go up there anyway. I look out at the crowd. It seems as if the only people in America not at this funeral must be the ones lying under all those headstones.

"All of you knew Nelson Carpenter in your own way," I begin. "Like everyone, he had his labels, and he wore them proudly and well. To many he was the District Attorney, a brilliant man whose devotion to justice was complete, and who would go to any lengths to ensure that everybody received fair and impartial treatment under the law.

"To many of you he was simply a friend, and when you

had Nelson Carpenter as your friend, you didn't need many others. Because he wasn't simply there if you asked for his help; he had a sixth sense that could see through you, and a generosity that would provide that help without you ever having to ask.

"But I knew Nelson Carpenter as a father, and that makes me luckier than any of you. Because his family was his world, and let me tell you something, there was no better world to live in."

My throat feels like it is in a vise the entire time, but I don't cry, just like I didn't cry at my mother's funeral three years ago. But I remember having my father to share the pain with then, and I could focus on supporting him. Now it's just me.

Only child becomes even more only.

Afterward I'm walking toward the cars, nodding thank you to the remaining four or five million people who are just now approaching me. Philip Gant, U.S. Senator Philip Gant, soon to be ex–father-in-law Philip Gant, walks toward me.

Philip was my father's oldest friend, and though that friendship always struck me as rather unlikely, it was remarkably strong and enduring. Their relationship is what originally brought their offspring together. Philip was upset when Nicole left me; I always thought that she must have had a harder time breaking the news to him than to me.

Philip dominates every room he is ever in, even rooms with no walls, thousands of people, and rolling hills dotted with headstones. As he comes toward me, everyone else seems to melt away. He taps me on the shoulder with authority. Philip does everything with authority.

"Magnificent eulogy, Andrew. I knew Nelson longer than anyone here, and let me tell you, every word you said was true."

It is typical of Philip that even when he is trying to be nice, he secures the upper hand, this time by assuming I need his confirmation that I really knew my father.

This time he's gone too far. "Thank you, Philip. I appreciate that," I lash back.

"I spoke to Nicole," he says. "She was very upset."

I nod, since I know this must be true; Nicole was quite fond of her father-in-law. I am actually surprised that she wasn't here.

"Terrible," he says, shaking his head. "Just terrible. You just let me know if there's anything I can do."

I nod again, Philip heads off to a limousine the size of North Dakota, and his chauffeur holds the door open for him as he enters. I turn and see Laurie, who has been great throughout this. She takes my arm and squeezes it gently.

"You okay?" she asks.

"I'm okay," I lie.

I don't feel like going home, so we go to a sports bar named Charlie's. It is my favorite restaurant in the entire world; in fact, it is the best restaurant in the entire world. In fact, every single item on the menu is better than every item on any other menu at any other restaurant in the entire world. Some people think I overrate Charlie's. I think those people are stupid.

Anyway, Charlie's feels more like home than home, so this is where I want to be. We go to our favorite booth in the corner, the one next to the video trivia game. We order burgers and beer and I start planning my life as an orphan.

The first thing I'm going to have to do is go back to my father's house. I'll need to go through his papers and his personal possessions, and make sure that everything is in order. That's not going to be easy. Laurie promises to help, but I feel like I want to do everything by myself, like it's some rite of passage I have to go through.

Within a short time we're laughing and joking, punctuated every few minutes by my feeling guilty that I'm laughing and joking. But we're enjoying each other's company, and it feels good.

Laurie and I have only been sleeping together for two weeks, a total of four times. Each time has been better than the time before it, and the first time wasn't too shabby. She has blue eyes which she claims are green, and when you stare into them you feel like you're on a gorgeous beach on a gorgeous day drinking a gorgeous drink with an umbrella in it.

She's also the best investigator I've ever known, smart,

tough, and relentless, at least when she doesn't let her integrity get in the way. She's an ex-cop and I'm a lawyer, which probably explains why I think all my clients are innocent, and she thinks they're guilty. It's the difference between law school and the police academy. We bridge this gap by agreeing that the clients are all entitled to the best defense possible.

I hesitated a long while before letting things turn sexual, to say nothing of emotional, with Laurie. I've been married to Nicole since I was twenty-three, and I wasn't exactly a sexual dynamo before that, so even when I got separated I felt like I was cheating by being with another woman.

I also was leery of mixing business with pleasure, cognizant as I was of the difficulties that can result. But the main reason I hesitated to sleep with Laurie is because whenever I brought it up she said no. Two weeks ago she changed her mind, which coincidentally was the exact moment I stopped hesitating.

But tonight Laurie is not my lover, nor is she my investigator. She is my friend, and the time with her at Charlie's is comforting. She drives me home, pulling up in front of my house at around nine. I live in Franklin Lakes, an upscale suburban community about a half-hour northeast of New York City. Each house, including mine, has manicured lawns and perfectly maintained flowers, none of which are maintained by those of us who live here. I've never checked, but Franklin Lakes must have the highest number of gardeners per capita in the United States.

What it doesn't have is the feel of a neighborhood, at least not the ones I remember. I am on a waving relationship with my neighbors; it is the suburban equivalent of a nodding, elevator relationship for those who live in high-rise apartments.

"You want to come in?" I ask.

"I don't think I should. I think you might need some time alone."

I don't argue, because we both know she's right; her staying over tonight wouldn't feel right for either of us.

It's just as well that Laurie doesn't come in, because when

I go into the house Nicole is sitting on the leather sofa in the den, petting Tara and waiting for me.

"Hello, Andy."

"Nicole . . ." is the cleverest retort I can come up with.

"I heard about Nelson . . . I was in Seattle visiting my grandmother . . . I got here as fast as I could . . . oh, Andy . . ."

She comes over and hugs me, though it makes me feel awkward. I wonder if she feels the same, but there's no sign of it. Actually, I don't think "awkward" is something Nicole ever allows herself to feel. Feeling awkward would just make her feel awkward, so she simply avoids it.

"He was really crazy about you," I say, driven by a sudden need to make her feel better.

"And I felt the same way about him. Are you okay?"

"I'm hanging in. I'm not sure it's totally hit me yet."

She still has her arms around me, it's one of the longest hugs I've ever experienced. And there's no sign of it ending anytime soon.

"Andy, I've been thinking . . . even before this . . . I don't want to just give up on us."

I'm at a loss for words, not an everyday occurrence for me, which goes on for quite a while. The uncomfortable silence is enough to get her to break the hug.

"It's your turn to say something," she says, though I already knew that.

I give it my best shot. "Nicole, we've been separated for six months. In that time I have not become a big-time corporate attorney, nor have I decided to run for Congress."

"Andy . . ."

"And I still represent people who think Beef Wellington is a wrestler. In short, I'm not what you seem to want anymore."

"So maybe I can try and change. It's worth a try, isn't it?"

I'm not sure and I tell her so. She takes that as a qualified yes.

"So I was thinking we could start dating . . . have dinner or something?"

"You want to start dating?" I ask. "What's the matter, you

can't find anybody to take you to the prom?" This is meant to sound tough; it comes off as cutesy.

"Andy, let's start over." She renews the hug again, this time with certain body parts rubbing against certain other body parts.

"Am I going to have to get you a corsage?" I have now openly switched to cutesy. Even Tara looks disgusted.

Nobody's ever accused me of being a tower of strength, least of all Nicole. I think we're going to try. This would have been a good day for my father.

• • • • •

THE HOUSE OF MY FIRST EIGHTEEN YEARS WAS ON 42nd Street in Paterson, New Jersey. This is of considerable significance because of the manner in which Paterson has developed. There is a downtown area, economically poor and overwhelmingly African-American. Then there are the numbered streets, 1 through 42, ending at the Passaic River. The river is where 43rd Street would be.

The higher the street number, the more expensive and desirable the houses. For years, almost all of the people living in the streets above 20 were white. Gradually, though, African-Americans started moving "upward" to the mid-20s, then the early 30s, and on toward the heavenly 40s. The whites would then move further up, fearful that the mixing of the neighborhood was driving their home values down.

Looking at the big picture, it was as if the whites were being driven to the sea, in this case the river, and that it eventually would part and allow them to flee to the suburbs. This they did, in droves, and Paterson is now overwhelmingly African-American. The houses look exactly the same, but the people look different.

It is a source of great pride to me that my parents never followed the masses across the river, but a source of some shame that I did. But I love that house, and that neighborhood, and I love my parents even more for not abandoning it.

I drive to the house, with Tara sitting in the front seat and looking out the window at the neighborhood, checking it out as if she is thinking of buying property here. We arrive at the house, now empty of family, and I take a deep breath as we walk toward it. We walk up the steps where I covered myself in glory playing stoopball. We step up onto the porch from which I used to watch summer thunderstorms, mesmerized as the water hit the ground so hard that it bounced six inches back in the air.

And then we enter the house. You could blindfold me and I could describe every square inch of the house, tell you every piece of furniture that has ever been in it, yet I could barely remember what any house I've lived in since looks like.

Once inside, the pain begins inside my stomach and keeps boring inward. By the time I'm in the den it has reached previously unexplored depths, but I resolve not to give in to it. My resolve lasts for about eight seconds, and I start sobbing. Tara nuzzles next to me, letting me know that she loves me and is there for me. I wonder if she can comprehend how much that helps; I believe she can. The power of a dog's love is astonishing.

I compose myself and get started. My father kept everything in four file cabinets in his office, and for the next three hours I go through papers and documents. Everything seems characteristically straightforward and organized; my father would never have had it any other way. My unspoken (even to myself) dread that I would find something troubling (an old love letter to a mistress?) soon gives way to semiboredom as I plow through the material.

I seem to remember that there are a lot of things in the attic, so I take a stepladder and go up there. It's dusty; this area obviously was not a frequent place of visitation. There are boxes of old papers, books, photographs, and memorabilia, and despite myself I get lost in them. I realize with a flash of guilt that I have not similarly chronicled my own life, then I realize with a flash of sadness that there will not be anyone to notice.

Many of the items I see trigger old memories, though some

are literally before my time. There is a yellowed newspaper clipping from the day that my then thirteen-year-old father slipped through an ice crack in a local pond, along with a picture of Philip, dripping wet after heroically pulling him out. It is an incident my father related to me perhaps half a dozen times; he truly credited Philip with saving his life. Surprisingly, I never heard Philip mention it, though it would certainly have added luster to his political résumé.

I pick up a photograph of my parents at the beach. What strikes me about it is how comfortable they look together; I can never remember a time when it was any other way. Looking at their youthfulness, it seems amazing that they are gone, or even that they ever existed in this form.

The photograph is in a frame, and as I go to put it back, I see there is something behind it, as if hidden. I pry open the frame and pull out another picture, which is of four men, arm in arm, smiling and laughing as they pose for the camera. All of the men seem to be in their early twenties, and my father is one of them. There are two 1960s model cars in the driveway behind them, one sideways to the camera and one facing it.

The black and white shot was taken at night, and the young men seem jovial, perhaps intoxicated. In the background are trees and a large, manicured lawn, but I don't recognize the location.

I go to put down the photo, then do a double take and pick it back up. One of the men looks like a young Victor Markham, a very wealthy, very influential local industrialist. I've never met Markham, but his son's girlfriend was the young woman that my client, Willie Miller, was convicted of murdering years ago. Even though my father prosecuted the case originally, I until now was not aware that he knew Victor Markham as a younger man. It is a strange thing for him not to have mentioned.

It is the Miller case that finally draws me away from the house. I put the picture in my pocket and leave. I have to go out to the prison this afternoon and see my client, to keep him up-to-date about what is going on. He's the one who very well might receive the lethal injection, so I think he has a right to know.

After driving Tara home, I head out to the prison, which is about twenty-five minutes from Paterson, near Newark Airport. It seems a sadistic placement, as the prisoners must constantly listen to those living in freedom literally soaring off into the sky. It must make their cagelike existence seem that much more confining. On the other hand, they never have to eat airline food.

Visiting death row is something I don't think I'll ever get used to, and I don't recommend it at all. The first thing I notice about it, the first thing I always notice about it, is that it is so clean. It's ironic. The people housed here are deemed the filth of society, not even worthy of life, yet their "house" is kept clean with a zeal unmatched this side of Disneyland.

The place seems entirely gray, as if I am looking at it through black and white eyes. The stench of hopelessness is everywhere; it feels like the animal shelter in which I found Tara. Everybody in cages, just waiting until it's time to die, knowing no one is coming to set them free.

I go through the process of checking in and wait until the guard, Danny, comes to bring me to the cell block. Danny and I are by now familiar with each other, and I am struck by his ability to maintain a sense of humor in these surroundings. He's not Jerry Seinfeld, but he's okay.

We walk down a corridor flanked by cells on both sides, just like you see in the movies, and the prisoners call out taunting comments about the legal profession in general and myself in particular. None of it is flattering, some is positively brutal.

Danny is amused by it. "They're getting to know you pretty well."

I just nod and walk faster; I'm not in the mood for banter.

I'm finally brought to Willie Miller's cell, the small iron box where he has spent the last seven years. He is heavily muscled and keeps himself in outstanding shape by working out. I don't have the discipline to exercise even though I know it will help me lead a longer, healthier life. Willie's about to be put to death and he never misses a day.

Willie never acknowledges my arrival until I'm inside the cell, and this time is no exception. I'm waiting for Danny to open the door, but instead he pulls over a metal chair and positions it outside the cell.

I'm puzzled, so I give him my puzzled look. He explains, "No direct contact with visitors during the last two months." He's referring to the time left in Willie's life, and on Willie's behalf I'm thoroughly irritated.

"I've been frisked and put through a metal detector. You afraid I'm going to slip him my teeth so he can bite through the bars?"

"Rules are rules, Andy."

I can tell that he feels bad, and I feel bad for making him feel bad. But I keep going, 'cause Willie feels worst of all.

"Are you sure? Rules are rules?"

"That's right."

"Have you got a pen? Because I want to write that down. 'Rules are rules,' " I repeat. "What a great line. Is it okay if I use it at cocktail parties?"

He's not in the mood for my bullshit. "Call out if you need me," he says, and then walks away.

I turn to Willie, who is on his cot all the way across the length of his home, which means he's eight feet away from me. "How are you doing today, Willie?" It is an innocent question, but it presses a button.

He stands up and walks toward me, challenging. For a brief second, I'm glad Danny didn't let me in the cell.

"What the hell is the difference? You think next year anybody is going to say, 'Boy, I wonder how Willie felt fifty-seven days before they killed his ass?' "

"What is it about death row that makes people so damned cranky?"

Willie looks at me for a moment, then starts to laugh. The weird thing is I knew he would. I know and like Willie, plus I think he's as innocent as the rest of my clients.

"Man, you're a lunatic, you know that? Of course, if I had me a lawyer, instead of a lunatic, I wouldn't be here."

This has become a familiar refrain, and I respond in kind.

"Need I remind you that I was not your lawyer when you were sent here? I have merely been handling your appeal. A small but significant point."

Willie looks around at the cell. "You don't seem to be appealing too well," is his logical reply.

"That's because the Supreme Court has become a major pain in the ass in this area."

"More white bullshit," he says.

"Did you ever hear of Clarence Thomas?" I counter.

"No, who's he play for?"

I laugh so loudly that it rattles through the corridors. Willie knows damn well who Clarence Thomas is, he's been reading up on everything about his case, including who might someday be ruling on it.

As if satisfied that he got me laughing, he gets right to the point. It's a point we've gone over before.

"We gonna get the new trial?"

"The Court of Appeals ruling should come down at any time."

"We gonna win?"

"I think so," I say. "But even if we get it, we're still in deep shit."

"I'll just lose again?" he asks.

I pretend to be puzzled. "Lose? Did somebody say 'lose'? I know I've heard that word, I'm just not familiar with it."

"Make sure it stays that way."

The specifics of Willie's case really haven't come up between us, since all I've had to concern myself with is the technical aspect of the appeal. We're pursuing a number of arguments, but our best one is the fact that one of the jurors on Willie's case openly lied in concealing the fact that her brother was a cop. More significantly, that brother had been killed in the line of duty six months earlier. That does not tend to make one friendly to the accused.

But if we get a new trial, we're going to have to move quickly. I decide to put my toe in the water, mainly because there's not much else to talk about. "You know, you're going to have to help me more than you helped your last lawyer."

His antennae are up. "What the hell does that mean? I got nothing more to tell you than I told him."

"That's because I haven't started my subtle, probing questioning yet."

"Why don't you just ask your father? He was damn sure he knew everything that happened that night."

It is not exactly unprecedented for a death row inmate to hold a grudge against the prosecutor that put him there, and Willie has been open about his hatred for my father. Because of those feelings, it took longer than usual for Willie and me to establish a mutual trust.

He obviously has not heard about recent events, and I see no reason to conceal them. "My father died last week."

Willie's face reflects his feelings, or lack of feelings, at hearing this news. No guilt, no triumph, no nothing. "I'm sorry for you, man," is what he says.

I nod my thanks. "Are you ready?"

"Ready."

"Okay," I say. "Let's start with an easy one. Did you kill her?"

I almost never ask this question, since if the client says yes, I am then prohibited from allowing him to say no at trial. It's called suborning perjury. The reason I ask is because I know what his answer is going to be. That doesn't make it any easier to hear.

"I don't have the slightest fucking idea."

It goes downhill from there. Willie was totally drunk that night, with no memory of anything that happened. But he had never committed a violent act in his life, except for a few street fights. He wouldn't, couldn't, murder a woman.

We don't get very far, which right now is not a big problem, since we don't even know if we'll ever get another trial. The only fact that the conversation reaffirms in my mind is that Willie is never going to testify in any trial in which I am his lawyer. The "I was too drunk to remember if I did it" defense isn't generally a winner.

After twenty more minutes of getting nowhere, I head home, where I find Nicole preparing dinner. This is in itself a rare event; Nicole can make three types of food, the best of which is a tuna fish sandwich. But here she is making spaghetti, which means she's trying to "change," which means I'm going to get stuck eating some really terrible spaghetti.

Outside the kitchen, things seem to be going reasonably well between us. We're both aware that we're testing the waters, which doesn't make for spontaneity, but I agree with her assessment that we're making progress. We haven't had sex yet, which shows how limited that progress has been, but I think we might be getting there.

If we had no history together, I'm not sure that we would fall madly in love. But we do have a history, and I'm just not ready to abandon it. I haven't mentioned this to Laurie yet, and I tell myself it's because I haven't seen her. I also tell myself that I don't owe her anything, that we have no commitment to each other, but I can't quite get myself to stop feeling like a shithead.

• • • • •

THE NEXT MORNING I HAVE TO STOP AT

Roger Sandberg's office. Roger is known as "the attorney's attorney," and for years he has personally represented many of the top lawyers in the area. He and my father had been close friends for twenty years, and my father trusted Roger with his life. Since he doesn't have his life anymore, here I am.

The purpose of this visit is to go over matters of the estate and learn the terms of my father's will. I arrive ten minutes early and start reading one of the ancient magazines from the rack in the waiting room. For some reason, every doctor's, dentist's, or lawyer's office I am ever in only has magazines more than four months old. Where do the magazines go when they first arrive? Is there a publication purgatory that they are required to inhabit until their information is no longer timely?

I pick up the current one in the office, a six-month-old *Forbes*. It predicts that the stock market will go up, a prediction which has turned out to be wrong. I'm glad I didn't read it six months ago.

The door to Roger's office opens and he comes out to greet me. Roger is a very distinguished-looking man, with a kind smile and smooth manner. He is the definition of "unruffled," a neat trick to have pulled off since he's been married five times. I've had only one troubled marriage, and I am thoroughly ruffled.

"Sorry to keep you waiting, Andy."

Roger shakes my hand and then hugs me, just like he hugged me at the funeral. I'm not a big hug fan, but I hug him back.

"No problem."

We exchange pleasantries about his wife and children, all of whom I vaguely know, and he inquires about my practice. I talk briefly about it, at which point his eyes start to glaze over. Criminal law is not Roger's thing.

We go into his office and he suggests that I sit on the couch. He goes to his desk and starts to gather the paperwork he is going to show me. He handles legal papers like a Las Vegas dealer handles cards . . . smooth, with no wasted motion.

"Roger, before we start, there's something I want to ask you. Did my father ever mention knowing Victor Markham?"

He seems surprised by the question. "Of course, don't you remember? He prosecuted that murder a few years ago . . . when the young woman was murdered in that bar. I believe the victim was Markham's son's girlfriend."

"I know. I'm handling the appeal."

"Really? Did your father know that?"

I nod. "Definitely. He encouraged it."

"Anyway, as far as I know, that's how Nelson knew Victor Markham," he says.

"I was talking about much earlier. Almost forty years ago. I'm pretty sure he was one of the people in a picture I found up in the attic. Dad was in the picture as well."

"He never mentioned it to me. But there was apparently a great deal about your father that I didn't know."

Roger has just lit a fuse; and all I can do is wait for it to reach the dynamite and explode. He doesn't make a comment like that unless he has something significant to tell me. I get a strong feeling that I'm not going to like it. I know for sure that I'm dreading it, so I take a breath so deep it sucks most of the air out of the room.

"What do you mean by that?"

He looks me right in the eye. "I was very surprised by the amount of money in your father's estate. Very surprised."

It's exhaling time; I'm relieved to hear that it's about money. I'm comfortable enough, and I really have no need to live off an inheritance. But I'm still surprised.

"Really? Dad was always so careful with his money."

He nods. "That he was."

"How much is left, Roger?"

He takes a deep breath and presses the detonator. "Twenty-two million dollars."

"Twenty-two million dollars!" I choke.

"And change." He reads from the papers. "Four hundred thirty-two thousand five hundred and seventy-four dollars' worth of change."

My mind immediately registers three possibilities, listed in order of likelihood. One, Roger made an error. Two, Roger is joking. Three, I'm rich! I'm rich! I'm rich!

I find myself standing up, though I'm not sure why. "Can't be, Roger. It's an appealing thought, but it's simply not possible."

"You had no idea he had this kind of money?"

"He didn't," I say firmly. "I knew he made some good investments over the years, but not like this. He would have told me. He would have raised my allowance."

"I don't know what to say, Andy. But it's all real."

My legs seem to give out from under me, and I sag back down on the couch. Roger brings the books over to me and takes me through them, every square inch of them, and there is no doubt about it. I am, in fact, rich.

It isn't immediately clear where the money came from, but it doesn't seem to be the result of particularly shrewd investments. The money is sitting in long-term tax-free municipal bonds, earning much less interest than it could be elsewhere.

None of this makes any sense, so I decide to investigate, and make the logical decision to assign my investigator. I call Laurie from Roger's office and tell her what I've learned, and the extent of my wealth.

"You've suddenly become far more attractive, you big adorable hunk, you," she gushes.

Since I haven't told her about Nicole, this doesn't seem to be a good time to engage in sexual/romantic banter. So I don't, and she promises to get to the bottom of this quickly. I have no doubt that she will.

When I get home I tell Nicole the news, and her astonishment matches mine. My father would be the last person you'd expect to keep a momentous secret like this from his family, and I have to assume my mother had been in the dark about it as well. She was biologically incapable of keeping a secret; she would have told me without any prompting at all.

There are ordinarily no circumstances under which I have trouble sleeping. My ability to fall asleep on a moment's notice is a blessing I have never taken for granted. But tonight I toss and turn for half the night.

I don't even have Tara in bed for me to pet; since Nicole's return Tara has been reduced to sleeping on a comforter on the floor. I could pet Nicole, but she might read more into it than she should. So I just lie there, eyes open, staring at the ceiling. Becoming an orphan, a husband, and a multimillionaire in the same week must be causing me some stress.

The next morning I go to the office for the first time since the funeral. When I arrive I find my secretary-receptionist, Edna, doing a crossword puzzle. Edna is sixty-six and she proudly and often proclaims that she has worked every day of her life since she was a mere child, yet she hasn't done a real day's work in the five years she's worked for me. If you think I'm about to tell her that, you don't know her or me.

Edna, to hear her tell it, has what must be one of the largest extended families in the United States. There is nothing one can mention, be it an experience, an occupation, a talent, an affliction . . . anything . . . that isn't shared by a member of Edna's family. The only thing they all seem to have in common is that all are constantly advising Edna that she doesn't need to work. If I could speak to all of them, and a venue the size of Yankee Stadium would be necessary, I would reassure them that their advice has been taken to heart. Edna does many things, but work is not one of them.

But whatever one might say about Edna, she is the greatest crossword puzzle talent this country has ever produced. It's amazing; she can go through the *New York Times* puzzle in less than twenty minutes. She often waxes eloquent about the injustice of it all. Here Michael Jordan made millions because he was better at basketball than anyone else, while she gets nothing for being at the peak of her chosen avocation. She vows she will live to see the day that crossword championships are held at Madison Square Garden before screaming multitudes, and she's signing huge pencil endorsement deals.

I get in early and set about trying to relax, which for me means a good sock basketball game. I take a pair of rolled-up socks (I keep some in the office for just this purpose) and shoot at a ledge above the door. I have to pretend to dribble, since rolled-up socks don't really bounce, and I create fantasy games to play in.

Right now I'm in the middle of an intense game, made all the more difficult by the fact that I also serve as commentator.

"Carpenter fakes left, the shot clock is off, the game clock is down to ten, his teammates have cleared out, giving him room . . . Carpenter loves to take the final shot . . . a two will tie, a three will win. The crowd is on its feet."

Edna watches this with no apparent emotion, unimpressed by my prowess, since she has previously told me that sock basketball was invented by her Uncle Irwin. The door opens and Laurie comes in, carrying a huge watermelon. Even this isn't enough to hurt my concentration.

"Carpenter backs in, three on the clock. He turns, jumps, shoots . . . and hits!" The shot has actually gone in, but I'm not finished. I wait a few moments for effect.

"And a foul!"

I go up to my nonexistent opponent and get right up in his nonexistent face.

"In your face, sucker! In your face!" I snarl.

Laurie has finally managed to put the watermelon on a

table, and she turns to me and my imaginary opponent. "I think you've got him intimidated."

"Her. I've got her intimidated," I say. "I combine my sports and sexual fantasies. It saves time."

Laurie looks around the office, as she always does, her face reflecting her displeasure at the mess I've made.

"This is a dump," she says with some accuracy.

"So is that why you brought in a four-hundred-pound watermelon? To class up the place?"

We both know that Sofía Hernández, the owner of the fruit stand downstairs, has given us the watermelon as partial payment for defending her son. I would have preferred peaches, but they're not really in season.

"Someday you might want to take payment in actual money. Although as rich as you are, you don't need to."

This interests me enough to put down the sock basketball. I walk toward her, throwing out questions along the way.

"Did you check out the money? Where did he get it? Is it really mine?"

"Yes. I don't know. Yes."

I focus in on the negative. "You don't know where he got it?"

Laurie takes a diet soda out of the small refrigerator and pops the top before she answers. "Correct. But I do know *when* he got it. Thirty-five years ago. It started as two million."

This has now moved smoothly from the very strange to the totally bizarre. Thirty-five years ago my father was in his mid-twenties and in law school. How the hell could he have gotten hold of two million dollars?

Laurie continues. "It gets even stranger. He never touched the bonds, not once in all these years. The principal just grew from interest."

"But he loved to play the stock market. When he retired he used to sit by the television all day and watch that stupid ticker go across the screen."

She shakes her head. "Not with this money. The brokerage was instructed never to suggest new investments . . . they were told never even to call him . . . to pretend the money didn't exist."

"You spoke to them?"

She nods. "Not the same people who were there back then, but the instructions were passed down, and nobody ever questioned them. Not a single person in the place had ever spoken to your father about the money."

"I've got to find out where he got it in the first place."

Laurie has an annoying habit of dribbling out information, and she is dribbling away now. "The plot thickens. The brokerage records show it was a single cashier's check . . . so there's no way to trace it from this end."

This is incredibly frustrating, so I spend the next ten minutes brainstorming ideas with Laurie about how to go about getting more information. We collectively come to the conclusion that she already had come to: The only way to find out more is to look back into my father's life.

Laurie thinks I should drop it, that there's nothing to be gained by going further. The unspoken concern is that there's something to be lost, that my father did something to acquire that money that was so untoward that he could not bring himself to tell anyone about it or even touch it for thirty-five years.

The prospect of going further is frightening, but I have no choice. I don't want to feel like I didn't know a big piece of my father, though the evidence clearly shows that I didn't. We discuss how to proceed, and I'm thinking that I want to take the lead in this rather than Laurie.

The phone rings and we wait for Edna to answer it. By the fourth ring it is clear that she's not going to; 48 across must be requiring all of her considerable powers of concentration. I pick up the receiver and am jolted by the voice of Judge Henderson's clerk. Hatchet wants to see me about the Miller case. It can only mean that the decision has come down from the Court of Appeals.

I grab my jacket and start heading for the door, but Laurie walks along with me and asks if we're still having dinner tonight. It's the moment of truth, and I almost choke on my tongue.

"Laurie . . . Nicole's back in town . . . we . . . the situation . . ."
The actual words, when spoken, are even wimpier than they
look on paper.

Her tone is instantly challenging. "Talk, Andy. Nicole's back
in town and that means what?"

"I'm not sure. Part of me says it's over and part of me feels
like I should see where it goes."

"And you think I'm going to hang around while your parts
fight it out? Forget it, Andy."

"I know this is difficult . . . but if you'll just try and understand . . ." I'm dying here and she shows no sign of letting me
off the hook.

"Oh, I understand. I understand that your wife, the wife
who walked out on you, has decided she might give you a second chance, and you're jumping at it. Well, you can jump
through this particular hoop without me."

I start to blabber some more, but she dismissively points
out that Hatchet Henderson doesn't like to be kept waiting.
Her saying this is both true and at the same time an act of
mercy, and I'm able to leave with what little dignity I have left.

Even though I'm not actually going into the courtroom, but
only into the judge's chambers, I decide against risking pissing
off the superstition god, and I stop at Cal Morris's newsstand.
I've already gotten the paper today, so I pick up a *Baseball
Weekly,* which I will never read. Cal and I go through our conversation in a perfunctory fashion; I'm too nervous to hear
what the judge will say to put my heart into it.

Judge Walter Henderson, better known as Hatchet Henderson, is a large, imposing hulk of a man who stays in shape by
adhering to a no-carbohydrate, no-fat, all-lawyer diet. He ter-
rorizes all who appear before him, though me less than most.
I've developed the ability to step back and view him as a car-
icature of the "mean judge," and my reaction is usually amuse-
ment. He instinctively knows that, and it drives him crazy.

Hatchet absolutely refuses to engage in the small talk that
constitutes social relationships between normal human beings.
"Hello" is to him meaningless and wasteful chitchat; every
word he says or allows himself to hear must provide informa-

tion. Right now that's fine with me, because information is what I'm waiting for. I'm going to learn whether Willie Miller is going to die or be granted another trial.

Hatchet's clerk ushers me into his chambers, which is famous for how dark Hatchet keeps it. The drapes are drawn and the Great One reads a brief at his desk in the sparse light of a table lamp.

He doesn't look up, but he knows I'm there. He also knows that I know the game, which is to stand there like an idiot and wait for him to speak. It can go on for a while, and this time it goes on for ten excruciating minutes.

Finally, he talks without looking up. "Speak."

I'm now free to open my mouth. "Nice to see you again, Judge."

"Sorry about your father." For him that is an amazing burst of humanity.

"Thank you," I reply.

"Top man. Top man." He's positively gushing. "One of the best."

"Thank you," I reply again.

"You said that already." Hatchet is back in character. "The decision is coming down today from Appeals. You're getting your retrial."

There it is. Willie is saved, at least for the time being. Hatchet said it with such a lack of emotion that it took me off guard, though of course I would have expected nothing else.

I'm going to be humble about this. "That's good news. It's the right decision."

"Bullshit."

I nod agreeably. "That's another way of looking at it."

He takes off his glasses and stares at me, peering through the darkness. This is not a good sign. There is a possibility I will never be heard from again.

"You got the retrial on a technicality." He says "technicality" with such intense disdain that his teeth are clenched. It comes out "technically," but I don't think I'll point this out. What I think I'll do is just listen.

"You'll need a hell of a lot more in court," he continues.

"There was enough evidence to convict Miller ten times over, and that's not going to change."

"Well . . ." I begin.

"Bullshit." I wonder how he knew what I was going to say?

"Your father did a good job prosecuting that case, but Daffy-fucking-Duck could have nailed Miller. And your courtroom stunts, should you be crazy enough to risk contempt and try them, won't help."

A question forms on my lips, but I hesitate to ask because I dread the answer. I can't help myself. "Has a judge been assigned?"

"You're looking at him," he says with obvious relish.

"Wonderful," I lie. Other than the fact that I just got twenty-two million dollars dropped in my lap, and my client isn't going to be executed anytime soon, this has been a rough couple of days.

"You know," he says, "there are some people that refer to me behind my back as Hatchet Henderson."

"No!" I'm flabbergasted. "Why would they do that?"

"Because I cut the balls off lawyers in my courtroom who piss me off."

"As well you should."

"Trial is set for four weeks from today. I want your motions filed within ten days."

This is simply unacceptable. Four weeks is not nearly enough time. I don't care if they call him Hatchet, I'm not going to let him walk all over me. "Judge, I need more time. The preparation involved will take—"

He cuts me off. "You've got four weeks."

I'm raging with anger now. There is no way this asshole is going to railroad me and my client into this. "Four weeks," I nod.

I realize that Hatchet is looking back at the papers on his desk. He's effectively dismissed me.

"Nice talking to you, Judge." He doesn't respond; I have ceased to exist. Without saying another word, I turn and leave, closing the door behind me. I don't say goodbye. That'll teach him.

My next stop is out to the prison to tell Willie the good news in person. It's the first one of these visits I've looked forward to, although I'm already starting to focus on just how difficult this trial is going to be.

On the way to the cell, Danny asks me if I've gotten any news on Willie's appeal. He obviously can sense that I have.

"I really want to talk to Willie about it first," I say.

He nods. "I understand. I hope he gets the new trial."

I just nod, still noncommittal. It would seem a betrayal of Willie to tell anybody else before I tell him.

Danny continues, "I don't always root for the prisoners, you know? But I like Willie. I don't know what he did, or didn't do, but I judge 'em on how they are in here. And I like Willie."

Willie is waiting for me, but trying to act nonchalant. He can't quite pull it off, but it doesn't matter. I get right to it.

"We heard from the Court of Appeals. We got the retrial."

Willie sort of flinches when he hears it. I was nervous waiting to hear what Hatchet would tell me, and I'm just the lawyer. Willie was listening to hear whether he would live or die. He's going to live, at least for now. I can't imagine what this moment would have been like if I had to tell him the appeal was turned down. I don't know how I could have done it.

I call Laurie and tell her the good news. We agree to meet the next morning at eight o'clock in my office. There's going to be about three months of work to do in the next four weeks, and Laurie is going to be responsible for a great deal of it. She doesn't mention Nicole or the situation between us, but neither does she whisper sweet nothings into the phone. It's going to be the longest, shortest four weeks of my life.

• • • • •

NICOLE AND I HAVE DINNER PLANS TONIGHT. I'M
still feeling guilty about Laurie, so I exact my revenge on
Nicole by taking her to a sports bar that I've never been to. It's
a sign of how hard she's trying that she doesn't voice a com-
plaint about the choice.

The only sports Nicole tolerates are sports cars, and occasionally sports shirts. It was a problem in our marriage. One
time I planted myself on the couch and watched football for so
long that she came over and watered me. Tara licked it off my
face and I didn't miss a single play.

This place actually turns out to be pretty cool, with nine
large-screen TVs and headphones that plug into the table so you
can hear whatever game you want. Unfortunately, the only game
on is a hockey game, which doesn't interest me. I have this rule:
I'm only a fan of sports in which I can pronounce 30 percent of
the players' names. I don't think Nicole is a big hockey fan either; she glances at the screen and asks me what inning it is.

Nicole doesn't seem terribly impressed by the place. She
has this hang-up about wanting edible food when she goes to
a restaurant, and her meal doesn't seem to measure up. I make
the mistake of inquiring as to how her salad is.

"Actually," she says, "I've never said this about salad before . . . but it's too tough."

I nod with characteristic understanding. "Same thing with the burgers. It's good for your teeth."

She smiles and takes my hand. "It's just good to be together."

At this point I'm thinking that she might be right. Things are getting more comfortable, more like old times. Of course, old times led to our separating, but I'm willing to overlook that right now.

I've known Nicole since I was fourteen; my father and Philip Gant were old friends who had gone on to Yale Law School together. They both then went on to work in the District Attorney's office. Though it became my father's life and passion, it was a résumé-builder for Philip, and after four years he left crime fighting behind to fight for votes.

Tevye would have been thrilled with our courtship; it was the closest thing to an arranged marriage as the United States Constitution permits. We were introduced at a charity ball at Nicole's family's country club, an important enough event that my mother bought me a new navy blazer and khaki pants. I went reluctantly, much preferring to waste time hanging out with my friends than to meet this ritzy prep school girl. I was cool, my friends were cool, the ice cream stand we hung out at was cool, and the country club was said to be very definitely uncool.

For an uncool place, it had some of the coolest things in it I had ever seen, and one of the coolest was Nicole. She was gorgeous, five foot eight, with curly black hair, bare shoulders sloping down from a perfect neck, and a smile that brightened up the entire room. But most importantly, most significantly, most amazingly, she had cleavage! Yes, actual cleavage! And she wore a dress that revealed it! In retrospect, there wasn't that much of it, but at that age, on that night, it felt like I was staring into the Lincoln Tunnel.

I almost choked on my tongue when we were introduced, but as the night wore on things became more comfortable. I regaled her with stories of my baseball prowess, and she told me about her trip through the Orient with her family. She had a slightly rebellious air about her, and a smile that said she realized how absurdly ostentatious these surroundings were, but that was tough, because she was damn well going to enjoy them. She was funny, smart—and she touched my arm when she talked.

I think we both knew from that night on that we were going to wind up together. School and family obligations conspired to keep us mostly apart over the next eight years, but we never lost touch. We'd even talk about our respective relationships, as if they were just passing, unthreatening fancies until we got back to the real thing. Each other.

When I was in my third year of law school it somehow simultaneously dawned on us that the time was right, and we started dating seriously. Less than ten months later we were married, followed by a wedding reception, the cost of which could have fed Guatemala for three months.

It seems too simplistic to say that we grew apart, that our respective lifestyles finally lost their capacity to blend together. But as near as I can tell, that's basically what happened, and when Nicole finally left me, the dominant feeling I was experiencing changed from sadness to relief.

But now she's telling me that it's good to be together, and I'm buying into it. I made a lifelong commitment to this woman, and that is what I'm trying to fulfill. What this world needs are more honorable, responsible people like me.

Now she has said that this feels right, and I raise my bottle of beer. "I'll drink to that. How's your father?"

"Very busy. They're still hassling over that crime bill . . . trying to pass it before the summer recess. But he's really happy we're working things out."

A few days ago she said we were "trying" to work things out. I guess we must have succeeded while I wasn't paying attention.

"My father would have been just as happy. It must be a father thing."

She nods as if that is sound wisdom. "Any luck with Nelson's mysterious money?"

I shake my head. "Not yet. You know, all those years I

thought I married you for your money, and now it turns out you married me for mine."

She laughs. "Twenty-two million dollars? To us Gants, that's tipping money."

She's joking, but not that far off. Nicole comes from real money, money so old it was originally called wampum.

She leans forward seductively. It's a lean she has mastered. "But you rich men do excite me."

I give her a sexy lean of my own, but I'm not quite as good at it. "When I stand on my wallet I'm six foot four."

"What about when you're lying down?" she purrs.

We haven't had sex since she came back, so there's more excitement here than I remember. We're like two kids teasing each other, but both knowing where it will wind up.

"How about coming back to our place?" is my clever response. It seems to work pretty well, because the next thing I know we're back home, standing next to our bed, slowly undressing each other.

Tara's outside the room, pawing at the door. Nicole has always felt uncomfortable having Tara in the room when we have sex. Right now I don't even hear Tara's whimpering; Nicole has my undivided attention. This is not feeling like a husband-wife thing, and I can sense she's a little nervous. Join the club.

"Andy, I haven't been with anyone else since we separated."

"I know," I respond. "I've had you followed."

I have this problem; I joke at inappropriate times. Also at appropriate times, though there don't seem to be that many of them anymore.

"What about you?" she asks. "Have you been with anyone?"

I nod, though she can't see me in the dark. "The Olympic girls' volleyball team, Michelle Pfeiffer, the women's division of the Teamsters, the White sisters, Vanna, Betty, and Reggie—"

She interrupts, which is just as well, since there's no telling how long I would have babbled on. "I had forgotten that about you," she says.

"What?"

"You never shut up."

With that she prepares to shut me up, except for an occasional moan. She does a really good job of it, but hell, somebody had to.

I have a great night's sleep, which carries right through the usually effective wake-up call planted in my brain. I gulp down a cup of coffee and some M&M's and head for the office. I'm feeling good for the first time in a while; the idea of diving headlong into the Miller case is actually appealing.

I stop off at Cal Morris's newsstand, not for superstition purposes, but rather to read what the media is saying about Willie's prospects. For the time being they're buying the prosecution line about this being merely a technicality, and that the result will be the same the second time around. I know in my gut they're probably right, so I bypass my gut and make a mental note to meet with the press and push our point of view. That is, as soon as we come up with a point of view.

On the way into the office I'm stopped by Sofía Hernández, standing and waiting for me in front of her fruit stand. She hands me two cantaloupes, the second installment on her son's legal bills.

"Thank you," I say. "You know, the best thing about being paid in cantaloupes is that they don't bounce."

She doesn't come close to getting the joke. If a joke is told in a fruit stand and nobody gets it, did it make a sound?

As I enter the office, I see Laurie sitting there, waiting for me. The smell of annoyance is in the air.

"Good morning," I cheerily volunteer. It doesn't get the response I hope for. Actually, it doesn't get any response.

I look at my watch. Uh, oh. "You're pissed off because I'm late."

"Forty-five minutes late. Which wouldn't mean much if the meeting were called for three P.M. But since it was called for eight A.M., forty-five minutes is a very long time."

"Sorry. I had a late night." I can see Laurie react, but it's too late, the words have already left my mouth. Maybe I've said stupider things in my life, but I can't remember when. This isn't pouring gasoline on a fire, it's more like pouring freon on a frozen tundra.

Laurie, to her credit, doesn't say anything. Which means the ball is still in my court. "Okay . . . you're right . . . I'm a shit-head."

"Let's not let that obvious fact interfere with our work, okay? And let's keep each of our personal lives personal."

She's right, at least for now. The strain between us is not likely to go away, and eventually it will have to be dealt with. We both know that. But this is not the time, not with the Miller case staring us in the face. Edna is of course not in yet, so I make some coffee and we get right to work.

Laurie has spent the previous night reading the transcript of the first trial, which makes me even guiltier about how I spent the night. Her reaction is rather predictable.

"It's a disaster. Open-and-shut," she says.

This is Laurie's style. She's an optimist in life, a total pessimist in work. Not only does she assume that all clients are guilty, she assumes they are going to be found guilty as well. One would think it would then fall to me to be encouraging, to be a motivator, but it's really not necessary. Laurie is a total pro; she'll do the best that can be done for the client, despite her personal views.

We start talking about the case, and she asks why Willie's lawyer, a man named Robert Hinton, didn't plead it out last time. It's a question I've wondered myself, and I make a note to ask Willie about it. Maybe Willie adamantly refused to plead down for a crime he didn't commit in the first place. It's also possible that my father wouldn't go for it. Even though he wasn't the death penalty type, he may well have been under a lot of pressure to take this one all the way.

I ask Laurie if she's ever heard of Hinton, but she hasn't and neither have I. We're going to have to find him; he should be able to give us some insight that the cold transcripts don't provide.

What the transcripts do provide is a version of the fateful night that appears devastating to Willie's case. According to the prosecution, Willie Miller left work an hour before the murder, went on a drinking binge, and came back through the alley and into the back door. He went into the ladies' room, where he came upon Denise McGregor. Willie allegedly hit Denise over the head and dragged her out into the alley, where he slashed her with a steak knife from the bar.

Cathy Pearl, a thirty-five-year-old waitress from a nearby diner, came through the alley on the way home from work and saw Willie standing over the body. He ran off, dumping the knife in a trash can three blocks away, before settling into a doorway and collapsing in a drunken stupor.

As if that weren't enough, there were scratch marks all over Willie's face, and his blood and skin were found under Denise's fingernails. Just to add another positive character trait for the jury to consider, there were needle marks in Willie's arms. It is such an airtight case that I am suspicious of it.

Laurie believes every word of the government's case, while I say that is for a jury to decide.

"They already have," she notes.

"The conviction has been set aside," I point out.

"He admits it."

"No, he doesn't dispute it. He can't remember anything. He was too drunk."

"Andy, read the transcript. This is not exactly a major whodunit."

"It reads like a frame-up to me."

She laughs derisively. "You're amazing," is what she says, but what she means is that I am an asshole.

"Thank you, but enough about me. What do we know about the victim?"

Laurie recites the facts that I already know. Denise McGregor worked as a reporter for a local newspaper, the *Newark Star-Ledger*. No information was ever turned up to show that she had any enemies, anyone who would have had reason to kill her. According to testimony, she had been dating Edward Markham for about three months, and she was out with him on the night of her death. This reminds me of the picture I found in the attic, so I take it out of a drawer and show it to Laurie.

"Isn't that Victor Markham?"

"I have no idea what Victor Markham looks like," she says. But then she points at the man standing next to him in the picture. "But I think I recognize him."

He doesn't look at all familiar to me, and Laurie tells me that she thinks it's Frank Brownfield, a real estate developer who has built ugly malls all over the New York metropolitan area. Laurie has a friend who works for him, and she had met Brownfield about a year ago. All this does is add to the puzzle; my father never mentioned knowing Brownfield either.

Laurie turns the picture over and reads the date, June 14, 1965, off the back.

"Now, *that's* weird."

"What?" I ask.

She digs a piece of paper out of her purse and confirms her recollection. "The cashier check your father got for the two million. It was deposited on June 17, 1965."

Less than a week after my father posed for a picture with the future Who's Who of American industry, all of whom he never admitted knowing, he received two million dollars, which he never admitted having. If these two facts aren't related, then we're talking serious coincidence here.

Laurie asks if she should check further, but I've got to get my priorities straight. I tell her I need her working full-time on the Miller case, and we agree she'll find Hinton, Willie's lawyer, to get his notes and impressions from the first trial. Meanwhile, I'm going to kill one witness with two stones and have a chat with Victor Markham.

• • • • •

MY GUESS IS THAT VICTOR MARKHAM NEVER GETS LOST on the way to work. First of all, he no doubt gets into the back seat of a car and says to the chauffeur, "Take me to my office." But if by some chance he were left to fend for himself, he would just have to look up. There, towering over the office buildings in Paramus, are the huge words "Markham Plaza" emblazoned across the top.

If he got to the underground parking lot and was somehow still unsure that he had reached the right place, he would be reassured as he took a ticket from the machine. A computer-generated female voice would say to him, "Welcome to Markham Plaza. Please take a ticket. Have a good day."

"Thank you, I will," I reply graciously when the machine welcomes me. I think that perhaps this particular computer-generated female might have a crush on me, but when I pull into the lot I hear her welcoming the guy in the next car just as warmly. Women.

I take the elevator up to the lobby, which is large enough for the Knicks to play their home games. I enter another elevator, and this time a computer-generated male voice addresses me. "Welcome to Markham Plaza. Please press the floor of your choice."

"Will do," I say. "By the way, there's a gal in the parking lot you might like. Short, a little metallic-looking, but a good personality."

Unfortunately, a couple is getting on the elevator behind me, and they hear my conversation.

I smile lamely at them. "The elevator talks." Heh, heh.

They don't respond, and we have an uncomfortable ride up, especially for them. They're the ones trapped in an elevator with a lunatic.

The reception area outside Victor's office is nothing short of spectacular. I'm pondering the cost of the paintings on the walls, when I realize that I could probably afford them. I've got to get used to the concept; I am the most nouveau of all the nouveau riche in the country.

Victor's secretary, Eleanor, appears to have a permanent scowl on her face. Clearly her job is to protect Victor, and I doubt that Norman Schwarzkopf could lead a battalion past her without an appointment. Fortunately, I have one, and she buzzes me through.

I enter Victor's office, which makes the reception area look Third World. Victor is at his desk. He's tall, graying at the temples, wearing a three-piece suit which strains slightly to contain his rather bulky midsection. I don't think I've ever sat at my desk without taking off my jacket, but there's Victor wearing all three pieces, sitting back in his deep leather chair, staring out at the world as if he hasn't got a care in it. And there's really no reason that he should.

"Mr. Markham, my name is Andy Carp—"

He cuts me off. "I know who you are. I'm sorry about your father. Good man."

"Yes, I wanted to talk—"

He does it again. "You wanted to talk about that killer." He means Willie Miller, but I doubt he even knows his name. "I won't help you with that," he goes on. "You shouldn't have gotten a new trial. It's a waste of taxpayer money. End of discussion."

Since this hasn't really been a discussion, I consider his announcement of its ending to be premature. "Actually, I thought that since—"

And again. "Since I have influence, and since the victim was my son's girlfriend, I could talk to the governor, get that scum's sentence reduced to life in prison. Forget it. As I said, end of discussion."

This is getting annoying. "I like beer," I say quickly.

"What the hell is that supposed to mean?" he demands.

"Nothing. I just wanted to see if I could get in one complete sentence without you interrupting, and 'I like beer' was the quickest sentence I could think of."

This is the point where the gruff, overpowering type usually laughs grudgingly and warms up. Victor, unfortunately, doesn't seem to be familiar with that stereotype. He looks at me with the same respect he would a roach that he just found in his Rice Krispies.

"You're as big a wiseass as I've heard."

"Thank you very much." That's my second sentence in a row, so I'm feeling pretty chipper.

"What do you want? I'm a busy man."

I had been planning to talk to him about the Miller case, but he's made it clear that the only way I'll get any answers about that is to take his deposition under oath. I smoothly switch to plan B, taking out the photograph and laying it on his desk. "I was curious about when and where this picture was taken."

For the first time, I see a human reaction. I can't tell what it is, maybe a gas pain, but something has gotten through his outer crust. A moment later it's gone, and he's back in control.

"Where did you get that?"

"My father had it."

"Who are those people?"

"The second one from the left is you."

He shakes his head a little too hard, and doesn't bother to look at the photo again. "That's not me."

I'm surprised, because it is clearly him. "You're saying it's not you? That's the position you're taking?"

This annoys him; human reactions are rapidly becoming

commonplace to Victor Markham. "Position? I don't have to take a position. It's not me."

"Did you know my father back around . . . oh, thirty-five years ago?"

"No. Now if that's all, my girl will show you out."

"Your girl is older than you are."

He is already on his intercom, calling for Eleanor.

I keep at him. "Why are you so upset that I have this picture of you?" I look at the picture again and then at Victor. "Maybe it's because you've had a few snacks since then."

He doesn't answer, pretending to no longer be paying attention. The door opens and the ominous Eleanor arrives. I can either follow her out the door or she'll throw me through the glass wall.

"By the way, Victor. I will be deposing you about the McGregor killing. You can do it the easy way, or I can get a subpoena. Let me know."

I wink at Eleanor and keep talking to Victor. "Have your girl call my girl."

I go downstairs, taking out my annoyance on Victor by refusing to converse with the elevator. I call my office from a pay phone in the lobby, catching my girl, Edna, with her mouth full, and I wait while she swallows to get my messages.

"Mr. Calhoun from a company named Allied called. He says it's about your car."

I'm terrible paying bills; they sit on my desk until collection agencies call with reminders.

"Forget it. He's from a collection agency. I'll take care of it later."

"My cousin Shirley's husband, Bruce, worked for a collection agency. He could tell you—"

I interrupt her. "Edna, did anyone else call?"

"Cal Morris."

"Who?"

"Cal Morris from the newsstand. He said if you don't recognize his name, I should tell you that they're hanging really low today."

Cal has never called me before; I didn't even realize he knew my full name. "Did he say what he wanted?"

"He wouldn't tell me," Edna says, "but he said it was urgent, and he sounded really upset."

I stop off at the newsstand on the way back, and sure enough, Cal has been anxiously waiting for me to contact him. He closes up the stand and takes me to the diner next door for a cup of coffee. We sit at a booth, and he lets it spill out.

"It's my daughter, Andy. She's been arrested. You got to get her off, there's no way she could have done this."

"Take it easy, Cal. Start at the beginning."

Cal doesn't know much, just that his only daughter, Wanda, has been arrested on prostitution charges. She's only sixteen, and until today Cal has assumed she's a virgin. In fact, he still does.

Cal knows that I have contacts in the local justice system. He is desperate, and he offers to pay me whatever it will take. Since money is not my biggest problem these days, I shrug it off, mumbling something about free newspapers and magazines. I don't mean it, though, since paying for the papers is part of my superstition.

I've got about an hour before I'm supposed to meet with Laurie, so I tell Cal that I'll stop off at the police station and see what I can do. He's so grateful I think he's going to cry, and it makes me feel good to be able to help. That's if I'm able to help.

I go down to the station and am lucky enough to run into Pete Stanton. Not only is Pete a pretty good friend of mine (we play racquetball together), but he is a lieutenant, and he owes me a favor. That doesn't mean he won't give me a hard time, it just means he'll eventually give in.

By a coincidence, Pete was the detective originally assigned to the Willie Miller case, and he ran the investigation. He assumes that is what I'm here to see him about, and is surprised when I tell him about Cal's daughter, Wanda.

Though Pete does not have anything to do with Wanda's case, he tracks down her file and looks through it. I tell him that Wanda Morris is a troubled kid, but after a quick read he dismisses her as a hooker.

I correct him. "An alleged hooker."

"Who do I look like?" he sneers. "John Q. Jury? She allegedly propositioned a cop. Vice has allegedly got it on tape."

"An obvious case of entrapment."

Pete laughs and shows me his nameplate on his desk. He points to the word "Lieutenant." "See that?" he says. "That means I'm hot shit around here."

I nod. "You're a goddamn legend, a combination J. Edgar Hoover and Eliot Ness. Which means you spend your time walking around in a dress looking for alcohol."

He ignores that. "Come on, Andy, why are you talking to me about a hooker? I deal in big stuff, like homicides. If this hooker screws a guy to death, come talk to me."

"You owe me." I didn't want to have to use my ace this early in the conversation, but I don't want to be late again for my meeting with Laurie. I represented Pete's brother on a drug charge in a nearby town. I got him off and kept Pete's name out of it. His brother is doing well now, turned his life around, and Pete remembers. Pete's the type who will remember it until the day he dies, and maybe even a few years afterward.

That doesn't mean he'll cave easily. "You calling in your chit on this? A hooker case? You know as well as I do she'll be back on the street in a day anyway."

"Her father's my friend."

Pete nods; no more explanation is necessary. Pete is a guy who understands friendship.

"I'll call McGinley," he says. "I'll get him to plead it out to probation. She stays clean and it comes off her record."

"Thanks. Now, on to more important business."

He's surprised. "There's more? You got another friend whose kid is a bank robber? Or an arsonist? Why don't you just give me a list of your friends and we won't arrest anybody with those last names?"

I haven't met the sarcasm that can stop me, so I push on. "What do you know about Victor Markham?"

"He's a rich scumbag." He reflects for a moment. "That might be redundant."

As a rich person, I'm offended, but I don't show it. "What did Markham have to do with the Miller case?"

"You want me to tell you what you already know? The victim was his son's girlfriend. They were out together when it happened."

"Were you aware of any special connection between Victor Markham and my father?"

Pete shows me a flash of anger. "Your father did not have special connections. Except to the truth."

"Don't you think I know that?"

He nods. "Yeah, of course you do. Sorry."

I wait for him to continue, to tell me what he knows. I don't have to wait long.

"Markham's son, Edward, was a loose cannon," he says. "I had the feeling that Victor was pulling his strings, like he was worried what the kid might say or do on his own. No big deal, just a feeling I had."

I take this very seriously. Pete is an outstanding cop; there are a lot of people making license plates and saying "Pass the soap, Bubba" in the shower because of feelings Pete has had.

"Where's Edward now?" I ask.

"He works for his daddy. Big job."

I nod. "He must interview really well."

I thank Pete and leave, stopping off at the newsstand on the way back to the office. I tell Cal that Wanda is to be in court three days from now, and if she behaves everything will be fine. For now. Cal is so grateful I think he's going to cry or, even worse, hug me. But since deep emotion is not really a part of our relationship, I'm glad when he doesn't.

I get to the office early, and Laurie hasn't yet arrived. I get a message from Richard Wallace, a Deputy District Attorney. Wallace is the best lawyer the department has to offer; if he is the one handling the Miller trial, an impossible job just got tougher.

Wallace is friendly when I call him; he and I have established a good working relationship over the years. Of course, he can afford to be nice; he's beaten me two of the three trials in which we've gone against each other. And I don't get the feeling he's too worried about this one.

The other factor that leads to us having a good rapport is that he used to work for my father, who was the District Attorney and head of the department. My father was a mentor to Wallace, and they shared a mutual respect. Some of that has transferred to me.

Basically the call is to discuss discovery, that process during which both sides turn over their evidence in advance, so that the other side is not ambushed and has time to prepare. It's not as big a deal in this case for two reasons. We already have everything that came out at the first trial, so there's not much for them to give us. And we've got nothing whatsoever to give them.

Richard informs me that additional DNA tests are being taken from the skin under Denise's fingernails, so as to more closely link Willie to the crime than the technology at the time of the murder was able to accomplish. Our response will be to attack the evidence as unreliable and incompetently gathered, but the problem is it isn't and it wasn't. I make a note to think about getting our own expert to refute what they are going to say.

"When will you have the results?" I ask.

"Just in time for opening statements."

"Why is Hatchet rushing this?"

I can hear him shrug over the phone. "You know Hatchet. He's not a big fan of technicality appeals. This is probably his way of showing it. I asked for more time myself; it's screwing up my vacation."

Near the end of the conversation, Richard brings up the possibility of discussing a plea bargain. He does this with a minimum of subtlety.

"You want to talk about a plea bargain?"

"Sure. We'll take a dismissal and an apology from the state. Something humble, but not cloying."

He laughs the laugh of the gracious winner. We agree to talk at his office tomorrow, though I can't imagine it going anywhere. There will be too much public pressure on Richard to right the wrong that the technicality appeal represents. Besides, Willie has said he absolutely won't cop to anything he didn't do, or as is the case here, something he can't imagine he could ever have done.

Laurie arrives, and her manner is cold but professional. It feels like I need to do something to resolve the situation, but I'm at a loss to know what. Her attitude is completely appropriate, which makes it all the more frustrating.

We set out going through all the files on the case, though we've both already been over them at least three times. I start letting my mind roam, not tempering my thoughts with logic. I often find it leads me to places I want to go, though just as often it leads me nowhere.

"What if Denise wasn't just a random victim? What if the killer had a motive?"

"Like . . ." she prompts.

"I don't know . . . she was a reporter . . . maybe she was going to write a story which would hurt the killer. He got rid of her to prevent the story."

"Why would she write a story about a loser like Willie Miller?"

I challenge her. "Who said the killer is Willie Miller?"

"A jury."

I'm starting to get frustrated by her pessimism. "Don't you get suspicious when there's all this evidence? Don't you think the prosecution's case might be a little too strong?"

"Actually, no," she says. "I tend to find evidence convincing. More evidence is more convincing."

I am about to challenge this logic when there is a knock on the door; it is the Chinese food Laurie has ordered for us. She hadn't asked me what I wanted, but I let it go because I figured she was lashing out at me, culinarily speaking. She also lashes out financially speaking, by signing for a big tip and telling the delivery guy to charge the whole thing to my account.

She starts to unpack the food, so I ask her what she's ordered.

"Steamed broccoli, stir-fried asparagus tips, and broiled sea-weed with tofu."

This is not exactly making my mouth water. "Are you cater-ing a rabbit convention?"

"It's good for you, unlike that greasy poison you always order." She takes two bites, then looks at her watch. "Are we almost finished here? Because I've got plans."

Uh, oh. The dreaded plans. I get a pit in my stomach the size of Argentina.

"Plans?"

"Yes, plans," she says. "Like in, I have a life so I make plans."

"Okay. I deserve that."

"No. If I gave you what you deserve, I'd be in the same sit-uation as Willie Miller."

I'm getting annoyed, and my level of annoyance has always been directly proportional to my level of courage. Actually, it's a theory of mine as well. I believe that all real heroes demon-strated their bravery only when they got angry. You think Nathan Hale liked the guys who put the rope around his neck? You think Davy Crockett considered the Mexicans coming over the Alamo walls his good buddies? I'm no different. Piss me off enough and before you know it they'll be writing songs about me.

Here goes. "Look, we started to get involved. It was nice . . . really nice . . . but we never took an oath."

She's ready for this. "Right. You and Nicole are the ones that took an oath."

"As a matter of fact, we did. And one of us may wind up breaking that oath, but we won't know that for a while."

She stands up. "I'm happy for you, but I've got plans. Now what is it you want me to do next?"

I guess she's not going to eat the Chinese food next, leav-ing it all for me. Yummm. I'll have enough left over to make broiled seaweed sandwiches tomorrow.

"Check out the eyewitness . . . Cathy Pearl. Maybe we can shake her. Maybe she did it, for Christ's sake."

"Great idea!" she enthuses. "I'll also ask people I meet at

the supermarket if by any chance *they* killed Denise McGregor. Maybe we can shake someone else into confessing."

"Aside from our personal situation, what is your problem with this case?"

She looks me straight in the eye, though that is what she always does. She's an inveterate eye looker; I on the other hand look at people's mouths when they talk.

"My problem is that we're defending a brutal murderer, Andy. If we're successful, which we won't be, he goes back on the street."

"And if he didn't do it, then the guy who did is *already* out on the street."

She sighs with resignation, as well as the fact that down deep she knows I'm right. We've been over this ground before. We have a role to play, and if we don't play it to the hilt the system doesn't function.

"Okay. It's a job and we do it. Where are *you* going to start?"

"With Denise McGregor."

• • • • •

VINCE SANDERS IS A GRUFF, UNKEMPT, VERY
overweight man who has spent one hundred twelve of his
fifty-one years working on newspapers up and down the East
Coast. He's the type that you think must still be pounding stories out on his old Smith-Corona while all his colleagues are
using high-tech computers. When I show up at his office, he is
doing research at warp speed on the Internet. Oh, well.

Vince was Denise's boss on the *Newark Star-Ledger.* I ask
him if Denise was working on something at the time she was
killed, and he laughs. Not a hah-hah, friendly laugh, but any
port in a storm.

"Working on something? Are you kidding me? Denise was
always working on something."

I ask him if he knows what she was working on. He
doesn't.

"She wouldn't tell me, but she was really excited. And it
must have been good, 'cause she asked me to meet her in here
the next day, which was a Saturday. She knew damn well I
don't get off my fat ass on Saturdays."

I laugh, since it seems like I'm supposed to, but he calls me
on it. "What the hell are you laughing at?" he asks.

"I was thinking that based on the size of your ass, the rea-

son you don't get off it on Saturdays is because crane opera-
tors don't work weekends."

He looks at me for a few moments, as if deciding whether
to kill me. He doesn't have a gun, which means he would have
to get that same fat ass out of the chair to get up and strangle
me. He seems to decide that it's not worth it.

"You think insulting me is the way to get information?" he
asks.

"I'm hoping you'll admire my honesty."

He shakes his head. "I don't. Besides I'm on a diet. All fish."

"Yeah," I say. Try as I might to conceal it, I'm afraid my
skepticism shines through, although he doesn't seem to notice.

"You ever notice how all fish tastes alike?" he asks. "I think
there's really only one kind of fish in the world, but they use
different names to scam the public."

For the sake of our budding friendship, I think I'll go along
with this. "Come to think of it," I say, "I've never seen a sword-
fish and a flounder in a room together."

"Of course not," he says. "Nobody has. That's because
they're the same damn fish. I'm telling you, it's a fraud on the
public."

I nod. "That's probably where they got the saying, 'There's
something fishy going on.'"

"Damn right," he agrees. Then, "You come here to talk
about fish?"

He knows I haven't, so I get back to Denise. "Is it unusual
that Denise wouldn't tell you what story she was researching?"
I ask.

"Unusual, but it wasn't the first time. I gave her a lot of lee-
way, because I trusted her."

"Did she leave any notes?"

He shakes his head, as the memories come flooding back.
"That was the weird part; I couldn't find any. And Denise took
notes about everything. I mean, you say 'good morning' to her,
and she jotted it down. You know the type?"

I don't, but I nod anyway. "What about Edward Markham?"

This gets another laugh from Vince, this one a little happier.
"Denise brought him to a party. I talked to him for a few min-

utes, and then I told her he was an arrogant asshole. Boy, did she get pissed."

"Why?"

"He was standing there when I told her." He starts laughing again, and I join in. I'm starting to think we're buddies, but the next thing I know, he's looking at me like I'm some slime he just got on his shoes.

"Let me ask you something: Why would you defend the scumbag that killed Denise?"

I look him right in the mouth. "I don't think I am. I believe that the real killer is running loose."

He stares at me for a few moments, and a feeling of impending doom comes over me. Finally, he shakes his head and says, "It's your job to believe that."

I shake my head. "No. It's my job to defend him. It's not my job to believe in him."

"If you get any real evidence, let me know how I can help. Me and my fat ass can get a lot done if we want to."

"Thanks," I say. "When all this is over, I'll take you out and buy you a tuna."

That night I'm at home, literally ankle deep in paperwork. My work style is to sit on the couch, cover the rest of the couch, the coffee table, and the floor in papers, and wade through them. There's a basketball game on the television that serves as background music. The Knicks are playing the Pacers, and I bet on the Knicks minus three. Allan Houston just hit a jump shot. Once in my life I want to hit a backhand down the line like Pete Sampras and shoot a jump shot as smoothly as Allan Houston. The Knicks are up by eleven with a minute to go, my bet is locked, and as my mother used to say, "Money goes to money."

The doorbell rings and I yell up for Nicole to get it. She doesn't hear me, so I answer it myself, which is just as well, since Laurie comes in, all excited. The last time she was here, she was a different kind of excited, but that's ancient history.

She doesn't even say hello, just launches into what she has to tell me. This is a sign that she's into the case, and I'm pleased about that. As it turns out, her visit has nothing to do with the Miller case at all.

"You've gotta hear this," she says. "I ran into my friend, the one who works for Frank Brownfield, the developer? He agreed that the guy in the picture looked like Brownfield, so I gave him a copy of the picture, and he said he would check it out."

"And?" I ask.

"And I got a call back an hour ago . . . what's it, ten o'clock? . . . from my friend . . ."

At this point, Nicole comes downstairs and into the room. On the list of people I was hoping would join us at that moment, Nicole ranks just below Charles Manson.

"Oh, hello, Laurie. How are you?"

Laurie hesitates, then says, "Okay . . . I'm okay. I didn't realize I was interrupting anything."

"Oh, you aren't. I was just going up to bed. See you in a while, Andy?" That's Nicole, another gracious winner.

"In a while. Laurie needs to talk to me about something."

Nicole nods. "Nice seeing you, Laurie."

Nicole goes upstairs; it's my turn to speak. Too bad I feel like I swallowed the four-hundred-pound watermelon from Sofía Hernández.

"I should have told you. Nicole moved back in."

Laurie puts on a look of feigned surprise. "She did? You're kidding! I just assumed her car broke down and she stopped here to phone for help."

"Laurie . . ."

"Your wife is waiting for you. We can talk about Brownfield tomorrow."

"No, let's talk about him now. So your friend called you and said what?"

The enthusiasm is now gone from Laurie's voice, but she says, "He said the picture is not Brownfield, on second thought looks nothing like Brownfield, and Brownfield knows nothing about it."

"So?"

"So he didn't sound like himself, and he denied it so hard,

you'd think the guy in the picture was naked in bed with a goat. And then, just before he gets off the phone, he asks where I got the picture."

"What did you say?"

"That if it isn't Brownfield, what do you care?"

So now we have what seems to be a harmless picture of a bunch of guys, none of whom will admit to being in it. And we're no closer to finding out why.

Laurie leaves and I go upstairs. Nicole is in bed, waiting for me as promised. She's reading a book, but she looks up as I walk in.

"Break in that murder case?"

Nicole uses the word "that" as a distancing mechanism. "That" murder case. "That" friend of yours. It diminishes the importance of what she is talking about, and removes any connection to her.

"No. But the situation with the picture is getting stranger and stranger. Brownfield denies that it's him . . . vehemently."

"Maybe they were a group of men who got together to cheat on their wives. It does happen, you know."

"Except this time it may have ended with my father getting two million dollars."

"Where are you going with this, Andy? What will you do if you find out what happened?"

I have no real answer to this. I can't predict how I will react until I know what it is I am reacting to.

By this time I'm already undressed. I shed clothes faster than basketball players tearing off their warm-up suits as they enter a game. I get into bed, and Nicole drops the bomb.

"You and Laurie have been involved."

Uh, oh. "It's that obvious?"

She nods. "It's that obvious."

"We started to . . . and then we stopped."

"What happened?" she asks.

"You," I answer.

• • • • •

FOUR WEEKS IS SIMPLY NOT ENOUGH TIME TO PRE-
pare for a murder case. There are lawyers who take that long
to pick out what suit they are going to wear for their opening
statement. But it's all Hatchet has given us, so we have to deal
with it.

Things are already starting to fall between the cracks. There
are motions to be filed, evidence to be challenged, discovery
to be gone over, witnesses to interview, media to be spun, and
prayers to be prayed. I'm going to need help.

Ordinarily, I would discuss additions to our team with Laurie, but discussions with Laurie these days are less than comfortable. I grapple with this for a short while, but I decide that
not to get the benefit of her input is to cause my client to suf-
fer because of my personal situation. I can't let that happen.

Laurie completely agrees that we need help, and after
thinking for a minute, she comes up with a name I've never
heard before: Kevin Randall.

"He's as good as any attorney I've ever met," she says. "And
he can be trusted totally and completely."

Laurie doesn't exactly throw around praise indiscriminately,
so I'm intrigued.

"Where is he practicing?"

"He isn't," she says. "He quit."

"Why?" I ask.

"Because he has a conscience."

As Laurie goes on to say, Kevin graduated Harvard Law about twenty years ago, but rather than join his classmates on their march to corporate law stardom, he went to work for the District Attorney in Essex County. He was a talented prosecutor, insightful and intense, but he had the misfortune to recognize his ability. Kevin would win cases with his skill and work ethic, which caused him to worry that perhaps innocent defendants were going to prison because their lawyers were outgunned.

To counter this situation, Kevin decided to become a defense attorney. It didn't work out quite the way he hoped. Now, when he won a case, he began to worry that he was responsible for dangerous felons roaming the streets. This was confirmed to him when one of his victories wound up killing two people in an armed robbery a month after Kevin got him off a convenience store holdup charge. Kevin blamed himself for the deaths.

That, Laurie says, was the final straw. Having been both a prosecutor and a defense attorney, Kevin had now run out of sides to take. His only other chance to stay in the legal system was to become a judge, so Kevin Randall made the obvious choice.

He opened a Laundromat.

Laurie and I drive out to East Brunswick to see Kevin at his current establishment, set in a tacky strip mall. There's a 7-Eleven, a takeout-only Chinese restaurant, a check-cashing business, and the "Law-dromat," Kevin's place. The sign outside offers "Free Legal Advice While You Wash and Dry."

I look at the place and then at Laurie, who has perfected the ability to read my thoughts. She can tell that I can't believe we've even come here.

"Open your mind," she says. "Unclench your ass and open your mind."

Laurie has mentioned that she knows Kevin quite well, but she hasn't provided any specifics. Actually, I think she knows him more than quite well, maybe much more than quite well.

I've got a feeling she once may have known him in the biblical sense, and my suspicious mind concludes that is one of the reasons she recommended him. But I've agreed to give it a shot, so we go in.

The inside of the place looks like a Laundromat, which in itself is no major surprise, since that is what it is. There is only one patron in the place, a middle-aged woman who is talking to the proprietor, Kevin. He, to my immense relief, is five foot seven, thirty pounds overweight, and balding. He doesn't have a hunchback, and he doesn't drool when he talks, but his overall unattractiveness should be enough to keep my jealousy in check.

Kevin and the woman are having an animated discussion, which Laurie and I cannot hear from our vantage point, since the washers and dryers are making too much noise. The woman seems upset, and Kevin's gestures indicate he is trying to placate her. It doesn't seem to work, and she throws up her hands and leaves.

Kevin sees Laurie and waves us over. When we get there, he's still shaking his head over the encounter with the woman. Laurie gives him a big hug and kiss, causing me to briefly wonder if my initial jealous instincts had been right. Nah, she's three inches taller than he is. Can't be.

"Hey, Kev, meet Andy. Andy, Kevin."

We shake hands and say how nice it is to meet each other. I ask him if the woman that just left is a tough client.

"They don't come any tougher," he says.

Laurie asks, "What's the problem? Or is it privileged and you can't talk about it?"

"No, I'll tell you," he says. "She put in seventy-five cents and her towels didn't get dry."

We go to a coffee shop around the block to talk, and I describe the Miller case. Kevin has three pieces of pie and a bowl of fruit while I lay it out, and I have no doubt he is going to eat as long as I talk. Fortunately the case is not that complicated, or he would have to get his stomach pumped.

I ask him what he thinks and wait for his answer while he

swallows. He tells me we are in a difficult position. My God, Clarence Darrow lives!

Laurie asks him if he'd be interested in coming on board, and he says, "No thanks. Been there, done that."

I'm relieved, since I don't yet share Laurie's high opinion of this guy. But Laurie keeps pressing him, and he seems to be weakening, so I jump in with what I think is an obvious point. "No offense, I'm sure you're a dynamite lawyer, but you do run a Laundromat."

Kevin nods and turns to Laurie. "See? This is a smart guy. He wants somebody who doesn't fluff and fold all day."

We talk about it some more, and he actually starts to impress me with his take on the case and the law. Laurie uses her considerable powers of persuasion on him, and he finally and reluctantly agrees to join the team, but only in a very secondary role. He'll do the grunt work, filing motions and moving things along, but will not take an active courtroom role. This is fine with me, since I was not about to offer him one.

"I think we should discuss my fee," he says.

"The sign says your advice is free," I reply.

"My free advice is don't use too much detergent. My legal fee is one fifty an hour. You as rich as Laurie says you are?"

I glare a dagger at Laurie, who shrugs. "It slipped out," she says.

I shake my head, disappointed at the injustice of it all. Why can't we rich people be treated as normal human beings? "Okay. One fifty an hour. But you pay for your own pie."

"Done," says Laurie. Then they shake hands on it. Then they hug on it. It's a beautiful moment. There isn't a dry eye in the room, unless you count both of mine.

We agree that Kevin will come to the office the next morning, and Laurie and I make arrangements to meet later to go to the scene of the crime. I head down to the courthouse to meet with Richard Wallace, which is not something I relish.

If you watched Geraldo or Larry King or any one of a hundred cable shows that covered the Simpson trial or the impeachment debacle, then you noticed that ninety-five percent of all the legal pundits they use are dubbed "former prosecutor." It's sort of like being a baseball manager: Every day you're in the job you're one day closer to being fired. Except every day you're a prosecutor, you're one day closer to quitting. The overwhelming feeling in the profession is that "former" is the best kind of prosecutor to be.

The exception to this rule is Richard Wallace. He's been prosecuting cases for eighteen years, and if he has enough to drink he'll admit that he loves it. He's the number two man in the department, which is the highest nonelected position. That's exactly the way he wants it, since if he were to go any higher he'd have to trade in the courtroom for an executive throne.

From a defense attorney's standpoint, the good news about Wallace is that he doesn't bullshit; you basically know where he stands and why. The bad news about Wallace is he doesn't bullshit, which means you can't expose his bullshit and make him look bad.

My theory about prosecutors is that they are the dishwashers of the legal profession; their main goal is to clean their plates. The problem is that criminals keep dumping more and more food on those plates, and they never can get them clean. But they keep trying, and Wallace is no doubt hoping that I'll help him put the Willie Miller plate in the dishwasher.

We sit down at two-thirty, right on schedule, and by two-thirty-one he has finished chitchatting and made his offer. Willie can plead guilty to murder one and take life without the possibility of parole. "It's an excellent offer," he says with a straight face.

"Wow!" I say. "Life in a shithole cage for the rest of his natural life. He'd have to be crazy not to go for it. Damn, I wish you'd offer it to me. I'd jump at it myself."

"If he doesn't take it, you might as well tell him not to unpack his things. He'll be back on death row before he knows it."

"He won't take it."

Wallace shakes his head as if saddened by my response. "Andy, this trial has already taken place. You've read the transcript; it'll be like putting a tape in a VCR and replaying it."

"You're not allowing for my brilliance."

"Hatchet is not big on your kind of brilliance. He'll cut you up in little pieces and feed you to the bailiffs."

I'm not in the mood to be lectured right now, even if every word he is saying is true. Especially because every word he is saying is true.

"So this is what you asked me to come down here for? Life without parole?"

"That's it. And we'll get killed in the press for that, but we'll have to deal with it."

"You're a regular profile in courage."

He smiles. "That's why I get paid the little bucks."

"This time you're going to have to earn them," I say. "Willie is going to pass on your offer."

He's not surprised by my answer, but he's not pleased that he's still got this dirty plate. "Then I guess I'll see you in court, Counselor," he shrugs.

I growl at him on the way out, as a way of starting the intimidation process, but he's already talking on the phone, so it doesn't seem to have much effect.

Since I have a few hours before meeting Laurie, I go out to the prison to get the conversation with Willie behind me. Behind us.

Willie has been moved off of death row and into maximum security. It is a subtle distinction; you get to trade tension and dread and the stench of death for the right to be surrounded by twice as many murderers and rapists as before. Willie is already a celebrity of sorts, since not too many people come back from the other side. It doesn't seem to have put him in a great mood.

I tell him the offered deal and he tells me to go fuck myself. I realize that he is talking to me as a representative of the system, but I tell him that he shouldn't kill the messenger. He tells me that not only wouldn't he kill the messenger, but he also wouldn't have killed Denise, so he's not pleading guilty.

"Willie, there's a very good chance you're going to lose this trial."

"Why?"

"Look at it this way. Suppose Dinky University's football team goes down to Florida State and gets beat a hundred and ten to nothing. Then somebody says, 'Hey wait a minute, the water boy Florida State used wasn't eligible because his grades are shit and he used too big a bucket.' So they rule that the game doesn't count, and decide to replay it the following week."

"You gonna get to the point before the trial starts?" he asks.

I nod. "When they replay the game, you think Dinky is going to win?"

"That depends," he answers, "on whether Dinky is bringing the same team down there."

"Same team."

"But I ain't going back to trial with the same team. I got me a new coach. You."

"It won't be enough. Dinky is still Dinky. You get Bill Parcells to coach 'em, they're still Dinky." I may be carrying the analogy a bit far, but he's still into it.

"So you're asking me to crash the Dinky team plane before it even gets to Florida. Can't do it, Andy. I'm on that plane."

There is certainly no way I'm going to convince him, and I don't really want to, since I'd probably do the same thing. If I were put in prison without any chance of parole, the first thing I would try to do is kill myself. Might as well let the state do it. Besides, I'm not just doing this for Willie, and I'm not just doing this for me. I'm doing it for good old Dinky U.

I call Nicole and tell her I won't be home until very late, and she's disappointed, because her father is in town for summer recess and wanted to have dinner with us. I tell her that I can't make it, and that she should go with him. I leave out the part about meeting Laurie at an XXX adult movie theater.

• • • • •

DENISE AND EDWARD HAD GONE TO A
movie the night of her murder. In the years since, the theater
they attended has not exactly thrived in the face of competition
from the malls out on the highway. Back then it was called the
Cinema One and showed first-run movies; it is now the Apex,
and tonight is proudly presenting *Hot Lunch* and *The Harder
They Come*. I want to go in so that we can really re-create the
experience of the evening, but Laurie doesn't think it's necessary.

We stand in front of the theater, as Edward and Denise
must have. Just another couple out on a date, except one of
them only had about one hour left to live. Denise isn't here to
tell us about the rest of the evening, so all we have to go by is
Edward's testimony. So far I have no reason to doubt it. At least
not this part of it.

"So they leave here," I say, "just after midnight."

Laurie nods. "And they decide to go for a drink."

I point down the street. "They walk that way, although Edward had parked down there. Which means they didn't just
happen to pass the bar . . . they were intending to go there."

"Edward said it was a bar he used to go to when he was in
college."

Edward had gone to Fairleigh Dickinson University, less

than a mile from where we were standing. I nod. "Care for a drink?"

We walk the three blocks down to the bar. The inside seems to have made the transition from trendy to seedy, and the ten or so patrons do not look as though they're waiting for their book club meeting to start. The television above the pool table is tuned to wrestling, and it has captured the attention of most of the group.

The bartender is a burly guy, about forty, with a friendly but grizzled face. It is as if we called Central Casting and asked them to send us a bartender. He comes over.

"Help ya?" he asks.

I point to the television. "Any chance you can change that to CNN? There's a Donald Rumsfeld press conference coming on."

Laurie and I have developed a strange kind of synchronization between us. As soon as I open my mouth, she starts rolling her eyes. "Don't mind him," she says. "He can't help himself."

The bartender shrugs. "No problem." You would think he hears Donald Rumsfeld jokes every day of his life. He directs his next question at Laurie. "What can I do for you?"

"We're looking for a guy named Donnie Wilson."

"You found him."

Surprised, Laurie says, "The same Donnie Wilson that was working here seven years ago, the night Denise McGregor was murdered?"

He nods. "My career ain't exactly taking off, you know?"

"Do you remember much about that night?" I ask.

"Are you kidding? Like it was yesterday."

This is a mixed blessing. He'll be able to describe to us what happened, but he'll also look credible in front of the jury. When a crime has happened this long ago, one of the things the defense hopes for are faded memories by the key witnesses. This guy thinks it happened yesterday, which is not quite faded enough for our purposes.

I ask him to tell us about that night, and he jumps right into it. "Not much to tell. A preppie guy and a good-looking broad come in . . . didn't look much like they belonged here, but who knows, you know? This place was classier then. Anyway, the broad gets up and goes to the john. I was real busy 'cause Willie, that's the guy that killed her, had taken off an hour before."

"Did you hear a struggle?"

"Nah," he says. "In fact, I didn't even know what happened until the boyfriend told me. Then this older guy showed up. Turns out the preppie called his old man and the cops when he found the broad's body. When the cops showed, the place turned into a zoo."

Laurie leans over to talk to him, as if she had a secret they were about to share. "Listen, Donnie, don't take this the wrong way, but if you call Denise McGregor a broad again, I'm going to cut off your testicles and shove them down your throat."

Ever helpful, I tell Donnie, "I've seen her do it a number of times. It only takes a few seconds."

Donnie has enough sense to be nervous and respectful. "Hey, I didn't mean no offense."

Laurie gives him her sweetest smile. "None taken."

It's now incumbent upon me to get Donnie thinking about the night of the murder, rather than the prospect of swallowing his testicles. It's not an easy job, but I give it a try. "So Denise gets up to make a phone call. The phone is in the ladies' room."

"Right. The ladies' room . . . the ladies' room." Laurie has him unnerved.

"And that's the last time you saw her?"

"Well, I saw her in the alley afterward. You know . . . her body. The woman's body."

Laurie and I go to the ladies' room to check it out, and Donnie is really happy to see us go. The door has a faded drawing of Cleopatra on it, which identifies it as being for ladies. I start to push the door open, but Laurie grabs my arm.

"Where do you think you're going?"

"To check out the room, see where the phone is, solve the crime, whatever."

"Let me make sure it's empty," she says.

I shake my head in mock disgust. "Come on, this is business. Why do you have to turn everything into a sex thing?"

At that moment, even before Laurie has time to tell me what a pig I am, the bathroom door opens. A person comes out; I think it's a woman but I'm just guessing. She's at least two hundred fifty pounds, with tattoos all over her shoulders and arms. If she played for Dinky, we could kick Florida State's ass.

I take a deep breath and wait for my life to stop flashing in front of my eyes. In this case, if Laurie hadn't stopped me, I would have been alone in a bathroom with Queen Kong.

I'm nothing if not a quick learner. "Laurie, maybe you should go see if there's anyone else inside."

"Maybe I should."

Laurie goes inside and comes back out moments later.

"The coast is clear, macho man."

I nod and enter. Except for possibly with my mother when I was too young to remember, this is the first time I have ever been in a ladies' room. It turns out I haven't missed that much.

This particular ladies' room is as unenlightening as it is unimpressive. There had been specks of blood near the telephone, and the police version of the crime was that Denise was struck over the head, and then dragged outside into the alley. Since there was no evidence of sexual molestation, I'm not sure why the assailant didn't kill her right there, but he clearly did not. The blood would have been everywhere.

Laurie and I go out into the alley where the body was found, which is no more than fifteen feet down a hall from the bathroom door. The hall cannot be seen from the main area of the restaurant, so if Denise were unconscious and unable to scream, it makes sense that she and her assailant would not have been noticed. She most likely was unconscious, both because of the blood in the bathroom and the fact that there were marks on the back of her shoes indicating that she was dragged down the hall.

While there is obviously no good place to be brutally murdered, this alley is particularly without dignity. Various establishments throw out their garbage in and around a group of

Dumpsters against the far wall, and there are so many stray animals picking at it that they must be required to make a reservation. "Two rottweiler mixes, table for two? Yes, we're running a little behind. Care to have a drink from the gutter while you wait?"

One of the more puzzling aspects of this is what the eyewitness was doing here in the middle of the night. Willie's lawyer, Hinton, barely touched on this at trial, but then again, he barely touched on anything. He seemed to have no strategy, no coherent focus, and no desire to probe until he found weaknesses in the prosecution's case.

We hang out at the scene for a little while, not saying much, each of us lost in our own thoughts about how horrible that night must have been for Denise McGregor. I try to picture Willie Miller committing this crime, but I can't. I try to picture anybody committing this crime, but I still can't.

I drive Laurie back to the office, since that is where she left her car. She mentions the photograph, and I realize I haven't thought about it all day. I'm having lunch the next day at Philip Gant's club. He had called and invited me, saying that he wanted to "catch up," but really wanting to know how things are between Nicole and me. I'll take advantage of the situation to ask him about the photograph. I'll do this because I need to find out information about rich people, and Philip is the proverbial horse's mouth.

Nicole is asleep when I get home, and I realize with a flash of guilt that I'm glad about that. I need to get the upcoming days straightened out in my mind, so that events don't just whiz past me. I want to be alone with a glass of wine and Tara, not necessarily in that order.

As I sit sipping the wine, I reflect for the fifty millionth time on the fact that I discovered Tara in an animal shelter. She was two years old and had been abandoned there by an owner who was moving and had no room for her. She was going to be killed—"put down" is the term shelters use—and I adopted her on her last day.

I don't care if those people were moving to a phone booth; they should have made room for Tara. What they deserve for almost causing her death is to be put in a cell next to Willie Miller. But, of course, I'm glad they didn't keep her, since if they had I wouldn't be sipping wine and petting her. Life for Tara is extraordinarily simple; she wants to be with me and have me pet her head and scratch her stomach. Experiencing that simplicity helps me right now.

I plan my strategy, legal and personal, for about an hour, and then I fall asleep in mid-scratch. I'm in the same position two hours later when the phone rings. It's the warden's office at the prison, informing me that Willie Miller has been attacked by two knife-wielding inmates and is in the prison hospital.

I briefly consider whether to call Laurie and tell her what's going on, but decide against it. It would not serve any useful function other than to provide company and a slight easing of my discomfort at having to drive to the prison at three o'clock in the morning. I'm going to be a big boy and do this on my own.

A guard meets me at the main gate and takes me to the prison hospital. He does not know Willie's condition, and unless I am a terrible judge of human behavior, he couldn't care less.

He brings me to Willie's room and leaves me there to fend for myself. The room is darkened and Willie is asleep, so I find myself standing there, unsure what to do. I don't want to wake him; he might be badly injured and very weak. On the other hand, I don't want to spend the entire night waiting for him to wake up.

"What the hell you looking at?" It's Willie's voice, but in the darkness I can't see his lips move.

"Willie?" I ask. It's a short, dumb question, followed by another. "Are you awake?"

"Shit, yeah. You think you can sneak up on me in the dark? 'Cause there's two guys down the hall that thought they could sneak up on me too."

"Are you hurt badly?" I ask.

"Nah, just a few slices on the arm."

He proceeds to tell me that two men approached him in the rec room and attacked him with sharpened kitchen utensils. They were unaware, as I was as well, that Willie is a black belt in karate. Within moments they were unconscious, and Willie had only a few minor cuts to show for his troubles.

I'm upset that Willie had to go through this, which makes me the only one in the room who feels that way. Willie is positively giddy.

"Man, that was the most fun I've had in seven years," he says, cackling with laughter. "Those guys thought I was dead meat. You should have seen what I did to them. They had to get them off the floor with a shovel."

"I'm glad you had such a good time," I say. "It's really brightened my night as well."

The sarcasm is pretty much lost on Willie. As I'm leaving, he says, "And I've got you to thank, man."

I stop at the door. "How's that?"

"They mentioned your name. Said they were going after me 'cause you don't know when to lay off. That was just before I busted 'em up."

This takes me by surprise. "You mean they went after you for a reason? It wasn't just a random attack?"

Willie laughs at my prison naïveté. "Random attack? There ain't no such thing in here, man. Nope, whoever sent them had a reason, and I'll bet he paid big bucks to get it done. You must be gettin' somewhere, man."

I don't think I'll share this with Willie, but the only thing I'm getting is confused. Somebody tried to have Willie killed because I am uncovering something. I see three minor problems with that: I don't know who that somebody could be, I don't know why they would go after Willie, and I've uncovered absolutely nothing.

I offer to have Willie moved into solitary confinement for his own protection, but he acts as if I am trying to steal his bicycle. He promises he can take care of himself, which seems to be a promise he can keep.

I head home for a restful three hours sleep, knowing full well that I'll be just as confused in the morning.

• • • • •

KEVIN IS WAITING FOR ME AND CHOMPING ON

his second raspberry turnover when I arrive at the office in the morning. Edna has already drawn him into her morning crossword puzzle, and is showing off her skills. He is suitably impressed, as she knew he would be. I hear her tell him that he has a flair for crosswords; she says it in an offhanded way, like Joe DiMaggio might have said to a rookie, "Nice arm, kid."

I like Kevin's style. When his mouth is not too full of food to talk, he's got a dry sense of humor, but a straightforward way of working. His work style on this case is simple and as advertised; he wants me to give him assignments and he'll accomplish them to the best of his ability. Based on this experience, if I were running a big firm, I would do all my recruiting at Laundromats. The first task I give Kevin is to prepare a motion for change of venue.

Change of venue motions almost never succeed, and they almost never should. If the publicity around a crime is so intense as to make it impossible to empanel an impartial jury, then that publicity is rarely localized. Judges recognize this, and since they are naturally protective of their own turf anyway, they almost always deny the motion.

My reason for requesting the change in this instance has more to do with Hatchet than with the community. I would love to get Hatchet off the case, but I have no grounds on which to so move. If I tried, it would get me nowhere and would most likely piss him off. Requesting the venue change represents a way to remove him, without directly identifying him as the reason.

Kevin outlines for me what his argument will be, and it is a solid one. Willie's case did not get particularly intense media coverage at the time, so at this late date its awareness level in other communities would not be great. However, local people have heard of it, and more importantly they are aware that a jury convicted Willie the first time. The prosecution has already made its case to the local media that the trial was overturned on a technicality, leaving Willie with a presumption of guilt in the minds of potential jurors.

Kevin has also managed to acquire specific, detailed information showing how much attention the media has devoted to this case, and it demonstrates that the recent coverage has been almost entirely local. It is a good argument, Kevin will make it persuasively, and we will lose.

I'm exhausted from last night, and I'd love to cancel lunch with Philip. The problem is that nobody cancels lunch with Philip. So I head out to meet him at the Westmount Tennis Club in Demarest. It's a twenty-minute drive from my office, but for all intents and purposes it's in another world. There are thirty-eight courts, a mixture of hard surface, clay, and grass. The place is perfectly landscaped on seventy-one acres, has three gorgeous swimming pools, a world-class restaurant, killer daiquiris, and ballboys on every court. It also, as far as I can tell, has a membership that does not include a single decent tennis player.

Philip is sitting in the lounge, picking at a fruit plate, when I arrive. He seems pleased to see me, and introduces me to the assortment of rich people within introducing range. I briefly wonder how many of them have less money than I do, and I figure I'm only in the middle of the pack. Just wait until I get my fee from the Willie Miller case.

We engage in meaningless chitchat until we finish lunch, at which point I take out the picture and ask Philip if he recognizes any of the men. He initially only recognizes my father, so I mention Markham and Brownfield. He has spent time with both men on a number of occasions, and while these are much younger versions, he does think it could be them, though he's far from sure.

"Why is this important to you, Andy?"

I tell him about the money, which he's already heard about from Nicole, and how the picture may well be related to that. I tell him I'm interested because Markham and Brownfield denied it so hard. What I don't tell him is the main reason, that I need to learn about my father in death what I obviously never knew in life. To voice this would seem somehow like a betrayal of my father, and I'm not about to come close to that with Philip.

"So how can I help you?" he asks.

"Well, with your connections in the business community, and your access to information . . ."

"You want me to check out Brownfield?"

I nod. "And maybe learn something about what he and Markham were doing thirty-five years ago. See if there was a connection between them."

"Or with your father?"

There's no way around it. "Or with my father."

He promises he'll do what he can, and I have no doubt that he will. Then he gets down to his own agenda for the meeting.

"How are things with Nicole?"

"Good. Really good." I say this with sincerity, and in fact it may be true. Of course, if Nicole had attacked me the night before with a meat cleaver, I still would have told Philip, "Good. Really good."

He's pleased; this obviously confirms what Nicole had told him last night. "Excellent," he says. "I'd hate to have to break in another son-in-law."

He asks if I have time for a cup of coffee, and I tell him that I don't. I thank him for his help, and then I say something I probably shouldn't say to my father-in-law.

"I've got to take care of a hooker."

Philip asks me what the hell I am talking about, which forces me to stay there another five minutes as I explain about Wanda, Cal's daughter. But I finally get away so that I can drive to court to deal with Wanda's case. This seems like a particularly appropriate time to indulge my superstition, and I stop off at Cal's newsstand on the way. It is closed for the first time in my memory. I assume that Cal is going to be at court supporting his daughter.

I arrive at the court and arrange to meet Wanda in an anteroom. When I walk in, she is sitting at a table. She's all of sixteen, with a face at least ten years older and sadder. The sight of her jolts me.

There is one thing that virtually all of my clients bring to our first meetings . . . the look of fear. All but the most hardened criminals are genuinely afraid of the process they are about to go through, knowing full well that it can end with them being locked in a steel cage. Many of them feign a lack of concern, but if you look deep into their eyes, you can see the fear. In a weird way it's one of the things that I like about my job; if I do it well I take away the fear.

That fear is not present in Wanda. Her eyes tell me that this is a piece of cake for her, that she's faced much worse. Her eyes scare the hell out of me.

When I enter, Wanda looks at me as if a gnat had flown in through an open window.

"Wanda?"

"Yeah."

"My name's Andy Carpenter. I'm a friend of your father. He's hired me to represent you."

Wanda doesn't seem to consider this worthy of a reply. I clearly haven't charmed her yet.

"Is he coming today?"

"Who?" she asks.

"Your father."

She laughs a short, humorless laugh, which unnerves me a little more. "No, I don't think so." And then she laughs again.

I explain to her that I am her attorney, and I detail the charges facing her. She takes it in with a minimum of reaction, as if she's heard it all many times before. I don't think Cal's daughter is a virgin.

"Any questions so far?"

"How long is this going to take?"

"Not very long. An agreement has been reached already. You just have to show some contrition, and—"

She interrupts me. "I've got to show some *what?*"

"Contrition. It means you have to say you're sorry. Just tell the judge you're sorry and you won't do it again."

"Okay."

"And Wanda, when you say it . . . mean it."

She nods an unconvincing nod. I tell her that we're fourth on the docket, and she should be called in about an hour. She frowns and looks at her watch, as if she has theater tickets and is in danger of missing the overture.

I leave the room wondering how a father can be so blind as to not realize what his child has become. I feel sorry for Cal because getting Wanda out of this is not going to come close to turning her life around. And I feel sorry for Wanda, because she's never going to put on a corsage and go to the prom.

The county is considerate enough to provide defense attorneys with small offices in the courthouse so that we can productively pass the time while waiting for the wheels of justice to ponderously come around to us. I head for the office assigned to me, which is on the third floor.

When I get off the elevator, I run into Lynn Carmody, a court reporter for the *Bergen Record*. She tells me that she has been waiting for me, and asks if I've got some time to talk. I say that I do, since I've been planning to start speaking to the press about our side of the Willie Miller case anyway. I invite her into the office, stopping off at a vending machine to get some absolutely undrinkable coffee.

I've never really had a problem with reporters. I treat them as human beings, not as objects to be manipulated. I find I can manipulate them better that way. I've long ago learned that in dealing with the press, sincerity is the most important quality you can have. If you can fake sincerity, you've got it made.

Lynn is a particularly good reporter. She's been covering

the courthouse beat for almost fifteen years, without aspirations of going anywhere else. She recognizes the incredible human drama that takes place in courtrooms every day, and enjoys conveying that emotion to her readers. She and I get along pretty well, because we understand each other. She knows I will only tell her that which will further my agenda, and she'll do the same.

I'm not really sure what to tell her about Willie, so I mouth platitudes about our confidence at trial, hinting at new evidence by talking about how different this trial will be from the first one. The strange thing is that I don't have to answer a bunch of penetrating questions about the case, since she doesn't seem terribly interested in it.

Lynn asks as many questions about the reason I am here today as she does about the Miller case. I tell her about Wanda, though I leave out my connection to her through Cal. He doesn't need his name dragged through the papers, though I can't imagine why Lynn would want to write about this anyway. She asks me if she can go with me downstairs when Wanda's case is brought up, and I shrug and say that it's fine with me. She's obviously a courtroom junkie.

The call comes moments later, and Lynn and I go downstairs. We enter the courtroom, and I'm surprised by the number of press in attendance. Obviously there is a case after mine that has some public interest, and I consider the possibility of hanging out afterward to lobby the assembled reporters about Willie's prospects. I just wish I had a more compelling story to tell.

On the way down to the defense table, I pass Alex, who has been the bailiff here since the fourteenth century. Alex looks twenty years older than his seventy-one years. In this courthouse, the metal detectors are the first and last line of defense; it the bad guys get to Alex they win.

"Big case today, Alex? The press is out in force."

He turns around in surprise, as if he hadn't noticed them. The Russian army could sneak up on Alex. He shrugs. "Beats me. I ain't never seen that many of them here before."

I take my seat at the table, while Judge Walling finishes up a misdemeanor drug possession case. Walling is sixty-two years old, and is staggering toward retirement the way a once-a-year marathoner staggers toward the finish line. He is all but sleeping through this case, and I doubt that Wanda and I will provide him any more substantial stimulation.

Wanda's prosecutor, Barry Mullins, comes over to say hello and to go over the final arrangements for the plea. Wanda will plead no contest, Walling will lecture her on the evils of her ways, and she'll get two years probation. If she stays clean, it'll come off her record. My initial assessment is that she won't and it won't.

In any event, it's all straightforward and has been done a million times before; it is a safe bet that no future attorneys will be citing *New Jersey v. Morris* as precedent-setting law.

Finally, Wanda is brought in and our case is called. Wanda is no more friendly or animated than she was before, and she's also no more nervous.

Without looking up, Walling asks if the state is ready to proceed. "Yes, Your Honor," says Mullins.

"And the defense?"

"We are, Your Honor," I intone.

For the first time, Walling looks up, taking off his glasses so that he can see me. He seems surprised.

"Well, Mr. Carpenter, this is an unusual type of case for you to be involved with."

I bow slightly. "A return to my humble roots, Your Honor."

I sense something and turn around. The press has moved forward, en masse, apparently interested in this exchange. I'm glad my retort was characteristically clever.

Mullins, less concerned with putting on a show, gets to the point. "Your Honor, Ms. Morris was arrested on May 15 of this year for soliciting a police officer. The District Attorney's office and counsel for the defendant have agreed to probation in this case, if it pleases the court."

Judge Walling examines the papers before him, as if deciding whether he will go along with this arrangement. Waiting for his decision is not exactly nail-biting time. He's probably had this kind of case brought before him ten thousand times, and it's safe to say that the next plea bargain he refuses to accept will be the first.

When he's finished, he removes his glasses and looks at Wanda, catching her in mid-yawn. "Young lady, do you know what is going on here?"

"Yeah, I'm getting off." Good old Wanda, she must have been valedictorian of her charm school graduating class.

Walling isn't pleased by her answer or her demeanor. "You are possibly being put on probation. There is a difference." He looks at me. "Which I hope Mr. Carpenter has explained to you."

I nod. "In excruciating detail, Your Honor."

Walling turns back to Wanda. "You understand the difference?"

"Yeah."

"You will be expected to find proper employment, and to refrain from future actions of this kind."

Wanda jerks her thumb in my direction. "Tell *him* that, not me."

She is now officially getting on my nerves, and I think Walling's as well. He asks her, "Why should I tell Mr. Carpenter that?"

" 'Cause he's my pimp."

It takes a split second for the meaning of what she has said to penetrate. However, it doesn't take the press quite that long. There is an immediate uproar among them; and I realize in a horrifying flash that they have been primed for this.

Walling pounds his gavel to get quiet. "What did you say?" he asks.

"I said, he's my pimp." Then she looks at me, a puzzled expression on her face. "I thought they knew that."

Walling turns to me. "Mr. Carpenter, do you have any comment on your client's contention?"

I've been set up. I don't know why, or by whom, and I can't believe that Cal would do this to me.

"Your Honor, she clearly is using a different definition of pimp, from the Latin *pimpius*, meaning 'to represent.' " I'm floundering and trying to use humor to defuse the disaster. But Wanda will have none of it.

"He keeps me and a bunch of other girls out on the street. We pay him part of what we take in."

Walling turns to me. He's having so much fun I can see him reconsidering retirement. "Well, Mr. Carpenter, sounds like Webster's definition to me."

Before I can respond, Wanda drops another bomb. "And he gets free blow jobs whenever he wants."

The press is going berserk, laughing and cheering as if they are in a nightclub. I try and compose myself.

"Your Honor, this is bizarre. Ms. Morris's father is a friend of mine, and he called me, asked me to help his daughter. I have never met her before today."

Wanda cuts in with the crusher. "My real name ain't Morris, and my father's been dead for ten years."

Walling almost gleefully turns to me. "Mr. Carpenter?"

I look at Wanda, then at the hysterical reporters, then back to Walling.

"The defense rests," I say.

It goes downhill from there. With an accusation like this taking place in open court, Walling is obligated to turn the matter over to the District Attorney for investigation. A hearing is set for two months from now to hear the results of that investigation, and Wanda is directed to appear. She says that she will, but she won't. This was her closing performance.

When I finally get out of the courtroom, I run into Lynn Carmody. She tries to stop giggling long enough to talk to me. It's going to take a while, so I walk past her. She turns and walks with me, finally controlling her laughter.

"I'm sorry, I just couldn't tell you."

I stop and turn toward her. "So you knew about this?"

She nods. "My colleagues would have killed me if I tipped you off."

"Who set me up?"

"I don't have any idea." She holds up her hand as if taking an oath. "Honestly, I don't."

I believe her. If she were protecting a source she'd say she's protecting a source.

"And you're going to print the story?" I ask.

"Andy, are you kidding? It'll be page one."

I just shake my head and walk away, and she calls after me to tell me that if I find out how this happened, I should tell her and she'll print that also. Somehow I don't find this all that comforting.

I leave the courthouse and stop at the newsstand. It's still closed, and I have this unsettling feeling that it is never going to open again. What the hell happened to Cal Morris?

The next morning I get to the office and experience a first: Edna has the newspaper opened to other than the crossword page. Actually, the paper isn't really open at all, since Edna, Laurie, and Kevin are all looking at the front page. I don't want to look at it, but I can't help myself. There's a picture of Wanda and me, with the headline "A Different Kind of Client?"

I moan, and Edna tries to make me feel better by telling me that it's a good picture, that it makes me look like a slightly fatter version of her Uncle Sidney. Laurie chimes in with the revelation that she has been around a long time, and she's never seen a better looking pimp. I smile and try to seem good-natured about it all. I have as good a sense of humor as the next guy, but I generally prefer it when the joke is on the next guy.

This is disturbing on a level beyond the total public humiliation. Somebody has gone to an incredible amount of trouble to do this to me, and has demonstrated remarkable power in the process. If I'm right, they have even made a person, Cal, disappear. I don't think Cal even has a daughter, and if he did Wanda certainly isn't her. He was either frightened into doing this or paid off; this was no minor prank to embarrass me. This was designed to impress me with strength. It wasn't a severed horse's head in my bed, but it did the trick.

Once my staff finishes giggling, we kick around the possibilities. I come to believe Cal was paid off, and I further believe it would have taken serious money to do it. Since Laurie and I have been prying into the lives of Markham and Brownfield, people with very serious money, there seems a possibility that one or both of them are involved.

It's a long-shot hunch, but my instinct says I'm right. Representing the opposing view are Laurie and Kevin, who say I'm nuts. I hope they're right, because if they're not, then my father was somehow involved in something so bad that these people are desperate to conceal it.

After half an hour of unproductively debating all of this, Laurie offers to try and find Cal. I tell her that I will want her to do that, but not now. Now we have to focus all our attention on Willie Miller.

Kevin's brief on the change of venue is thoroughly professional and well reasoned. I make one or two nitpick changes, wipe off a couple of mustard stains, and then instruct him to file it with Hatchet. I also assign him to deal with the DA's office on all discovery matters. It's only been a couple of days, but I already have the confidence that I can turn something over to him knowing it will be done. It's a nice feeling.

Laurie reports on her progress, which is less favorable. I expected this; when a murder was committed this long ago there's little likelihood of turning up much new. More disturbing is her inability to find Willie's lawyer, Robert Hinton. His elusiveness is puzzling. Lawyers generally don't like to disappear; it causes them to have trouble attracting new clients.

Laurie is going to redouble her efforts to find Hinton, as well as arrange to interview the eyewitness whose testimony helped to bury Willie in the first trial. She's also recruited a DNA expert for us to possibly use to rebut the state's evidence, or to help us prevent it getting in. Like the change of venue and just about everything else involved with the case, it's pretty much a lost cause, but I agree to see him at three o'clock this afternoon.

We're wrapping things up when the phone rings. Edna, despite having been told not to interrupt us, does so anyway.

"I think you'll want to take this," she says.

"Who is it?"

"It's your wife. It sounds like an emergency."

I pick up the phone and conduct a ten-second conversa-

tion during which Nicole tells me what has happened. I hang
up and start walking toward the door.

"Is everything okay?" Laurie asks.

I tell her. "Nicole found a threatening message on the
downstairs answering machine."

"What did it say?"

I shake my head. "I don't know yet. But whatever it says,
that's not the worst part."

"What's the worst part?"

"We don't have a downstairs answering machine."

I make it home in record time. Nicole was borderline hysterical when I spoke to her, and she's not likely to have calmed
down before I get there. She's also not likely to calm down
after I get there.

I pull up to the house, and I see that she is peeking out
from behind the drapes, watching for me. She opens the door
and leads me to the answering machine, which is hooked up
in the den. It is not a machine I have ever seen before.

So as not to smudge any fingerprints, and so I could appear
to know what I'm doing, I use the point of a pen to press play.
The voice is computer-generated, effectively concealing the
speaker.

"Think of your embarrassment in court as just the beginning . . . a small sign of our power. We are bigger than you,
Carpenter . . . much bigger. We can do what we want . . . when
we want. So drop your crusade, before it is too late. The past
is past."

Nicole looks at me, as if I can say something that will take
away her fear. Something like, "Oh, is that all? Don't worry. I
had told a friend he could break into the house and drop off
a threatening answering machine."

She sees I have nothing comforting to offer, so she says,
with great drama, "Andy, they were in here. While we were
sleeping. They were in our house."

My mind flashes to Michael Corleone, speaking to Pentan-
geli after gunmen shot up his house. "In my bedroom, where
my wife sleeps! Where my children come to play with their
toys!"

I decide not to mention the *Godfather* reference to Nicole. Instead I ask, "Did you check the doors and windows?"

"No, I didn't," she says before she explodes. "I'm not a policeman, Andy. I don't want this to happen in my house!"

"Of course you don't, Nicole, and neither do I. But . . ."

She's now more under control, but with an intensity in her voice that I don't think I have ever heard. It strikes me that I've never seen Nicole afraid. She did not grow up in a world where she ever had reason to be afraid.

"I do not want the awful people that you deal with in my life. Not the murderers, not the prostitutes, nor the other animals. I don't want it and I don't deserve it."

"We don't know who did this. Or why."

She shakes her head; as if I'm not getting it. "That doesn't matter. What matters is that it does not happen again."

I start looking around, but I can't imagine that I'm going to find a clue. Tara sniffs around with me, though if she were going to be active in the case I would have preferred that she had barked during the break-in. My mind starts trying to put it all together: the debacle in the courthouse, the picture, the twenty-two million dollars, the attack on Willie Miller, the trial . . . somewhere in there is the answer, but I'll be damned if I know where.

I'm now talking out loud, but to myself. "It's all blending together."

"What?"

I tell Nicole, "All the various elements, the photograph . . . the trial. It's like they're pieces of the same puzzle. But it doesn't make sense. How the hell could a picture my father took thirty-five years ago have anything to do with Willie Miller?"

"Whatever it is, it's not worth it. These people are dangerous. Andy, we don't need this."

She's right, of course, but after all these years living with me, does she really think I can just drop it? Could she not know me at all?

"It might be a good idea for you to get away for a while."

"Where to?"

"I don't know . . . one of your father's homes. Cannes, Gstaad, Aspen . . . pick a home, any home."

"Why? Because you're afraid for me? Because you're not going to stop what you're doing? Because you're going to be a martyr? Because you're a bullheaded son of a bitch?"

"E. All of the above."

She makes her decision. "No, Andy, I'm not leaving. I'm not the one who caused this problem, and I'm not the one who has to fix it."

• • • • •

I HATE DNA MORE THAN I HATE OPERA. I HATE IT more than I hate lizards. I hate DNA more than I hate meaningless touchdowns by the underdog that cover the spread when I'm betting the favorite. I recognize that it is the greatest invention since fingerprints, and that it is an incredibly valuable tool to help justice to be served, but none of that carries any weight with me. I hate DNA because it's boring, because I will never understand it, and because it almost always works against me.

My meeting this afternoon is with Dr. Gerald Lampley, a part-time professor of chemistry at William Paterson College. Dr. Lampley used to be a full-time professor, a career which lasted until the justice system discovered DNA.

Once the people in criminal justice start using something, they need experts to explain that something to them. They pay those experts very well, hence Dr. Lampley's sudden loss of his burning desire to teach chemistry to college kids. And it's certainly not just DNA. There are people out there making a fortune because they understand and can explain to a jury how and why blood spatters. It's a crazy world we live in.

Experts generally testify for the same side each time, and Dr. Lampley is known as a defense witness. In other words, he tends to testify that DNA, his area of expertise, is unreliable. He doesn't take the position that the science is bogus, of course, since if he ever convinced the justice system of that he'd be back teaching chemistry full-time. So Dr. Lampley confines himself to testifying that the DNA is unreliable in the specific case at trial.

Dr. Lampley has had time to read the prosecution's brief on their intentions regarding DNA in the Willie Miller case. They are planning to use a new type of test, in addition to the PCR and RFLP tests they have been using. I ask Dr. Lampley in what way this new test is supposed to be better.

"The government claims that it is considerably more accurate." He says "the government" as if he is talking about the Führer and his henchmen.

I ask him to explain, and he tells me that if this new test turns up Willie Miller as a match, it would be a one in six billion chance that it is wrong. The old tests are down around one in three billion.

It would be amusing if it weren't so depressing. "One in three billion isn't enough for them?"

"The goal of science and scientists is to strive for absolute certainty."

The basic issue here is whether or not we want to ask Hatchet for a Kelly-Frye hearing. Such a hearing would determine whether this new test is reliable enough to present to a jury. The earlier type of tests do not require such a hearing, since they've had Kelly-Fryes in the past, so Hatchet has his ass covered when he admits those tests as evidence.

A Kelly-Frye hearing takes the form of seven to ten days of excruciatingly boring and detailed testimony by scientists. They might as well be speaking Swahili, since the people listening are lawyers and a judge, none of whom have the slightest idea what the scientists are talking about. But the lawyers lawyer, and the judge judges, and the prosecution wins.

Five minutes into our conversation I make my decision about the Kelly-Frye: I'm not going to request it. We would lose anyway and it would be a total waste of time, but that's not why I'm not seeking it. If we ultimately lose the trial, and Willie is sentenced to death, I want to give his future lawyer an appeal based on the fact that his idiot lawyer Andy Carpenter never even asked for a Kelly-Frye hearing.

I'm more interested in talking to Dr. Lampley about the evidence collection in this case. It is in this area that DNA can often be attacked, and a case like this provides more opportunity than most. The evidence was collected at a time when DNA was in its relative infancy, and less sophisticated collection techniques were used. If we can show that this collection was faulty, then the results are useless to the prosecution.

Dr. Lampley agrees to study the case and the police work involved. This is not a particularly generous offer, since he's charging us three hundred an hour, but I agree. I don't tell him yet that I'm not going for the Kelly-Frye, since I'm pretty sure that would dampen his enthusiasm. With preparation and presentation, the Kelly-Frye would be worth twenty grand to him. It beats the hell out of grading final exams.

With the boring torture of talking about DNA at least temporarily out of the way, it's time to focus on Willie Miller's story, assuming Willie Miller has a story. I take Kevin and Laurie out to the prison with me, so that they can hear it firsthand.

Willie is already back in the main section, with only a small bandage to show for his fun in the rec room. His eyes almost pop out of his head when he sees Laurie. After I introduce everyone, Willie makes a finger-wagging motion back and forth between Laurie and me and says to me with a lascivious grin, "Uuuhhh . . . you and her?" When he does this, I become an instant proponent of the death penalty.

"Don't start, Willie. We're here to talk about you."

Still eyeing Laurie, he says, "Man, your life is a hell of a lot more interesting than mine."

I finally get him back on track, and we discuss the night of the murder. He thinks he remembers showing up for work that night, but everything after that is an alcohol-induced blank.

"Do you remember when you started to drink?" Laurie asks.

"You mean that night?"

She nods, and he says, "Nope. I wouldn't have, that's what's so weird. But I guess I did, huh?"

"According to the blood tests," I say. "Have you ever had problems with alcohol?"

"Nope."

"How long had you been working at that bar?"

"About six months."

"Any problems before that night? Any incidents? Were you ever reprimanded for anything?"

He shakes his head. "Nope. I did my job and didn't bother nobody."

"What about the needle marks on your arms?"

Willie reacts to this, tensing and flaring up. "I never took no drugs. Never."

This, of course, doesn't make any sense. I saw the marks on the police photographs. "Then where did the marks come from?"

"You know what 'never' means? I *never* took no drugs. I don't know nothin' about no needle marks. Tell them to stop trying to peddle this bullshit, man."

We question Willie for another hour, but it basically gets us nowhere. He never saw Denise McGregor before, has no idea what happened that night, but can't believe that he could have killed someone. It's not exactly a compelling case to present to a jury.

I arrive at home to something less than a standing ovation. Tara seems happy enough to see me, wagging her tail and graciously accepting her evening biscuit. Nicole is somewhat more reserved, having not yet gotten over the answering machine incident. I have to admit that I'm not quite over it either, and I double-check all the doors and windows to make sure they are locked.

We eat in, since Nicole doesn't seem anxious to go to a restaurant with the most famous pimp in New Jersey. That's fine with me, since I've got a briefcaseful of work to do. I'm still doing it at one o'clock when I fall asleep on the couch, Tara's head on my thigh. A boy and his dog.

I take stock of the situation the next morning, and I'm not pleased. I've learned almost nothing to help Willie Miller, and the trial is fast approaching. I also have no idea what secrets lie behind the picture and my father's money, nor do I know why I'm being harassed and threatened. So far, so bad.

The one germ of a clue so far is Vince Sanders's mini-revelation that Denise was working on something secretive and exciting to her when she was killed, and that for the first time in her career seemingly didn't take notes. It's not a stunner, but it is interesting and probably worth checking out further. At least until something better comes along.

I go back to Vince Sanders's office, not bothering to stop at the reception desk since I now know the way. I enter through the open door and find Vince throwing paper airplanes into a wastepaper basket. I should teach this guy sock basketball.

"A dedicated journalist," I marvel, "working tirelessly to preserve the people's right to know."

He keeps throwing the planes. "Next to the right to hire a hooker, it's one of our most sacred traditions."

"You know that was a setup," I lamely respond. "I thought I was helping out a friend."

"Really? That's too bad. It made a good story. Sold a lot of newspapers."

"You are a media leech."

He nods. "Always have been. Always will be. By the way, could you get me a pair of twenty-one-year-old coed twin hookers for tonight? Figure about ten o'clock?"

"No problem. I'll take care of it."

"Great. And tell them to call me Lord Sanders. No, change that. Dress them in Indian outfits and name them Little Feather and Babbling Brook."

"Okay."

"And tell them to call me Chief Broken Rubber."

"Done. Now you owe me one."

I take out my father's picture and put it on the desk. "Let's start with this."

"What about it?" he asks.

I point to my father. "That's my father almost forty years ago. I want to know who the other three are."

He looks at it for a moment. "No sweat. We'll just run it through our super-duper face computer."

"This is important," I tell him. "If my hunch is right, it might even have something to do with Denise's murder."

He stares at me for a few moments. "I think you're just about the dumbest pimp I've ever met."

"Thanks for your support."

I prepare to cajole him to use his sources to check into this further, but I don't have to, since he looks at the picture again and points to the fourth person.

"You know, that guy looks real familiar."

"Who is it?"

He doesn't answer, just goes to the intercom and presses the button. A female voice asks what he wants.

"Ask Carl to come in, will you?" Then, to me, "Carl will know for sure."

There's no sense asking Vince who he thinks it is, since Carl's on the way in anyway, and Carl will "know for sure."

Carl comes in. He's in his late fifties and wears a suit and tie. Isn't anybody in the newspaper business ink-stained anymore?

Vince doesn't bother to introduce me, and Carl doesn't seem to notice I'm even there. Vince hands him the picture.

"Does this guy look familiar to you?" He doesn't even have to tell him which guy he's talking about.

Carl takes out a pair of glasses thicker than the Hubble Telescope. He puts them on and peers at the picture for no more than three seconds.

"He should. I used to work for him. That's Mike Anthony."

Vince smiles at me triumphantly. "I told you so."

"Who's Mike Anthony?" I ask.

Vince says, "He used to be an editor at a small paper in Essex County. Let me tell you something, he was a little nuts, but one hell of a newspaperman."

Carl nods his agreement. "One of the best."

"Is he retired? Where can I find him now?" I ask hopefully.

Vince says, "At that great newsroom in the sky."

"Dead?" Why can't we catch a break?

Carl jumps in. "He committed suicide. I think we ran the piece maybe six, seven years ago."

I look to Vince to understand what piece Carl is talking about. He explains. "Carl runs the obit page. We write them and hold 'em until the person kicks off. Wanna read yours?"

"No, thanks," I say.

Carl says, "Are you sure? I'm working on it today anyway. I'm adding the pimp thing as the lead."

"Turns out he denies it," Vince says.

"Lucky I don't have to include the denial. Dead guys don't sue much."

Carl laughs at his joke and leaves. I can still hear him laughing as he walks down the hall. I'm glad that my pain can bring some joy into his life.

I ask Vince where I can find Denise McGregor's family, on the off chance that they can tell me something. That's if they agree to talk to the scumbag representing their daughter's killer.

"I think her father lived in South Jersey somewhere; I should be able to get you the address from personnel. I don't think she ever mentioned her mother."

"Is her father still alive?"

"I don't know, but . . ." He seems to drift off, lost in thought.

"But what?"

He says, "Maybe it's a coincidence, but I remember Denise asking me a bunch of questions about Mike Anthony. At the time I figured he had offered her a better job, and she was checking him out, deciding whether to take it."

"Was it around the time that she died?"

He nods. "I think so."

I pump him for a while, trying to get more information, but he doesn't have any more memory to jog. I feel like he's given me a major piece of the puzzle, though I'm still not sure how it fits in. But one thing I'll bet on: Denise sure as hell *was* checking out Mike Anthony. It is the first factual link between the Willie Miller trial and the photograph. It confirms my instincts, which doesn't make me feel that great, since I still have no idea what the hell is going on. But the more I learn, the stronger my hunch gets that the people in the photograph are somehow related to Denise's death.

Before I leave, Vince gets me the address where Denise's father lived when she worked there, as well as copies of every story she wrote in the year before her death.

"Thanks," I say. "I owe you."

Vince tells me that if I can get the coed twins to sing the naked version of the Doublemint jingle, then we're even. He also says that he's got a feeling I'm on the right track, and he'll help in any way he can. I thank him without mentioning that I'm nowhere near the right track.

As I leave, I run into Laurie in the parking lot. My keen lawyerly mind has a feeling that this is not a coincidence.

She confirms it. "I'm glad I caught you."

"What's up?"

"I've been tracking down Hinton . . . Willie's lawyer."

"You find him?"

"In a manner of speaking," she says.

"Are we in a cryptic mood today?"

"The bar association doesn't have any record of him, he's never tried a case anywhere except for Willie Miller's, and he never graduated from a law school, at least not in this country."

"Are you telling me that Willie's lawyer never existed?"

"I'm telling you Willie's lawyer wasn't a lawyer."

This is stunning news, and in a way it's embarrassing. A revelation like this would obviously have been a slam dunk for getting a new trial, yet Willie's crack new lawyer, Andy Carpenter, never tracked this down until now. Had Willie not gotten the okay from the Court of Appeals on the juror misconduct, it would never have come out at all and he would have been put to death.

The next, more important question that comes to mind is: How did Willie wind up with Hinton? That and answers to other questions can only come from Willie.

"Come on, let's go see Willie."

"I can't," Laurie says. "I've got a lunch date."

I do a double take as I'm already starting toward my car. I

turn and for the first time notice that there is somebody in Laurie's car. Somebody that's male and good-looking, if you like the tall, well-built, and handsome type. Personally, I don't.

"With him?"

She nods. "With him."

"He looks familiar."

"His name is Bobby Radburn. You may have seen him on television. He pitches for the Yankees."

I would have much preferred she hit me on the head with a two-by-four, and for that matter so would she.

"I know who he pitches for. He's not even in the starting rotation." That'll teach her.

"It's only a matter of time," she says. "He's incredibly athletic. You want to meet him? I can get you his autograph." She's loving this.

"No thanks."

She nods. "Then I'll see you back at the office later."

I take one more stab. "You'd rather have lunch with a guy who has a pitiful strikeout-to-walk ratio than visit a maximum security prison?"

"That's a tough call," she says. "I'll think about it over lunch."

• • • • •

BEFORE I DRIVE OUT TO THE PRISON, I CALL
Richard Wallace to arrange a meeting. He tells me he's got a few
minutes and that I should come right over, that he had been
planning to call me as well. It's nice to be wanted.

When I arrive I get right to the point. I tell him about Hinton
not being a lawyer, and watch his reaction. He seems genuinely
surprised, and can't imagine how that could have happened. He
promises to check into it, and I tell him that this is evidence of
what I see as a conspiracy to convict a totally innocent Willie Miller.

He smiles. "What this is, if it's true, is a clear ground for getting a new trial. But you've already got the new trial, Andy.
And Miller already has a new lawyer."

"The system has failed Willie Miller. It railroaded him by ap-
proving a fraud and letting Hinton represent him. For all I
know the court may have appointed him; Willie didn't exactly
have a legal defense fund."

"So?"

"So I'm going to move for a dismissal and then I'm going
to sue the state for ten million dollars."

He laughs. "You want cash or a check?" He is unfazed, and
though it annoys me, I can't say as I blame him. We both know
I'm not going to get the dismissal.

Wallace then reveals why he had been calling me. He's

being pressured from above to reach a plea bargain, though he seems confused as to why. My hunch is that Markham and/or Brownfield are using their clout to lean on Wallace's boss, but I'll never be able to prove that.

Wallace's new offer is forty to life, with the possibility of parole in twenty-five years. Willie would be fifty-three before he'd have a chance of getting out. It's still terrible, but it's a lot better than life without parole or a needle in the arm.

I don't think Willie will take it, but it's his decision, and that's what I tell Wallace. He tells me that even though he had to offer it, he hopes Willie won't take it. Wallace believes that anyone who could slaughter Denise McGregor like that doesn't deserve to ever again taste freedom. On that we agree.

I promise to talk to Willie, and I leave to make the drive out to the prison to see him. I ask him where he found Hinton.

"Where did I get my lawyer? Where do you think I got him? From the fucking lawyer fairy?"

"If I knew where you got him, I wouldn't ask. So don't bust my chops, okay?"

He can tell that I'm annoyed, and he doesn't want to piss me off further. I'm the only lawyer he has; in fact I now know that I'm the only lawyer he's ever had.

"The court assigned the asshole to me."

"Are you sure?"

"That's what he told me. You think I had the cash to go out and interview lawyers?"

"*He* told you?"

Willie nods. "He did. He bullshitting me?"

I confirm that Hinton was indeed bullshitting him. Willie asks the obvious question. "Why would he want to be my lawyer if he wasn't getting paid?"

I evade the question, but the answer is pretty well set in my mind. Somebody else was paying Hinton. Somebody who wanted Willie Miller to lose. Very possibly the same somebody who paid off Cal Morris and the guys who attacked Willie.

Before I leave, I bring up Wallace's new offer. His answer is short and to the point.

"No."

"It's the best offer they are going to make," I say.

"Then go back and tell them to take their best offer and shove it up their ass."

"I'm not saying you should take it; but I am saying you should seriously consider it. If we lose at trial, it will turn out a hell of a lot worse."

"I already told you, we ain't gonna lose at trial," he says.

I'm not going to be able to convince him of our dire circumstances, so I leave and head back to the office. Laurie is back from lunch with Mr. Wonderful. I hope he tore a rotator cuff passing the potatoes. She has checked and learned that the court had in fact not appointed Hinton, and Wallace has also left a message confirming that fact.

My plan is to bring this up before Hatchet at tomorrow's pretrial hearing, but I'm going to need to get my facts in order. What this means is another late night tonight, and I grab all my papers and head home.

• • • • •

AN ENORMOUS LIMOUSINE WITH
a chauffeur waiting in the driver's seat is in front of the house
when I pull up. I go inside and find Nicole sitting in the
kitchen, drinking coffee. She does not look happy, which gives
us something in common.

"Hello, Nicole."

"Hello, Andy."

"Based on the size of the limo outside, either the President
of the United States, the Sultan of Brunei, or your father is
here."

"Right the third time," Philip says as he comes into the
kitchen, smiling but not exactly bubbling over with warmth.

"Daddy's heard about what happened." She takes Philip's
arm, which I suppose is her way of showing me who she
means by "Daddy." "He's concerned."

"Join the club," I say.

"What are you doing about it?" Philip asks.

"I called the police, made sure the windows and doors
were locked, got the alarm system fixed . . . but most importantly, I'm trying to find out what's going on and who might
have done it."

"Have you made any progress?"

"Not much." Nicole moans in frustration, but I keep talking

to Philip, who puts his hand on Nicole's head to comfort her.
"Did you check out Brownfield?"

He nods. "Yes. He was attending business school in London the entire year that picture was taken."

"Maybe he was back for one of the school breaks."

Philip smiles his condescending smile, as if I'm a backwoodsman trying to understand the big city. "I pulled a few strings and checked with Immigration. Their records show he was in London for fourteen straight weeks surrounding that date. If the date is right, then it certainly is not Brownfield."

This is another piece of distressing news placed on top of the pile I already have. Laurie and I were both sure it was Brownfield, and that his adamant denial came from his involvement in some criminal plot. If he was out of the country, then he loses his connection to the picture and to the date my father got the money. My face must show my disappointment and frustration, because Philip pounces on it.

"Can I make a suggestion?" he inquires. He doesn't do humble real well.

"Of course."

"Since we don't know what or who is behind this, I suggest that you eliminate the potential dangers."

"And how should I do that?"

"By giving up the murder case. It can't pay too well anyhow and in any event you no longer have any need for money. And it might be a good idea to stop looking into this photograph. Just in case."

I'm really annoyed, especially by the suggestion that I drop the Miller case. Does he think this is a video game? Can he not realize and respect that a real life is at stake?

"Philip, if you don't mind my saying so, that is ridiculous. I'm going to see this through to the end. My client is on trial for his life."

"He's already lost one trial. And you know as well as I do how little chance you have to turn that around. Hell, when I was in the prosecutor's office, I would have begged to handle a case like this."

I'm sure that's true, since publicity was the only reason

Philip was there. I'm about to answer him, but he's still going. "Besides," he says, "it's Nicole's life that has been threatened, Andrew."

"Actually, it hasn't. Mine has. But I get your point, and I have already suggested that Nicole go someplace safe until this is over. Maybe you can convince her that I'm right." We're talking about Nicole as if she's not there, and when Philip is around, she effectively isn't. It makes me sad that the disappearance of the Nicole I knew happened on my watch.

Then Philip delivers his roundhouse right. He tells me that I'm not thinking clearly, that if I were I'd realize that whatever I discover could have a negative impact on my father's memory.

"My father never broke a law in his life," I say.

He walks over and wraps his arms around my shoulder. I probably dislike shoulder wrapping even more than hugging. "Now look, we're all family here. I'm on your side. But Andrew, your father didn't earn the two million dollars delivering newspapers. If he had he wouldn't have kept it a secret and left it untouched all these years. You've got to face that fact."

Philip is right about that much, of course, and after he leaves I try to bury that truth in a mountain of paperwork. I don't succeed. So I try and get some sleep, since tomorrow is my first session with Hatchet in his ballpark, and I had better be ready, because he and Wallace certainly will be. But I don't succeed at that either; I can't stop thinking about my father never touching that money.

I can clearly remember back to a time when I was eleven. My bedroom was right off the kitchen, but it was past midnight and my parents believed I was asleep. I wasn't, and the strange tones in their voices, particularly my father's, kept me awake with my ear to the wall.

They were discussing my request, made earlier that day, to go to overnight camp in the upcoming summer. It did not seem an unreasonable request, my two best friends had gone there the year before, and they were returning. But camp cost over two thousand dollars, plus all the equipment and clothing, and it was this financial commitment that my parents were discussing.

"You've got to tell him, Nelson," my mother said. "He's a mature young man, he'll understand."

"I know he will," my father replied. "But I'm just not ready to give up on managing this."

My mother pointed out that they simply did not have the money now, and that in any event summer camp was an extravagance, not a necessity. Better to save the money for college, which she said was just around the corner.

My father was adamant. His voice cracking, he talked about wanting me to have this experience, wanting me to have every experience he was never able to have. He would somehow figure out a way to make it work.

The next morning, to my undying shame, I did not withdraw my request. I had the time of my life at camp that summer, and I know now that my father, so desperate for me to go that he was in terrible pain, had millions of dollars that he refused to touch.

Money that he did not make delivering newspapers.

• • • • •

HATCHET'S GAVEL POUNDS THE CASE OF *NEW Jersey v. William Miller* to order. Present for the prosecution are Richard Wallace and an assortment of Assistant DAs. At the defense table are myself, Kevin Randall, and Willie Miller.

This is the first time I have ever seen Willie outside of prison. He's wearing prison clothing and has his hands cuffed behind him, but I can still tell that he's enjoying this tiny taste of almost real life. I will get him normal clothing to wear when there is a jury present; prison clothing makes him look like he belongs there.

For some reason they have chosen to put us in courtroom three, which is the most modern and by far the least impressive of the six courtrooms in the building. It is as if the designer was taken to a typical Holiday Inn room and was told, "Give me this."

There is not much room for the public and press, which may be the intent behind choosing it. Hatchet likes a calm and controlled courtroom; if he could I think he would conduct the trial in a plastic bubble. Personally, I like commotion and disorganization. In this case especially, I want the jurors on their toes and willing to think outside their box.

What I do like about the room is that since it is fairly small, the lawyers are close to both the judge and jury. There is a good chance for interaction, for the little asides that can have a disproportionately large effect. Playing to the jury is going to be difficult with the vigilant Hatchet in charge, but I'm still going to try.

Hatchet gets the names of the attorneys on the record, and then says, "Before we go through these motions, is there anything we need to discuss?"

"Your Honor," I say, "I would request that my client's handcuffs be removed whenever he is in the courtroom. It is unnecessary, uncomfortable, and prejudicial to the jury."

Hatchet looks around. "Do you see a jury here, Mr. Carpenter?"

"No, Your Honor. But I expect there will be."

"Motion denied." Not a great start.

I persist. "Your Honor, could we at least have his hands cuffed in front of him? I am advised that it would greatly lessen the discomfort, while not providing too serious a physical danger to the members of the court."

"Mr. Wallace?" Hatchet inquires.

"No objection, Your Honor."

"Very well. Guard, please adjust the handcuffs so that they are in the front."

The guard comes over and does just that. When he is finished, Willie leans over and whispers to me. "Thanks, man. You're better than the last lawyer already."

I just nod as Hatchet shuffles through some papers. "We'll start with the change of venue motion. Mr. Carpenter, I've read your brief. Do you have anything to add to it?"

I stand up. "Yes, Your Honor. We believe that the prosecution, in speaking out to the press about their view of the new trial as the result of an inconsequential technicality, has prejudiced the jury pool, and—"

Hatchet interrupts me. "That's all in your brief. I asked if you had anything more to add."

"I'm sorry, Your Honor. The brief adequately represents our position, though perhaps understates the passion with which we hold it."

"I'm suitably impressed," says Hatchet. "Mr. Wallace?"

"Our response papers are complete, Your Honor." Wallace is the type who would go up to high school teachers and thank them for a fair and well-thought-out final exam. "We believe that cases with far greater public awareness have managed to empanel impartial juries without much difficulty."

"I am inclined to agree with that," Hatchet says.

"Your Honor," I jump in, trying to stem the tide. "Our papers demonstrate media coverage both inside and outside this community in great detail. We feel—"

He interrupts me. " 'Great detail' is an understatement. I would appreciate it if you would be more concise in the future. But look at the bright side, Mr. Carpenter. Every motion I deny gives you a future grounds for appeal."

"We would rather get a not guilty verdict in the first place, Your Honor."

"Then present your best case. What's next?"

"The matter of Robert Hinton, Mr. Miller's so-called counsel in the first trial," I say.

Hatchet nods and takes off his glasses. He's heard all about this, so he looks at Wallace.

"This can't be true, can it?"

Wallace replies, "I'm afraid our information shows that it is, Your Honor. We cannot find Mr. Hinton, but there is no record that he was ever a member of the bar."

"How could that happen?"

"We're still looking into it. But it appears that Mr. Miller hired Mr. Hinton independent of the court, and that his credentials were not examined."

Hatchet turns to me. "Is this consistent with your understanding of the facts?"

I take a quick look at Willie before I answer. "Yes, Your Honor, but our major concern is not with my client's representation, or lack of it, in the first trial, as terrible as it was. That verdict has already been set aside."

Hatchet seems surprised to hear this. "Then exactly what is your concern?"

Here goes. "Your Honor, we believe this is evidence that a conspiracy existed at the time of the murder, and continues to this day, so as to protect certain powerful interests. We would request substantial leeway to deal with this matter at trial."

"Do you have any other evidence of this conspiracy?" Hatchet is obviously skeptical, as I knew he would be.

"We are developing it, Your Honor."

Wallace chimes in. "Your Honor, granting the defense's request would be providing them a license to conduct a time-consuming fishing expedition. The state would suggest that when and if the information is *developed* that it be presented to the court for admissibility."

I expect Hatchet to agree with Wallace, but instead he turns to me. "Mr. Carpenter, was Mr. Hinton paid for his services?"

"Not by my client, Your Honor. Hinton represented himself as a public defender, assigned by the court. My client, *having never before been charged with a crime,* did not have the sophistication to realize that he was the victim of a conspiracy."

Hatchet seems very troubled by this. "Mr. Wallace, we have here an extraordinary circumstance in which a fraud was perpetrated on the court in a capital case. Since we can safely assume that most lawyers, even fake ones, have at least some financial self-interest, then it seems quite credible to surmise that Mr. Hinton was put up to this by a person or persons, other than the defendant, prepared to pay for his services."

"It is a long jump from that to evidence of the defendant's innocence," Wallace says.

Hatchet nods. "That's true, and Mr. Carpenter, I am not going to allow wild Colombian death squad testimony." This is a reference to the defense mounted in the Simpson case. "But I will be inclined to grant some leeway. We'll take it on an issue-by-issue basis."

"Thank you, Your Honor." It's not a victory, but it's a hell of a lot better than I expected, and Wallace looks a little surprised.

Hatchet continues moving things right along, turning to Wallace. "I believe there are DNA issues we need to address?"

"The state has submitted its intentions in this regard. Additional tests are being conducted right now."

Hatchet nods. "Mr. Carpenter, if you are requesting a Kelly-Frye, I suggest you do so as soon as possible."

"Your Honor," I reply, "we respectfully point out that we cannot begin to decide whether to challenge evidence until we see that evidence."

I've already decided not to ask for the Kelly-Frye, but by delaying announcement of that decision I might give us more time to prepare for trial.

Wallace will have none of this. "Your Honor, the Kelly-Frye, as the defense knows, is designed to challenge the technology itself, independent of the specific case. The results will not be in until almost the date of trial, and if the defense waits until then to decide whether to seek the hearing, the trial date you've set will almost certainly be delayed."

I chime in. "In the interests of justice, the defense is willing to allow a delay, though we would prefer that our client not have to sit in a jail cell while the prosecution gets its act together."

Wallace is getting annoyed, which is what I want, but Hatchet refuses to let the back-and-forth continue.

"Mr. Carpenter, your request to delay your decision is denied. Are you requesting a Kelly-Frye or not?"

"No, Your Honor." Wallace whirls around in surprise. "But the defense reserves its right to challenge the evidence when presented."

"No objection, Your Honor," Wallace agrees.

"Very good. What's next?"

"There is the matter of bail, Your Honor," I say.

"In a capital case?"

"The prosecution has not officially announced its intention in that regard."

"That's just a formality," Wallace says. "The paperwork is being prepared now."

"My client has already served seven years in prison for a crime he did not commit. Every single additional day is an intolerable imposition."

"Motion for bail denied. Anything else?"

Before Wallace or I have a chance to reply, Hatchet slams down his gavel. "See you at jury selection."

Kevin and I say our goodbyes to Willie and make plans to meet with him and discuss some specifics of the case. After he leaves, Kevin says, "The judge wasn't as tough as you led me to believe."

"Just wait," I say. "Just wait."

• • • • •

NEW JERSEY HAS ALWAYS BEEN A STATE WITH AN identity crisis. It is essentially divided into three areas: the part near New York, the part near Philadelphia, and everything in between. That middle part includes both fashionable suburban areas and lower- to middle-class towns and farmland. It is in the economically depressed farmland where Denise McGregor was raised, so it is where I am going today.

The trip down the Garden State Parkway is bumper-to-bumper because of beach traffic, compounded by the fact that it seems like there are tollbooths every twenty feet. I switch off to the New Jersey Turnpike and the drive goes much more smoothly. It gives me time to think.

I've learned that Denise's father still lives down here, but I've decided not to call ahead and prepare him for my arrival. It is likely that he will be disinclined to speak to me, since he no doubt believes that I represent his daughter's killer, and I think I have a better chance if I take him by surprise. I really have no preconceived notions of what I might find out from him, but if my theory is correct that Denise's murder was not random and served a purpose, then the more I can find out about her the better.

I soon find myself on a small, mostly dirt road in a very depressed area. I pass a series of small shacks, all with ani-

mals and trucks out front. I finally pull up to a ramshackle
trailer, which bears the address I have for Denise's father. I'm
glad that it's not part of a trailer park, since that seems to be
where tornadoes always pick to strike. I don't have time to
ponder the meteorological significance of this, because I see
an elderly man rocking gently on a rocking chair in front of
the trailer.

Sitting next to the man is a large German shepherd, quiet
but eyeing me as if lunch just arrived. I pull my car up fairly
close and get out, leaving the door open so that if the dog
chases me I might have an escape route.

I approach the man, who shows no signs of even being
aware that I am there.

"Hello, I'm looking for Wally McGregor."

"He's the blind guy in the rocking chair."

I look around to see if the person he is talking about is
there, and then I realize with an embarrassed flash that he's
talking about himself, and that he's already made an idiot out
of me.

"You're Wally McGregor?"

He laughs. "I can't fool you, can I?"

I return the laugh. "No, I'm much too sharp for that. My
name is Andy Carpenter."

"What can I do for you?"

"I want to talk to you about Denise."

I can see him tense up when he hears Denise's name;
there is no statute of limitations on emotions when a parent
loses a child.

"Why?"

I've been debating the idea of evading the truth, of not
telling him that I represent Willie until I've gotten information
out of him. In the moment, though, I can't do it. He has the
right to know, as well as the right to throw me out if he so
chooses.

"I represent the man that the police say killed her. I believe
they have the wrong man."

He doesn't respond, just rocks slightly back and forth,
thinking it through.

"I understand the feelings you must have," I say. "But I would very much appreciate your talking to me."

"I heard about the retrial . . . Mr. Wallace called me. I can't say I'm happy about it."

He thinks some more, and I wait. "But I want the real killer to be punished, and I can't see how talking to someone can hurt the chance of that."

"Thank you."

He invites me into the trailer for a cup of coffee, and I follow him in. His blindness certainly doesn't interfere with his ability to get around, and he gets the coffee up and brewing in a matter of maybe three minutes.

While he's doing so, I look around the place. There are some pictures on the wall. One of them is of a young woman, perhaps twenty-one years old, sitting on a horse. It is the first photo I have seen of Denise McGregor that wasn't taken by the coroner, and it makes the fact of her brutal death all the more horrifying.

"She was a very beautiful young lady," I say.

Obviously, Wally can't see where I am, so he asks, "Which picture are you looking at?"

"Denise sitting on a horse."

Wally nods. "She was beautiful, that's for sure. But that's not Denise . . . that's her mother, Julie. Everybody says how much they looked alike."

"Oh. Is Julie—"

"Alive?" he interrupts. "Can't say as I know. She left me and Denise when Denise was only a year or so old. Julie wasn't the family type; she couldn't be tied down. So when she found herself stuck with a husband and a child, well, she took off and never looked back."

Wally McGregor lost his wife, his daughter, and his sight, yet he has the knack of making a visitor feel completely comfortable. It's a great knack to have.

"And you raised Denise by yourself?"

He laughs. "Once I lost my sight, it was more like she raised me. There was nothing Denise couldn't do."

"Do you have any idea what she was working on at the time she was killed?"

"Sure don't. But Denise used to call me and read me all her articles once they got in the paper. I got such a kick out of that. She was some writer."

I had read her articles, and he is right. She was a terrific writer.

"And you have no idea why anyone would want to kill her?"

"No. Everybody loved Denise . . . it don't make no sense . . . you'd have to ask Miller why he did what he did."

"So you think it was him?"

He shrugs. "I just know what the police told me. But if you're looking for a reason for Denise to have died, there ain't none."

He shakes his head and relives the senselessness of it for the millionth time. "Damn, there just ain't none."

I can see that Wally is starting to get upset, and I give him time to let the pain subside. I know people that have lost children, and they tell me the pain never goes away, it's there twenty-four hours a day, but that after a while you develop techniques that can help to mask it. Wally manages to do that, and we have a conversation that steers clear of Denise.

Later I ask him about Edward Markham, and he tells me that they never met, not even at the funeral. Edward sent a large floral arrangement and a condolence letter, but did not show up personally. Wally doesn't seem particularly upset about the slight; Edward never really had any importance to him. Denise, in fact, had never mentioned Edward.

It's almost time for me to leave, and Wally knows he hasn't given me what I need. He brings it up himself. "So you think it could have been someone else that killed her?"

I nod. "That's what I think. It's not what I know."

"If you find out something, I want to know. Promise me that."

"I promise," I say. It's one I'm going to keep, no matter how this turns out.

It's too late to go back to the office, so I head home.

There's a pile of personal matters to attend to, not the least of which is dealing with my father's money. It's financially crazy to just let it sit in the low-interest bonds, but I'm somehow not inclined to touch it yet. Maybe a shrink can tell me why that is, and I can certainly afford Sigmund Freud if he's available. And if I had the time.

Nicole has warmed up considerably, and she greets me with a glass of Chardonnay and a kiss. It feels nice, and I appreciate it, but I know that I'm not going to have the time to pay attention to her, and it gives me a pang of guilt. I talk to her about it and she understands, so after dinner I retreat to the den with Tara and get back to work.

I have to wade through the latest of Kevin's briefs, which argues that the death penalty should not be considered in this case. The main point he makes is the obviously unfair way it has been administered throughout the country. Not only has racial bias been clear, but the number of death row inmates that have been exonerated is staggering. In Illinois alone, over a fifteen-year period, more death row inmates were exonerated than executed.

Once again, Kevin's work is professional and well reasoned, a clear, concise indictment of the death penalty, and I make very few changes. Unfortunately, Kevin and I both know that it is once again destined for failure, at least as far as Hatchet is concerned. He has long been a pro–death penalty judge, and with an election coming up next year we're not likely to change his mind.

I've also given Kevin the assignment of preparing our witness list, as well as the job of going over the witness list that Wallace has provided us. As is the norm, Wallace has given us a voluminous list, with every conceivable person listed on it. There is no way he is going to call even ten percent of these people, but he wants us to use our limited time and resources looking into people that will not appear in court. It's not terribly nice, but it's the way the game is played. I've told Kevin to come to me or even to Willie with anyone on the list whose role in the case we're not sure of, so that we can be prepared for any eventuality.

So much to do, so little time. The trial date is approaching like a freight train, and we are in deep trouble. I fall asleep around two o'clock in the morning, without having accomplished much of anything except making myself even more tired.

● ● ● ● ●

THE ALARM GOES OFF AT SIX A.M. DID

I go to school to be a lawyer or a dairy farmer? I take Tara for a quick walk, then shower and head for the office.

I'm in full work mode now, able to totally concentrate on the matter at hand. I find that when I'm in this mind-set, I can drive somewhere and not remember anything about the trip. It amazes me that I don't have accidents, but my instinct must take over.

This morning my mind is in total clutter, trying to juggle a million things that have to be done and examined. Kevin is coming in with a jury consultant for a meeting. I've never had much use for them, always trusting my instincts, but Kevin has convinced me to keep an open mind about it. After that, I'm going over to depose Victor Markham at his lawyer's office.

I arrive at my office at eight-thirty, which is too early for Edna to have gotten in, so I'm surprised when the door is unlocked. I'm also concerned that someone may have broken in during the night, but I look around quickly and don't see anything amiss.

A moment later I don't see anything at all, as either a fist or a baseball bat hits me on the side of the head. The rest is more than a little blurry, but I hear myself scream in slow motion, and fall to the ground.

I look up and see a man wearing a ski mask, and since it hasn't snowed in the office in quite a while, I instinctively cover up. That proves to be a good move, as he kicks me in the stomach and then punches me again in the chest and head.

My mind registers the fact that there is no one around to help me, that this monster can continue to kick and punch me for as long as he wants. Fortunately, he stops after a few more well-placed shots, all of which send shooting pains through my body. He leans over and snarls through his mask.

"You'd better learn how to take a warning, asshole."

I try to respond, but another kick silences me.

"Next time you're dead, asshole. Dead."

He moves away and out the door, a beautiful, blurry sight if ever I've seen one.

After a few minutes, I stagger to the phone and call the police. I ask for Pete Stanton and tell him what happened. Then I slump down to the floor and wait for the cavalry to arrive.

The first soldier in the door is Edna, who screams when she sees me. She's no beauty early in the morning either, but apparently I look worse. She responds to the crisis terrifically, getting cold rags to apply to my bruises and helping me to the couch.

The place is soon swarming with paramedics and police. The paramedics want to take me to the hospital, but I refuse. Nothing seems to be broken, although my entire body hurts like hell, and I just can't afford to give up the time. Instead they take me into the back office and attend to me, while the police survey the scene.

The paramedics finally finish, and I drag my bruised and bandaged body into the outer office. The only police officer left is Pete, who is on the phone. He signals for me to wait, mouthing that he's on an important call with his office.

I stagger to the couch and sit down, and after a few minutes Pete hangs up. Rather than come talk to me, he makes another call. I'm not paying much attention, until I hear part of it.

"I've got to stop at the cleaners, and I don't know if I'll have time to get the car washed. So figure me for about seven. Right. Goodbye." I've been waiting for this?

He hangs up the phone and turns to me. "Okay. Talk to me," he says.

"Talk to you? About what? About some seven-foot-eight, four-hundred-pound monster who beat the shit out of me? I don't think so. I admit it seemed important at the time, but it pales next to the possibility that you won't have time to get your goddamn car washed. That really puts everything into perspective."

He laughs; this episode doesn't seem to concern him as much as it does me. He tells me that I've got to answer some questions, as well as provide a description of the assailant.

"I didn't see him, Pete. The son of a bitch was wearing a ski mask."

"There's nothing you can give me? A distinctive voice, maybe?"

I search my recollection, but come up with almost nothing. "He's got big feet."

"Well now we're getting somewhere."

I'm really annoyed. "Look, my house has been broken into, I've been threatened, and now I've been beaten up in my office. Any chance you're seeing a pattern, Sherlock?"

"Andy, I see this every day. It happens all the time, and you defend most of the scumbags who do it."

I shake my head. "This is not supposed to happen to me. I'm a lawyer, for Christ's sake. When I piss people off they're supposed to stand up and object."

Pete asks me if I see anything missing in the office, or if there seems to be anything that the intruder had gone through. There is no evidence of that, and I tell him so.

"Hmmmm," he hmmms.

"What are you hmmming about?"

"Obviously, the intruder was here just to do what he did, beat and threaten you."

"That makes me feel much better."

"What time did you get in?"

"Early. Eight-thirty."

"Are you always the first one in?"

"No. When I'm due in court I sometimes don't come in until the afternoon."

"Somebody's been watching and following you, Andy. Any idea who it could be?"

"No."

"Maybe another pimp looking to take over your stable?"

"Kiss my ass."

"Believe me, right now it's a lot better looking than your face."

Pete asks me a lot more questions, and I answer them as best I can. Well, maybe not quite that completely, since I neglect to mention the parts about my father and the money and the picture. My shrink and I are going to have a lot to talk about.

Pete heads back to the office, promising to put his best people on the case. He also makes a reference to our next meeting, which is when he will be testifying as a key witness in the Miller case. It'll be my job to attack Pete in cross-examination, which won't be easy.

As Pete's leaving, Laurie arrives. She hasn't heard about the attack, and the first thing she sees is my battered face.

"Oh, my God. What happened?"

"Sort of a pretrial conference," I say. Hey, I used to sleep with her. I've got to act brave.

She touches my arm, and I can't help it, I wince in pain. "No touching. Please, no touching."

She's okay with that. I knew she would be.

I call Nicole and tell her what happened, since I'm afraid she'll hear it through the media. She's concerned and upset, though less so than when the house was broken into. I renew my suggestion that she move out until the danger has passed, and again she refuses.

Kevin shows up soon after and shows a hell of a lot more sympathy than Laurie had. We soon get back into the details of the case, and I almost forget the pain I'm in. Almost, but not quite.

The jury consultant shows up for our meeting. Her name is Marjorie Klayman and to my chagrin I take an immediate liking to her. My father brought me up to believe in the old school of trial lawyering, and jury consultancy is part of the new school. Marjorie is in her thirties, unpretentious in looks, dress, and attitude, and totally self-confident in her ability to help me pick a jury.

She explains what she calls the "science" of the process, which consists of conducting polls among sample jury pools, probing with sophisticated questions about attitude and lifestyle. The responses are then correlated with those people's attitudes toward information about the specific case. I'm not knocked out by what she has to say, but then again how many times can I be knocked out in one day? I hire her on the spot, and give her one week to get back to me. This is generous; jury selection begins in ten days.

I ask Laurie to join me for the Victor Markham deposition, and we head over to the office of one Bradley Anderson, Victor's lawyer. I bring Laurie with me because she's smart, and in this case two heads are better than one, especially since one has just recently been punched in.

Bradley Anderson is one of the few attorneys I've ever met for whom the moniker "Esquire" fits. His office is spacious and ornately furnished in an elegant prewar building in Ridgewood. The conference room would seem more appropriate for a state dinner than for a criminal law deposition, but that is what we're here to conduct.

There is a fruit plate set out for us to sample, along with cheese and crackers, except they are so thin and delicate that they're probably called something a lot classier than "crackers." There is also a silver coffee urn with cups smaller than your average test tube.

Victor feigns graciousness when we arrive, even expressing sympathy for my bruises. It is as if he has absolutely nothing better to do than have a little chat with us over coffee. Bradley is distant but polite, though my impression is that he feels like he's soiling himself by talking to us. Bradley explains that he does not usually do criminal law, but Victor is a dear friend, so if we can move this along . . .

Once the stenographer is ready, I ask Victor some preliminary questions about his business and family. Actually, I beat these questions to death with boring minutiae, and I can feel Laurie staring daggers at me, wondering what the hell I am doing.

What I am doing is trying to annoy Victor Markham, to get him out of his glossy little shell and dig under his skin. I accomplish this when I ask him for perhaps the fifth time about his son, Edward's, grades at Fairleigh Dickinson. Victor snarls his response and Bradley threatens to terminate the deposition. I threaten to bring Victor in front of Hatchet for unresponsiveness. Now that I've achieved the warm tone I've been looking for, it's time to get to the matter at hand.

The goal of a deposition, at least one of an adversarial witness, is not necessarily to accumulate information, and certainly not to trip him up. Rather it is to get the witness under oath, and thereby lock him or her into answers. Those answers then serve as a basis for cross-examination, and the witness cannot come up with a new story when painted into a corner.

"How well did you know Denise McGregor?"

"I didn't know her very well," Victor says. "But Edward hoped to marry her."

"Were they engaged?"

"No, I don't believe so."

"You don't know for sure whether your own son was engaged?"

"He was not engaged." He's annoyed, snapping out his words.

"Do you know what story Denise was working on when she died?"

"Of course not."

The questioning moves to the night of the murder. "Why did Edward call you from the bar?"

"As I would assume you can imagine, he was terribly upset. He always turned to his father in times of crisis. He still does. I encourage it."

"Where were you at the time?"

"At the club."

"Which club might that be?"

"Preakness Country Club. We have been members for many years."

"How did he know you were there?"

"It was a Friday night. I am always at the club on Friday nights."

"So when Edward called you, what did he say?"

"He told me where he was, and that his girlfriend had been murdered. He asked me to come there immediately."

"And you did?"

He nods. "I did."

I take out the picture that I found in my father's house. "Can you please point to yourself in this photograph?"

Bradley has obviously been primed for this. He jumps in instantly and advises Victor not to answer on the grounds that it is not relevant to the Miller case. No amount of badgering on my part, not even the threat of Hatchet, can get him to change his mind.

My last question for Victor concerns the current whereabouts of Edward, since Laurie has been unable to locate him.

Victor smiles. "He's in Africa, on one of those safaris. I'm afraid he's simply not reachable."

I return the smile. "Then we'll just have to talk to him on the stand."

• • • • •

TEN DAYS FLY BY AS IF THEY ARE TEN MINUTES, AND THE next thing I know the bailiff is intoning, "In the matter of the people versus William Miller, the Honorable Justice Walter Henderson presiding . . ."

"William" sits at the defense table in a new suit I had Edna purchase for the occasion, and he looks terrific. He also looks calm and collected; he's been a lot lower, and faced a lot tougher, than this and he thinks the momentum has turned upward. He's not thinking very clearly.

There is a special feeling, an excitement combined with queasiness, that hits me every time a trial is about to begin. The only thing I can liken it to is former Boston Celtics great Bill Russell saying that no matter how long he played, he still threw up in the locker room before every game. I don't think throwing up on the defense table is the right way to get on Hatchet's good side, so I control the impulse.

For me trials are about strategy and confrontations. Strategy is one of my strong suits, but in real life I don't do well with confrontations, so I have to deal with that in another way.

My father used to lecture me that a trial is serious business, not a game, but I have come to disagree. For me a trial and the investigation surrounding it is in fact a game. I turn it into one, so that I can handle and thrive in the midst of all these confrontations. In sports, every play between the participants is a confrontation, but I can deal with that because that is the purpose of the game. Once I can put trials into the same category, it becomes depersonalized and I'm home free.

Jury selection is especially difficult and dangerous for the defense in a capital trial. That is because each juror must be death-qualified, which is to say that he or she must be willing to vote for the death penalty if it seems warranted. Such juries are by definition more conservative and more favorable to the prosecution.

The first prospective juror is brought in for Wallace and me to question. Marjorie is at my side as we go through the tedious process, made more so by Hatchet's insistence on throwing questions in of his own.

Number one is a doorman who claims to know nothing about the case. He also claims to have an entirely open mind, to have no predispositions about the police or the justice system, and to be willing to consider capital punishment if called upon to do so. This is clearly a guy who'd rather sit in the jury box for a few weeks than open doors. Marjorie's okay with him, but Wallace challenges, and he's excused.

It takes us two days to empanel a jury of twelve and two alternates. There are seven whites, four blacks, and one Hispanic, five men and seven women. All twelve of them claim to have a completely open mind. I don't think I've met twelve people in my entire life with completely open minds, but I'm reasonably satisfied with this group. Marjorie is positively euphoric, but if she thought we had a bunch of turkeys, it would mean she did a poor job.

The real action in a trial begins with the opening statements. The prosecutor stands up and gives the jury a road map of the trial. He tells them what they are going to hear, what he is going to prove, and what it will all mean. His goal is to sound confident and to convince the jury that he has the goods on this guy, then his task will be to deliver a case that makes good on the promises he's made in the opening statement.

Richard thanks the jury for their willingness to serve, then talks for a while about their obligations under the law. It's all straightforward, boilerplate stuff, until he finally turns to Willie Miller.

"So he got drunk," Wallace says, pointing to Willie. "Happens to a lot of us, right? But what do you and I do when we have too much to drink?"

He laughs to himself as if remembering past nights at the frat house.

"Well, I have to admit, I fall asleep. Knocks me right out. But I'm a little unusual in that regard. Other people, maybe even some of you, get a little wild, have some fun, maybe even say a few things they shouldn't."

Most of the jurors are nodding along with him. This is starting to feel like an AA meeting.

Wallace turns serious. "But not Willie Miller. No, Willie handles his liquor a little differently. Willie kills people. And on June 14, 1994, Willie Miller killed Denise McGregor. She was a hardworking, intelligent young woman, a loving daughter, full of life, who is not here today because Willie Miller spent a night drinking and killing.

"Your job is a very serious one, have no doubt about that. But in this case it is not a particularly difficult one. That is because we will prove everything I am telling you about that night. Every single, ugly moment of it. We will show you who Willie Miller is, and what he did. We will present overwhelming physical evidence to you, and you will hear from an eyewitness to the crime. That's right, an eyewitness. Someone saw Willie Miller standing over the body, moments after committing the crime. She will come in here and tell you what she saw. And you will have no doubt that she is telling the truth.

"On behalf of the state, we will prove that Willie Miller is a cold-blooded murderer. We will prove it not just beyond a reasonable doubt; we will prove it beyond any doubt. Thank you."

Wallace finishes just before lunch, and Laurie, Kevin, and I have two hours to decide whether I should give my opening statement now or wait until after the prosecution's case is finished and it's time to present ours.

I include Willie in our discussions, as I always do with my

clients. It makes them feel better, even though I never listen to anything they have to say. Willie thinks I should speak now, since he's just been made to look like a monster by Wallace, and he thinks I'll provide him some vindication. Laurie feels I should hold off, that Wallace didn't go as far as he might have, and that we'll need our best ammunition after his case in chief, which she expects to be devastating. Kevin feels I should go now, since otherwise the jury will think I have nothing to refute what was just said.

My decision is to speak now, since it feels like there could be a steamroller effect if I don't. I want the jury to understand that there is a serious, other side to this argument, and if I don't tell them so right now, I'm afraid they won't get it.

When court reconvenes, I tell Hatchet that I want to make my opening statement now. I stand and face the jury.

"I'm going to start by answering a question that must be on your minds. You must be wondering why, if this murder was committed so long ago, and if Willie Miller was captured so soon after the murder, he is just being brought to trial now. Well, the truth is, he was tried once before, and found guilty. That verdict was overturned, and we're back here."

I can see Wallace almost getting up, trying to decide if he should object. This is information he should want included, and he doesn't know why I'm bringing it up.

I continue. "Actually, I shouldn't say that *we're* back here. I didn't represent Mr. Miller last time. In fact, his lawyer was not really a lawyer. He was a fake, brought in to ensure that Mr. Miller would lose. It is convincing evidence of a conspiracy that resulted in—"

"Objection!" Wallace leaps to his feet.

"—my client losing seven years of his life—"

"Objection!" Wallace is going nuts, and Hatchet slams down his gavel.

"Bailiff, remove the jury. I'll see both counsel in chambers."

I've accomplished my task, the jury has been shaken up and hopefully will now expect to see a fight between two competitive positions. It's put our side on a more equal footing, which is all we can hope for at this point.

Back in chambers, Hatchet doesn't come down on me as hard as I expected. Wallace complains that I cannot go making wild charges about alleged conspiracies, but Hatchet still wants to rule on it step by step as we go along. He knows I'm trying to develop evidence on the fly, and he may well be feeling guilty about rushing me to trial. He says that I can talk about a conspiracy and frame-up in my opening statement, but before I can give further specifics I have to clear it with the court. It's a reasonable decision and elevates my opinion of Hatchet.

Wallace is displeased with the result of this conference, but he and I both know he will be upset often during the trial. My style as a defense attorney is often to ridicule the prosecution's case, to make it look not worthy of serious consideration by the jury.

Lawyers, even those who know it is crazy to personally identify with their respective positions, have a tendency to become their case during the course of a trial. If their side loses, then they lose, and the key for the attorney is to allow objectivity and passion to coexist in his or her mind.

As I try to make Wallace's case look bad, he will have a knee-jerk reaction that I am making him look bad. He's a professional, and it won't destroy the level of his work, but it will be tough to deal with, and occasionally he will erupt in anger. It's unfortunate that I have to bring this out in him, but for me it's just part of the game.

When we return to the courtroom, I continue with my statement to the jury. "The interesting question that you will face is not whether or not Willie Miller committed this terrible crime. He simply did not, and the evidence will bear that out. The proof to which Mr. Wallace refers does not exist, no matter what he claims. He will present a manufactured proof, no doubt one in which he sincerely believes, but an illusion nonetheless.

"But the really fascinating part is why Willie Miller stands before you at all. Because there has been no accident here, no case of mistaken identity. Nothing in this case has happened by chance. Willie Miller has been framed . . . cleverly, diabolically, and ruthlessly. It is a frame-up that began the night of the murder, in fact well before that night, and which has continued to this very moment.

"Denise McGregor died tragically that night, but Willie Miller is a second victim, and the extent to which he has been victimized will astonish you."

I take a drink of water from my glass at the defense table, and nod very slightly to Kevin's cousin, sitting in the first row behind the defense table, right where we planted him. The word "astonish" was the trigger, so he gets up and walks the few feet to me, leaning in and pretending to whisper something in my ear. I nod, and he leaves the courtroom through the rear doors.

I turn again and face the jury. "When I finish, the prosecution is going to be presenting their case. I already know what it consists of, and take my word for it, the most significant part of that case is an eyewitness."

I stop, as if seriously considering the import of such a witness.

"An eyewitness. Sounds pretty momentous, doesn't it? The word almost sounds as if a drumroll should precede it. The average person thinks, well, he might as well plead guilty, because they've got an . . ."

I beat a drumroll with my hands on the railing of the jury box.

". . . eyewitness."

The jury laughs, which is what I'm looking for.

"Every moment of every day, we are eyewitnesses to what happens before us. Moments ago, a man got up from that chair, spoke to me, and left the court. Since there's not much else to do around here, I assume most of you watched him. You were eyewitnesses to it."

There is a slight murmuring among the jury, as Kevin reaches under the defense table and picks up a large piece of paperboard. He hands it to me, and I bring it over to the jury, after first registering it as a defense exhibit.

The board has six photos on it of six different men. They all look vaguely similar and are all dressed alike. Any one of them could be Kevin's cousin, as long as no one was watching closely.

"One of these pictures is of the man that just spoke to me. I wonder if any of you could identify him. And if you were to try, would you also be willing to say, 'I am so sure that was him, that I would send someone to be put to death, based on my certainty.'"

The look on their faces clearly reflects the fact that they have no idea which photo is the correct one, and they are afraid that they will actually be called upon to try and pick it out.

"I think not. And remember, there was no shock or excitement connected with this. You were paying attention, but nobody had a knife, no one was bleeding to death in front of you, and you weren't afraid for your lives. Do you think that would have made your job easier, or harder?"

A pause for effect. "I'd guess a lot harder."

Many of the jurors are nodding along with me.

"Tough, huh? And just think, you were all . . ."

Again I beat a drumroll on the jury railing.

". . . eyewitnesses."

I don't go on much longer, mainly because I don't want to screw up a good thing. Also, Wallace hasn't gotten deeply into the specifics of the evidence to be presented, so I don't have to go into how I will refute it. If I will refute it.

When I walk back to the defense table and sit down, Willie looks positively giddy. I'm afraid he's going to give me a high five and a chest bump, but he manages to stifle the impulse. I'm going to have to talk to him about looking impassive. My guess, however, is that Lee Strasberg couldn't teach Willie to look impassive.

Hatchet decides that it's too late in the day to start calling witnesses, so he adjourns. As we are filling our briefcases, with the jury already dismissed for the day, Wallace comes up to me, a slight smile on his face.

"Upper right," he says.

"Excuse me?"

He points to the board with the six pictures on it. "The guy who was in the courtroom is the photo in the upper right hand corner."

The truth is, I have no idea which is the correct picture. I look to Kevin, who has heard Wallace and who obviously knows which one his cousin is. Kevin nods. Wallace is correct.

I smile. "Lucky for me you're not on the jury."

He returns the smile. "You got that right."

• • • • •

MY WAY OF WORKING WHILE A TRIAL IS
in progress is to have nightly meetings with the rest of the defense team, so that we can prepare for the next day's court session. I sometimes have these sessions at my house, but in
deference to the Nicole/Laurie situation, we're meeting at the
office.

I have to assume that I am still in danger; the people that
broke into our house and who attacked me in the office may
well strike again, perhaps with more deadly results. I probably should get a bodyguard, but the stubborn side of me is resisting it.

The ironic thing about the threats is that I'm not sure what
they are warning me against. It might well be the Miller case,
except for the fact that it is illogical to think a lawyer would
just give up a case in mid-trial, especially since he would just
be replaced by another lawyer.

Besides, if I were someone looking to get Willie recon-
victed, I would want this to move along as fast as possible.
The more delay, the more attention that is brought to the trial,
the more chance to find exculpatory evidence.

The other possibility, of course, is the photograph. I
haven't exactly been relentless in hunting this down; all we
have done is ask Markham and Brownfield if they are in the

picture. If that is enough to trigger this violent reaction, the secret behind the picture must truly be incendiary. Then why is the picture so bland?

I'm still not positive that there's a connection between the picture and the Miller case; but I feel in my gut that there is. If I'm right, it means I have to step up my investigation into the picture before it's too late and Willie is back on death row. And if I do that, I'll likely be in more danger and more in need of a bodyguard. And round and round, "Like the circles that you find, in the windmills of your mind."

The meeting is short and to the point. Kevin and Laurie give me their impressions of the opening arguments (mostly positive). Kevin correctly believes that we have an uphill struggle ahead of us, and that we should be shooting for a hung jury. Therefore, with Marjorie's help he has isolated two jurors who are most likely to be on our side. One, a twenty-four-year-old African-American woman, is a college teaching assistant. The other, a thirty-four-year-old Hispanic, is an account executive at a direct mail advertising agency. Kevin feels that whenever possible I should speak directly to them, and I agree that, within limits, I'll do it.

Laurie tells me that she has located Betty Anthony, the widow of Mike Anthony, the newspaperman who we believe is the fourth person in the photograph. I had requested that she not make contact with Betty, since I want to do that myself. All I have to do is find the time.

The next morning, Wallace calls his first witness, Detective Steven Prentice. The prosecution always builds their case from the bottom up, establishing all the facts in a way that is incontrovertible. Prentice was a young patrolman at the time of the murder, and he was the first one to respond to the 911 call that Edward made.

"Can you describe the scene when you first arrived?" asks Wallace.

Prentice nods. "Ms. McGregor's body was lying facedown in the alley behind the bar. There was a significant amount of blood surrounding her."

Wallace introduces some horrific pictures of Denise and

the murder scene to buttress what Prentice had said. "And what was the first thing that you did?"

"I cordoned off the area. There were people around, curiosity seekers, and I wanted to make sure that they did not tamper with anything before the detectives arrived."

"Did you see a murder weapon anywhere?"

Prentice shakes his head. "No."

"Was there anyone present that you considered a suspect?"

"No, but there was an eyewitness there. She was pretty shaken up. I put her in a room upstairs from the bar to wait for the detectives, so that she could give them a statement."

"How long did it take for the first detective to arrive?" Wallace asks.

"About ten minutes."

"And who was that?"

"Detective Pete Stanton."

Wallace has him explain that once Pete showed up, his main function was over. Prentice obviously did his job professionally and by the book, and there is a limited amount I'll be able to get from him on cross-examination. I start by showing him police photographs taken of the rest of the alley on the night of the murder.

"Detective Prentice, are you married?"

"Yes, I am."

"Would you be nervous if your wife told you she was going to hang out in this particular alley tonight at around one A.M.?"

"I would advise her not to," he says.

"Why is that? Do you consider it dangerous?"

He tries to evade the question. "There are a lot of places that are not very safe at night."

"Thank you for that. Is this one of those places?"

"Yes, I would say so."

"Was there a homeless problem in the area at the time?"

"I believe there was, yes."

"In your experience, is one of the reasons for the proliferation of the homeless mental illness?"

"Objection. Mental illness is not an area of the officer's expertise."

I reply, "I am simply asking the witness to speak to his beliefs based on his experience."

"Overruled. You may answer."

"I believe mental illness is one of the causes of homelessness, yes," says Prentice. "There are others as well."

"Was the back door to the bar locked?"

"No. The bartender said it was always left open when the bar was open."

"So anyone walking through the alley could have entered the bar through that back door?"

"Yes, I suppose so."

"And if they did, would the first inside door they come to be the ladies' room where Denise McGregor was?"

"There is a storage closet first and then the ladies' room."

"So there was nothing about Willie Miller's job which gave him a unique access to that room?"

Wallace objects. "It is beyond the witness's direct knowledge to make conclusions about the defendant's unique access." Hatchet sustains the objection.

"But anyone could have entered?"

"Yes."

"Would you say the alley at the time you arrived was clean?"

"Well, there was a great deal of blood."

"I understand, but I mean in addition to the evidence of the murder. Did the alley look as if it had been scrubbed recently?"

"No, I wouldn't say so."

"So the scene was already dirty. Trash, food from the restaurants, animal waste?"

"Yes."

"Detective Prentice, you said the first thing you did was cordon off the scene. Why did you do that?"

"To prevent people from tromping around on the evidence and contaminating it. To preserve the evidence."

"Were you successful at that?"

"Yes, I believe that I was."

"Did any people enter that specific area?"

"Not after I was there. I made sure everyone stayed clear of the scene, so that the forensics people could do their work."

"I'm not an expert on this kind of thing, so perhaps you can tell me . . . is there a law of contamination that says it can only take place after the police arrive?"

"Of course not," he says. "Contamination can take place at any time."

"Well, was anybody on the scene before you arrived?"

"Yes."

I feign surprise. "Who?"

"Well, Edward Markham, his father—"

I interrupt. "Edward Markham's father was there? Was this some kind of a family outing?"

"No, he had called his father as well as the police."

Under prodding, Prentice is forced to admit that there were also a group of people from the bar that had been on the scene.

"So there were at least a half-dozen people walking around that alley before you got there?" I ask.

"Yes," he concedes.

"Just hanging out, contaminating away?"

He won't concede that, but he doesn't have to. I've gotten the idea in the jurors' minds, and that's all I was going to manage.

Wallace next calls the on-scene technician who supervised the gathering of the blood and other evidence. She comes off as thoroughly professional and confident that she had done her job well. The most I can get her to admit is that techniques have improved since then, and that DNA was not on her mind when she was doing the collecting. She leaves the stand unscathed.

The next to escape any damage from my cross-examination is Donnie, the bartender. Wallace leads him through his story, and his recollections remain crystal clear. I make little effort to attack him, since his information is factual, but not terribly harmful to Willie. But I need to make some points, so that the jury will remember that we are a force to be reckoned with.

"How long did you work with Willie Miller?"

"About six months."

"Was he a reliable employee?"

"He was okay. As long as he did his job, we didn't have too much to do with each other."

"So to your knowledge he was never reprimanded? Never threatened with termination?"

"No."

"Did you serve liquor at this establishment?"

Donnie laughs. "Of course. It was a bar."

"Did Willie Miller have access to this liquor? Was it within easy reach for him?"

"Well, sure. I mean, it wasn't that big a place."

"Did you ever see him drunk before that night?"

"No." He quickly qualifies it. "Employees aren't allowed to drink on the job."

"That's a rule?" I ask.

"Yes."

"So Mr. Miller followed that rule? He did not drink on the job?"

"If he did, I don't remember it."

"Would he have been reprimanded if he were caught drinking on the job?"

"Sure."

I switch the focus. "When Edward Markham told you what happened, what did you do?"

"I went out to the back, and I saw the . . . young woman's body." Donnie says "young woman" with a wary eye on Laurie. This is a man who has a strong testicle-preservation instinct. "He said he had called the cops, so I just waited with him."

"When the police came, did you tell them you thought Willie might have done it? I'm talking about before the eyewitness said what she had seen."

"No."

"So you had no reason to suspect that he would have committed this murder?"

"No."

I let him go and turn the momentum back to Wallace. He is doing what he is supposed to do: getting the witnesses necessary to build his case on and off quickly. Each represents a building block for the prosecution, and by the time they are finished they expect to have a house that cannot be blown over by the windbag defense attorney, me.

Next up is Edward Markham, who clearly did not spend his recent trip to Africa on a hunger strike to protest the granting of a new trial to his girlfriend's accused killer. He is at least forty pounds heavier than pictures show him to have been at the time of the murder, and though he is only in his thirties, he's already captured the look of an aging playboy.

"Had you and Denise McGregor been dating long?" asks Wallace.

"About three months. We were pretty intense."

"Any plans for marriage?"

"I certainly had some," says Edward. He grins. "But I hadn't gotten up the nerve to ask her."

Wallace brings him to the night of the murder, and Denise McGregor's fateful trip to the rest room.

"How long was she gone before you started to worry?"

Edward appears to consider this, as if it is the first time he's been asked this question, and he's trying to comb through his memory. I would bet twenty-two million dollars he and Wallace rehearsed every word of this testimony at least twice.

"I'd say about ten minutes or so. And even then I wasn't that worried. I mean, you don't think about something like this. But I thought there might be something wrong."

"So you got up to check on her?"

"Yes," says Edward. "I went to the rest room door, and it was ajar, you know, not fully closed. I didn't know if I should go inside, or maybe find another woman to go in and check up on her. I thought she might be sick or something."

"What did you do?"

"I called into the room a few times, just yelling 'Denise,' but there was no answer. So I pushed the door open a little more and looked in."

"What did you find?"

"Well, at first nothing. I looked around, and she wasn't there, so I started to go back to the table. I really didn't know what to think. Then I saw the blood."

"Blood?"

"It sure looked like it, and it was still wet. It was splattered on the floor near the phone. And the phone was hanging off the hook." Edward is doing a good job, he's been rehearsed well.

"What did you do next?" asks Wallace.

"I got real worried . . . panicky . . . and I started looking around. I went out into the hall, and I saw that the exit to the alley was right there. So I went out there, and . . . and . . . I saw her."

Edward acts as if he is trying to keep his emotions intact as he relives what happened. "It was the most horrible moment of my life."

Wallace gives him a few seconds to compose himself; I can use the time to get over my nausea.

"What happened next?"

"Well, I went to her . . . I touched her to see if she was breathing, but she wasn't. So I went back into the bar and called 911, and then I called my father. And then I told the bartender, and we just waited for everyone to get there."

Wallace turns Edward over to me. I don't want to do too much with him, because I'm going to call him during the defense case. I just want to put some doubts in the jury's mind, and maybe take away this image of Edward as the grieving near-widower.

I start off on his relationship with Denise.

"Mr. Markham, what is Denise McGregor's father's first name?"

He's surprised by the question. "I . . . I don't remember."

"How about her mother's name?"

"I don't know . . . it's been a long time. I don't think her parents lived near here."

"Have you seen them since the funeral?"

"No, I don't believe so."

"Did you see them *at* the funeral?"

"No, I was very upset, sedated . . . I've felt guilty ever since about not going, but I was in no condition—"

"You didn't go to Denise McGregor's funeral?" I'm so shocked, you could knock me over with a legal brief.

"No, I just told you, I—"

I cut him off. "Do you know what Denise was working on at the time of her death?"

"No. I know it was a story."

"Yes, Mr. Markham, that's what she wrote. Stories." My voice is dripping with disdain. "But you don't know which one she was working on?"

"No."

"Do you have a favorite story that she ever wrote?"

"Not really. She was a terrific writer. All of her work was great, but she didn't talk about it very much."

"Tell us about any one of her stories."

Edward looks stricken, so Wallace objects. "This is not going anywhere remotely relevant."

"Your Honor," I respond, "Mr. Wallace took the witness through a soap opera about how close he and the victim were, how he was about to propose. I believe he referred to their relationship as intense. If that was relevant, certainly my demonstrating that it is nonsense is equally relevant."

"We *were* close," insists Edward. "No matter how you try to twist things around."

Hatchet admonishes Edward. "The witness will only speak to answer questions posed by the attorneys."

Edward is chastened. "Yes, sir. Sorry."

"Let's move it along, Mr. Carpenter," says Hatchet.

"Yes, Your Honor." I have a little more fun with this area of questioning, and then move on to the night of the murder.

"Was there a great deal of blood near her body when you found her?"

"Yes, it was everywhere."

"And when you touched her skin, was it cold?"

"No, not really. But I could tell it was terrible . . . that she was dead. She wasn't breathing."

"How did you know she wasn't breathing?" I ask.

"I put my hand on her chest . . . here." He puts his hand on his sternum, so as to demonstrate. "It wasn't moving at all."

I nod and walk over to the defense table. Kevin hands me a piece of paper, which I bring over to the court clerk. I introduce it as a defense exhibit and then hand a copy of it to Edward.

"Mr. Markham, this is a police report regarding the night of the murder. Can you read the second paragraph from the bottom out loud for the jury?"

Edward locates the paragraph and begins to read. "Markham's clothing, including shirt, sweater, pants, shoes, and socks, was examined and was found to be free of any traces of blood."

"Thank you," I say. "Could you please tell the jury how you managed to walk through the pools of blood surrounding the victim, then put your hands on her skin and chest, and not get any of her blood on you?"

A flash of worry crosses his face, which is strange, because the same lack of blood that is causing his credibility to be questioned provides him a clear defense against being the murderer himself. There is no way he could have stabbed Denise to death in the manner this was done and not have blood on him.

"I don't know . . . I guess I was just very careful. I've always been really squeamish about blood, so I probably avoided it. Everything was happening so fast."

"What was happening fast?"

"You know, I found the body, called the police and my father . . . it just seemed like a dream."

I nod as if he has just cleared up everything. "A dream where you don't dirty your clothes."

"Objection."

"Sustained."

"No further questions, Your Honor," I say. "But the defense reserves the right to recall this witness in our case in chief."

Based on the look on Edward's face, I don't think he's looking forward to being recalled.

• • • • •

BETTY ANTHONY LIVES IN A SMALL GARDEN
apartment in Lyndhurst. There are maybe five hundred units in
the complex, and if any one is different from any other, it is a
very subtle difference. Since I have only an address and not an
apartment number, I have absolutely no idea in which specific
apartment she lives.

I stop five or six of her neighbors, none of whom has heard
of her. I'm forced to go to the rental office, where I wait as the
lone agent preaches to an elderly couple the benefits of the
tram that goes directly from the apartment complex to the supermarket. This is clearly *the* place to live.

Finally, the agent looks up Betty's apartment number, and I
go there. Betty obviously takes care of her small slice of this
earth with loving care; there is a small flower garden in front
that looks like it is a very pampered piece of real estate. Betty
is not in, and I'm trying to decide whether to wait when I finally
catch a break. Her next-door neighbor comes home, and tells
me that Betty would still be at Carlton's Department Store,
where she sells lingerie.

The lingerie department is on the third floor of Carlton's,
and is clearly not a place for males. Female customers look at
me as if I am an alien visitor, while a few smile a condescending "isn't that cute, he's buying something for his wife" smile.

The first thing I notice about the place are the mannequins, dressed in flimsy, sexy bras and panties. They are incredibly shapely; if I were a woman concerned about my figure I would throw out all the diet books and find out what they feed these mannequins.

I can't speak for other males, but the hardest thing for me in these situations is knowing who works for the store and who doesn't. Customers and salespeople look exactly alike. I try three people before I hit on an actual storeperson. I ask her if she can help me.

"Unless you want to try something on."

My guess is that she's used that joke on the last five hundred males that she's encountered in this department, so I smile a semi-appreciative smile, and ask if she knows where Betty Anthony is. She does.

"Betty! Customer!"

Betty is standing at the cash register, finishing a sale, and she motions that she'll just be a minute. I nod that I'll wait, and in a few minutes she comes over. She's in her early sixties, with a pleasant face and a slightly tired smile. She'd like to be off her feet, and she deserves to be.

"Can I help you?" she asks.

"I'd like to talk to you about your husband."

She tenses exactly as Wally had when I mentioned Denise. That's apparently my mission, to go around the state and re-open old wounds in people that deserve better.

Finally, she nods, slowly, the nod of someone who has been expecting this visit, and who has been dreading it. I instinctively feel that if I can find out why, I'll have found out everything.

Betty agrees to have a cup of coffee with me, and I wait the thirty-five minutes until she is finished with her shift. We go to a small diner down the street, the kind with little jukeboxes on the tables that never work. I tell her that I'm representing Willie Miller, and watch for her reaction.

There isn't any. She has no idea who Willie Miller is, and can't imagine what her husband could possibly have to do with him. It's not good news.

I tell her about the picture, and my suspicion that there is something about it that has changed a great many lives, possibly Mike's included.

She tells me that "Mike had many friends. He was the kind of person that people naturally liked."

Then I tell her that the woman Willie is accused of murdering is Denise McGregor, and I think I see a small flash of fear in her eyes, which she quickly covers up.

Her response is that "Mike was a wonderful man, a terrific husband and father. He loved his work."

Platitudes like this aren't going to do it for me; I know I have to somehow pierce this armor. "Look, I'm defending a man on trial for his life. I think you have information that can help me, but maybe you don't. The only way I'm going to find out for sure is by being direct."

She nods her understanding, but seems to cringe in anticipation. This is not going to be fun.

"Why did your husband take his own life?"

For a moment I think she is going to cry, but when she answers, her voice is clear and strong.

"He was a very unhappy man. Haunted, really."

"By what?"

"I loved my husband very much," she evades, "but I couldn't really help him, at least not the kind of help he needed. And now all I have is his memory, and I'm not going to destroy it. Not for you, not for your client, not for anybody."

Sitting across this table from me is the answer; I can feel it, I know it. I have to go after it, even if it means badgering a woman who is clearly suffering.

"Something happened a very long time ago, something I believe Mike was a part of. But whatever it was, it's over. It can't be changed. My client shouldn't lose his life to protect the secret."

"I can't help you," she says.

"You *won't* help me."

She thinks for a few moments, as if considering what I'm saying. Then her eyes go cold and she shuts off, as surely as if somebody flicked a switch. The window of opportunity has shut, leaving me to wonder if there's anything I could have done to keep it open. I don't think so; I think this decision was made a long time ago.

"I'm not going to argue with you," she says. "You're not going to get what you want here."

One last try. "Look, I know you want to protect your husband's memory . . . his reputation. Believe me, I want to do the same thing for my father. But a man's life is on the line. I need to know the truth."

I've lost her. She stands and prepares to leave. "The truth is I loved my husband." She says that with a sadness, an understanding that her love did not prove to be enough.

She walks away and out of the diner. I guess I'll pay the check.

The next day is devoted to DNA, and Wallace puts on Dr. Hillary D'Antoni, a scientist from the laboratory where the tests were done. She goes through a detailed but concise definition of the process, and then on to the results of the tests done on the skin and blood under Denise's fingernails.

"Dr. D'Antoni," Wallace asks, "what is the mathematical likelihood that the skin under the victim's fingernails was that of the defendant, William Miller?"

"There is a one in five and a half billion chance that it was not."

"And what is the mathematical likelihood that the blood under the victim's fingernails was that of the defendant, William Miller?"

"There is a one in six and one quarter billion chance that it was not."

My cross-examination focuses mostly on not the science but the collection methods. I get Dr. D'Antoni to agree with the "garbage in, garbage out" concept. In other words, the results her lab can achieve are only as good as the samples they are sent. My problem is I have no legitimate basis on which to challenge the samples, and if the jury has one brain among them they will know it. Besides, I'm going to challenge the physical evidence later, in a different context.

"Dr. D'Antoni," I say, "you raised some very impressive odds

concerning the source of the material under the defendant's fingernails. In the area of one in six billion."

"Yes."

"You are positive that the blood and skin actually belonged
to the defendant, are you not?"

"I am. The tests are quite conclusive."

"Is there anything in those tests that leads you to believe the
defendant was not framed?"

"I don't understand the question."

"I'm sorry. If I gave you a hypothetical that the defendant
was framed, and that the material you tested was in fact planted
before it was sent to you, is there anything about your testing
which would prove me wrong?"

"No. We test the material we are given."

"Thank you."

Wallace's next witness is Lieutenant Pete Stanton. This is not
something I look forward to. Pete is an experienced, excellent
witness, and what he is going to say will be very negative for
Willie. It will be my job to try and rip him apart, something I
don't relish doing to a friend. The only thing worse would be
not to rip him apart.

Wallace takes Pete through the basics, starting off with
Pete's status in the department at the time of the murder. His
goal is to show his rapid rise, lending credibility to his abilities.

"I was a detective, grade two."

"And you've been promoted since then?"

Pete nods. "Three times. First came detective three, then
four, and then I made lieutenant two years ago."

"Congratulations," Wallace says.

"Objection," I say. "Did Mr. Wallace bring in a cake so we
can blow out the candles and celebrate the witness's promo-
tions? Maybe we can sing 'For he's a jolly good detective.'"

"Lieutenant Stanton's career path is relevant to his credibility," Wallace says.

I shake my head. "He is not here interviewing for a job. He's
presenting evidence of his investigation."

"Sustained," says Hatchet. "Let's move along."

Wallace soon gets to the meat of his testimony, which involves the murder weapon.

"Where was the knife recovered, Lieutenant Stanton?"

"From a trash can about three blocks away from the bar. It was in an alley behind Richie's restaurant on Market Street," Pete answers.

"Do you know whose knife it was?"

Pete nods. "It was one of a set from the bar where the murder took place, and which was subsequently reported missing by the bartender."

"Now this knife . . . what was found on it?"

"Blood from the victim, Denise McGregor. And a clear fingerprint match with the defendant, Willie Miller."

Wallace asks him some more questions, but the damage has been done. If I can't repair it, nothing that follows is going to make any difference. I stand up to face Pete, who digs in as if he were making a goal line stand.

"Good morning, Lieutenant Stanton."

"Good morning, Mr. Carpenter."

Thus ends the pleasantries of this particular cross-examination. From now on it's no-holds-barred.

"How did you happen to focus on Willie Miller as a suspect?"

"He was identified by an eyewitness, who saw him standing over the body before he ran off. Her name is Cathy Pearl."

"This eyewitness, Cathy Pearl, did she say to you, 'I saw Willie Miller'?"

"No. She was not familiar with his name. She described him, and the bartender told us that it sounded very much like the defendant."

"So at that point he became your prime suspect?"

"Obviously, it was very early in the investigation, but he became someone we were interested in finding and questioning."

"And where did you find him?" I ask.

"He was lying in a doorway about two blocks away from the scene."

"Did he resist when you took him into custody?"

"No, he was incapacitated from alcohol."

"So he stood up and walked to the car and you took him down to the station?"

"No, as I said, he was incapacitated from alcohol, so he was unable to walk. We called paramedics, and he was taken on a stretcher to the hospital."

I'm puzzled. "So he ran away from the scene, but couldn't walk to the car?"

"An hour or so had gone by, so he had time to drink more alcohol during that period."

"Did you find an empty bottle?"

"There were plenty of empty bottles in that area."

"Any with Willie's saliva on them?"

"We didn't look for them or test them. The alcohol was obviously in his system; there was nothing to be gained by finding out which bottle he drank from."

"Lieutenant, when you are assigned a case like this, you develop theories, do you not? You try and re-create, at least in your own mind, what happened?"

"I have theories, but first I go where the evidence takes me. My theories follow from the evidence."

"Fine. So let's talk about that evidence. We'll start with the knife. Now, you testified that it was from a set of knives at the bar where the murder took place, and where Willie Miller worked as a busboy. Is that correct?"

"Yes, it is."

"How, exactly, do you know that?"

Pete is becoming impatient. "It was identical to the ones used at the bar, and one was missing."

I nod, as if that makes sense. Then I tell Hatchet that the bailiff has two packages that I gave him, and that I would like to use as evidence. Hatchet is suspicious, but allows it, and the bailiff gives me the packages.

I open one of the packages and take out a knife. I ask if I can hand it to the witness. Hatchet allows it.

"Detective, the knife you are holding is one of the knives currently used in the bar where the murder took place. Would you examine it, please?"

Pete looks at the knife, warily eyeing me the whole time. I

then open the other package, and take out six additional knives, all apparently identical to the first, and show them to Pete as well.

"One of these six knives is from the same set as the first one, and was also used at the bar. Please tell the jury which one."

Pete of course cannot, and he is forced to admit so.

"So," I ask, "the fact that one knife seems identical to another doesn't mean they are from the same restaurant?"

"Not necessarily, but it certainly increases the chances, particularly when one is missing."

I move on. "You testified that you found a knife, wherever it was originally from, three blocks from the bar, where it was sitting in a trash can."

"That's correct."

"So let me get this straight," I say. "Since you just told this jury that your theories follow the evidence, is it your theory that Willie Miller took a knife from where he worked, used it to murder a woman, and then didn't wipe off either her blood, or his fingerprints?"

"Yes."

"It's rare when murderers are that stupid, isn't it?"

"You don't have to be a college graduate to murder someone."

"Thank you for making the jury aware of that, Lieutenant. I'm sure they had no idea." Sorry, Pete, but it helps me if you look arrogant and uncooperative.

He glares at me, but I keep boring in. "Now, Lieutenant, you'll admit it would have to require both stupidity and a poorly developed self-preservation instinct to have done all this?"

Wallace intervenes. "Objection. The witness is not a psychologist."

Hatchet says, "Overruled. You may answer the question."

Pete has a ready answer. "When people are drunk they often have a tendency to be careless. And as I said, he was very, very drunk. There is no way he could have been thinking clearly."

I nod as if he has just cleared everything up for me. "Right.

He was smashed. So smashed that he could run from the scene, but not walk to the car. So smashed that he couldn't think clearly enough to wipe off his prints, but sober enough that he could make a conscious decision to hide the knife three blocks away."

I can see a flash of concern in Pete's eyes; he wasn't prepared for that.

"Murders and murderers aren't always logical."

"You're absolutely right, Lieutenant. Sometimes things aren't what they seem to be."

He's getting angry. "I didn't say that."

"I wouldn't expect you to. Your job is to justify what you've done in this case, no matter how little sense it makes."

Wallace objects, and Hatchet sustains, instructing the jury to disregard.

"By the way, Lieutenant, how did you happen to locate the knife?"

"A phone call was made to 911. Somebody reported finding a knife with blood on it."

"Somebody?"

Pete is getting more and more uncomfortable. "A man. He didn't give his name."

My tone is getting more and more mocking, and I'm making more eye contact with the jury, especially the two people Kevin had picked out. I'm trying to draw them to my side so that we can doubt Pete's credibility together.

"I see. Somebody who didn't give his name called to say he found a bloody knife while browsing through a trash can in the middle of the night."

"It happens."

"Apparently so," I say. "Did this human metal detector touch the knife? Were his own fingerprints found on it?"

"No. No other prints were found."

I seem surprised, although I knew what his answer would be. "So, somebody was browsing through the garbage, saw a knife with blood on it . . . by the way, would you describe it as very unusual for a steak knife to have blood on it?"

"Not human blood."

"Did this mysterious somebody conduct a DNA test on it while it was still in the garbage?"

"Objection."

"Sustained."

"Do you think the average person who spends his evenings going through garbage cans can tell the difference between human blood and steak blood? In the dark?"

"Objection. The witness couldn't possibly know the extent of other people's knowledge."

"Sustained."

I've made my point. "But this anonymous person was smart enough not to touch the knife, is that right?"

"There were no other prints."

"So this person wasn't looking to take things from the trash can. He was just making sure that everything was in order. Maybe conducting an inventory?"

"I don't know what his intentions were."

"Does any of this seem unusual to you, Lieutenant?"

"Unusual, but not impossible."

"Did you ever think to question any of it?"

"I question everything."

I've gone as far as I can down this road, so I veer off.

"Then let me ask you a hypothetical question. Supposing this was a frame-up?"

"Objection." It's becoming a steady chorus from Wallace.

"Overruled."

I continue. "Just for argument's sake, let's say it was a frame-up. Let's say that somebody wanted you to arrest Willie Miller. In that context, wouldn't all these 'unusual' things make sense?"

"No."

"No?" I'm incredulous. "Is it really no, or is it just that if this turned out to be a frame-up, then it would mean that your entire investigation has been an incompetent joke? That you helped cause Willie Miller to spend seven years of his life in prison for a crime he didn't commit?"

"Objection."

"Sustained. Jury will disregard. Mr. Carpenter, if I hear a

speech like that again, you will be held in contempt of court, a crime which you did commit."

I apologize and plow on, not wanting to lose momentum. "Isn't it true that you found Willie Miller and said case closed, let's get on to the next one?"

"No," he says firmly, "it is not."

"Isn't it true you saw all these clues laid out in front of you and followed them just like you were programmed to?"

Hatchet is in the middle of sustaining Wallace's objection while I'm yelling at Pete, and he tells Pete not to answer. He also admonishes me for being a pain in his ass, just not in so many words.

"No further questions."

Pete is asked a few questions by Wallace to rehabilitate him, and he stares at me the entire time. My friendship with Lieutenant Pete Stanton just took a shot. I'm not happy about making him look bad; but it's what I do for a living.

I set the evening meeting with Laurie and Kevin at the office for seven o'clock, but only Kevin is there when I arrive. I've come to trust his instincts and judgments. He thinks I did well today with Pete, but recognizes what our problem is. Wallace has a mountain of evidence: the knife, the skin, the blood, the eyewitness, etc. I can attack each one, but if the jury believes any one of them, Willie is finished. Because each one is by itself capable of carrying the day.

Tomorrow Wallace will have his forensics expert on the stand, and Kevin and I set about planning our cross-examination.

Laurie comes in uncharacteristically late, but with very interesting news. Utilizing her contacts, she has uncovered the fact that Edward Markham had two arrests for beating up women prior to Denise McGregor's murder.

At least as disturbing is the fact that, though the records of these assaults have since been expunged, my father should have been aware of them back when he was prosecuting Willie Miller. Yet there is no evidence that he ever followed up on it. Did he think it was unimportant, or was he repaying a favor to his apparent friend Victor Markham, who may have paid him two million dollars? But how could Markham have anticipated a murder trial that wasn't to take place for nearly thirty years after the payment?

Laurie asks if we can use the arrests at trial, and Kevin correctly points out that we cannot, that Hatchet would never let them in. The law is clear; the previous violations, even if they were proven, have to compare almost identically to the offense that is the subject of the trial. These don't.

"Too bad," says Laurie. "The bastard might have done it himself."

I do a double take. "I thought you were positive that Willie Miller did it."

"I was. And now I'm not."

This is a major concession for Laurie, but I'm not about to lord it over her.

Around ten o'clock, Kevin leaves and Laurie hangs around for a while as I finish my preparation for court tomorrow. As she is getting ready to leave, she walks toward me and says, "You're doing really well, Andy. No one could be doing more."

I shake my head. "You know," I say, "my father said I couldn't win this. I think he was right."

"He was goading you, and he was wrong. Good night, Andy."

"Good night, Laurie."

We just stand there, about a foot away from each other. We both know that we are dangerously close to kissing, but after a few seconds the moment passes. She leaves, and I'm alone with my thoughts.

When I was married, or at least before our separation, I did not come close to kissing other women. It sounds corny, but I rarely ever thought about other women, so ingrained in me was the sanctity of the marriage bond. That's now been changed, and I don't think it's going to change back any time soon. What's left for me is to figure out what that says about my marriage or myself.

I'll figure it out after the trial.

• • • • •

NICOLE HAS REALLY BEEN QUITE UNDER-standing about the trial, and the impact it's having on our time together. She waits up for me to come home at night, and gets up every morning to watch me make breakfast. She talks about us getting away after the trial is concluded; maybe to the luxury hotel in the Virgin Islands where we spent our honeymoon. That was in another lifetime, a time and place that I no longer have any connection to at all. I desperately wish I did.

I've been able to put the romantic-emotional aspect of my life on hold while I deal with the Miller case, but I know it's back there, in the dark recesses of my mind, waiting to cause me aggravation. I've always thought a main component of love is wanting, needing, to share things, good as well as bad, with the person that you love. I'm not feeling that with Nicole.

On some level I know that Nicole and I can never recapture what we had, or seemed to have had. I keep hoping that will change, but it doesn't feel like it ever will. I don't believe it is Laurie's presence that is causing this. She is not what is standing between Nicole and me.

Fortunately, I don't have very much time to agonize over these questions. Our whole team is putting in eighteen-hour days, and adrenaline is keeping us raring to go at the nine A.M. start to each court day. Another reason I'm able to be on time each morning is that I no longer even pass by the newsstand on the way to court; it is closed down and a symbol of my humiliation. Today I even arrive a few minutes early, and I use the time to get ready for the next witness, forensics expert Michael Cassidy.

As Henry Higgins would say, Cassidy "oozes smugness from every pore, as he oils his way across the floor." I find him to be thoroughly pompous and dislikable, and I hope the jury has the same reaction. He is basically there to testify about the material found under the fingernails of Denise McGregor, as well as the scratch marks on Willie that those fingernails obviously caused. Wallace has a lot of ammunition here, and he doesn't leave a single shell unexploded.

There is a large poster board with a full-color shot of a dazed and scratched Willie Miller, taken shortly after his arrest. The only way he could look more guilty in the picture would be if he were holding up a sign saying "I did it."

Wallace is questioning Cassidy about the photograph, and Cassidy has a wooden pointer, the type teachers used to have in class before they got the Internet wired in.

Wallace asks, "Where were the scratch marks?"

Of course, Stevie Wonder could have pointed to the scratch marks on the photograph, but Cassidy does so as if the jury really needs his help to see them.

"They are here, and here, on the left and right cheeks on the defendant's face."

Wallace then takes maybe thirty questions to elicit the information he could have gotten in two. Not only were the blood and skin under the fingernails of Denise McGregor that of Willie Miller, but Cassidy has determined that the scratch marks on Willie's face were made by those same fingernails.

Wallace turns the witness over to me. If I can't get the jury to doubt Cassidy, it's game, set, and match.

"Mr. Cassidy, what other foreign material besides Willie Miller's blood and skin did you find under the victim's fingernails?"

"What do you mean?" he asks.

"Which part of the question didn't you understand?"

Wallace objects that I'm being argumentative and badgering. Damn right I am. Hatchet sustains the objection. I restate the question, and Cassidy answers.

"We didn't find anything else."

I feign surprise. "To the best of your knowledge, was Willie Miller naked when he was arrested?"

"I wasn't there, but I believe he was fully clothed."

"Is there any reason to think he was naked when he committed the crime?"

"Not that I'm aware of."

I bore in. "Were there scratches anywhere other than on his face?"

"No, those were the only scratch marks. But there were needle marks on each arm."

The medical examination of Willie had shown needle marks on both arms, but since a blood test revealed no drugs in his system, the prosecution was precluded from bringing it out in direct examination. Wallace smiles slightly, assuming that I ineptly opened the door through which that information reached the jury.

"Yes, the needle marks, we will certainly hear more about those," I say. "Now, what was the defendant wearing when he was arrested?"

"Objection," says Wallace. "The answer is already in the record. His shirt and jeans, *with the victim's bloodstains on them,* have been submitted into evidence."

Hatchet sustains the objection, and I bow graciously to Wallace. "Thank you. It's so hard to keep track of all this conclusive evidence."

I ask Cassidy, "His shirt was cotton, wasn't it?"

"Yes."

"But there were no traces of cotton under her nails?"

"No."

"So she went after his face only?"

"It was only his face that she actually scratched," he says. "I can't say for sure what she went after, I wasn't there."

"No. Neither was I. Can I borrow your pointer? It's a beauty."

He would like to hit me over the head with it, but instead he grudgingly hands it to me, and I walk over to the large photograph of Willie in all his scratched glory.

"By the way, did you find a ruler near the body?"

"A ruler?"

"You know what a ruler is, don't you? It's like this pointer, only smaller, flatter, and straighter."

Wallace objects and Hatchet admonishes me; business as usual.

"The thing that puzzles me," I say, "is that I personally cannot draw a straight line, yet the victim managed to scratch two of them."

I point to the scratch marks on each cheek, which are in fact close to perfectly straight and perpendicular to the ground.

"There are no normal patterns for this. Every case is different." He's getting more smug as he goes along. It's time to de-smugitize him.

"No normal pattern? Isn't the existence of any pattern at all by definition abnormal?"

"I don't know what you mean."

"Then let me explain it to you, Doctor," I snarl. "Here we have a woman who is being beaten and stabbed to death by a drunken man, who must be pretty unstable in his own right. So she's flailing away, desperately trying to defend herself, trying to stop the knife from penetrating her, trying to stop his other hand from hitting her—"

"Objection!" yells Wallace. "Is there a question somewhere in this speech?"

"Sustained."

I push forward. "Okay, here's a bunch of questions. Why didn't she touch his clothes? Why didn't she touch those hands? Why, in her panic, did she choose to scratch two perfectly straight marks on each side of his face?"

The smugness is gone. "I can't say for sure, but it's possible—"

I interrupt. "It's possible that someone held her hands, after she was dead, and scratched Willie Miller's face, when he was too drunk to even know it."

Wallace stands again. "Objection, Your Honor. Must we continue to listen to Mr. Carpenter's ramblings about his visits to Fantasyland?"

I turn and address Wallace directly, which is something Hatchet will come down on me for. "If I'm in Fantasyland, you should visit it. Things seem to make more sense here."

After court is over, I find myself alone with Wallace in the men's room. We exchange typical standing-at-the-urinal small talk, and then I ask him a question which has been on my mind.

"Richard, you were in the office at the time . . . why did my father prosecute Willie Miller?"

"Come on, Andy. Don't believe your own speeches. There's a mountain of evidence here."

"No," I say. "I mean, why did he handle the trial himself? He was the DA by then; he hardly ever went into a courtroom."

Richard thinks for a moment. "I don't know; I remember wondering about that myself at the time. But he was adamant about it. Maybe because it was a capital case. Maybe with Markham involved, your father wanted to be the one to take whatever political heat would result if the trial went badly."

I nod. "Maybe."

Wallace zips up, says goodbye, and leaves me to ponder all the other possible maybes.

Hatchet adjourns for the day and I go back to the office. Nicole has called and left a message reminding me of a promise I had made to go to Philip's estate after the evening meeting at the office. He is throwing a fund-raiser for a local congressional candidate that I wouldn't vote for if he were running against Muammar Qaddafi.

We convene our evening meeting early, at five o'clock, mainly for the purpose of discussing tomorrow's cross-examination of the eyewitness, Cathy Pearl.

Laurie is not coming to the meeting; she has gone to see Betty Anthony, to try and do what I couldn't—get her to talk about her deceased husband, Mike.

Kevin and I go over how I will handle Cathy Pearl's appearance tomorrow, and we believe that we can be reasonably effective. The exciting, nerve-racking, dangerous thing about cross-examination is that there truly is no way to accurately predict how it will go. There is an ebb and flow that develops between all the players in the courtroom that is volatile and can lead in various directions.

The lawyer conducting the cross is most like a point guard in a basketball game. It's his or her job to set the pace, to try and dictate the way the game will be played. But like in a basketball game, the lawyer cannot determine what defense, what tactics, the other side will employ.

Most important, unlike in basketball, it's not a four-of-seven series; there's not another game in two days. Cross-examining a witness takes place once, and it's generally winner take all. It can be scarier than the Lincoln Tunnel.

Kevin has been a little down lately; his enthusiasm has seemed to wane even as we have had some success challenging witnesses. I ask him about that, and he reveals that his conscience is rearing its ugly head. In short, he thinks Willie Miller is probably guilty, and while he wants us to win, Kevin worries that we might cause the release of a brutal murderer out into society.

"So," I ask him, "you think we might be better than the prosecutors?"

He responds, "I think you might be the best defense attorney I've ever seen."

That's a subject I could talk about for hours, but I try to keep the focus on Kevin. He's in some pain over this, and I might be able to help. He believes I could be so good that there could be a wrong verdict reached.

"What if we didn't represent him?" I ask.

"Then he'd get someone else."

"What," I ask, "if that someone was better than we are? Or not nearly as good as Wallace? Couldn't a wrong verdict result just as easily?"

He nods. "Of course."

"I'll tell you how I see it. To me a right or wrong verdict isn't a question of accurately judging the defendant's guilt or innocence. To me the verdict is right if both sides are well represented and get their fair day in court."

"You might feel differently if you were wrongly convicted," he says. "Or if someone you loved was murdered, and the guilty man went free."

"I might, but I would be thinking about myself, and not about society. Society needs this system. Look, you're a terrific lawyer, and if you had a hundred cases, maybe you'd get a few guilty people off. But what if you didn't take those cases? A good portion of them would get lesser attorneys, and some of the innocent ones might be convicted."

He smiles. "But none of them would be on my conscience."

"Didn't they tell you to leave your conscience in a locker at law school?"

We're not going to resolve his doubts tonight; they've been hounding him for too long. But I think, make that hope, that we've taken a step. Kevin is a hell of a lawyer, and an even better person.

I invite Kevin to go to the fund-raiser at Philip's, but he begs off, since he has to go to the Laundromat and empty the quarters from the machines.

I drive out to Philip's estate in Alpine. He has eleven acres of prime real estate in the most expensive area of New Jersey, all magnificently landscaped and including a huge swimming pool, tennis court, putting green, and, believe it or not, a helicopter pad.

There is also an extraordinary three-bedroom guest house, about a hundred yards from the main one, that would qualify as a dream house to most families. Philip calls this "Nicole's place," since he built it shortly before she was born, in the hope that she would someday move in.

In fact, back when Nicole and I were about to be married, Philip mounted a campaign to get us to live in this guest house. He correctly pointed out that it was considerably nicer than anything we could afford to buy, and promised that it was separate enough that we would have our privacy. After all, he reasoned, he was in Washington most of the time anyway.

My father cautioned me against accepting the offer, but I

was smart enough on my own to turn it down. If we had moved into the guest house, Philip's dominance over us would have been total.

The party tonight is outdoors under the stars, in the area between the guest house and the pool. It is part of a concerted effort by Philip to actively help others in his party. Philip has used his prominent position as head of the crime subcommittee to get himself talked about as a possible vice presidential candidate in the next election, and he earns political markers by raising money for his colleagues.

I arrive, the only male in the entire place, including the staff, not in a tuxedo. Nicole comes over to me, not seeming to notice the fact that I'm underdressed, since I'm sure she is used to it. She takes my arm and leads me to hobnob with the rich, semifamous, and powerful.

We hobnob for about an hour, each minute more excruciatingly boring than the one before it. Finally, I can't stand it anymore, so I tell Nicole that I really need to get home and get some sleep. She seems disappointed, but understands. It hits me that she actually enjoys being here; this is where she is in her element. It's a scary thought.

• • • • •

THE EYEWITNESS, CATHY PEARL, HAS BEEN A
single mother since she was eighteen, supporting her daughter
by working until one A.M. each night in a run-down diner. That
daughter, as Wallace lets her proudly reveal, has just won a
scholarship to Cornell University. Cathy is the type of person
that juries believe, and very definitely not the type of person
they like to see dismantled on the stand.

Wallace takes her through her history, right up to the frightening moment when she saw Willie Miller standing over the
bloody body of Denise McGregor.

"How did you happen to be in that alley that night, Ms.
Pearl?"

"The diner I work at is on the next block. I cut through the
alley on my way home from work. It saves about ten minutes,
and at one o'clock in the morning, every minute counts."
Everybody, jury included, chuckles at this comment. Everybody except me.

"Please describe what you saw."

She proceeds to describe the scene in graphic, stark terms.
She saw Willie standing over the body, and he saw her as well,
but instead of attacking her he ran off. She thanks God for that
every day, and she especially thanks God that she was able to
pick him out of a lineup the next day.

Cathy is a very credible witness, and based on the jury's re-action to her I don't know whether to cross-examine her or ask for her autograph.

"Ms. Pearl," I begin, "was it unusual for you to cut through this particular alley?"

"No, I do it every night."

"Every night? At the same time?"

"Yes. I got off at one o'clock, and I sure didn't hang around. At one sharp, I was out of there. Every night."

"So anybody watching your pattern over some time would have known you were going to be there?"

"Why would somebody want to do that? I don't think any-body was watching me."

"I understand that. But if somebody *were* watching you, even if you were unaware of it, they would know that you go by there every night just after one o'clock?"

She looks at Wallace for help, but there is none forthcom-ing.

"I suppose so, yes."

"Thank you. Now, you testified that you didn't actually see the defendant stabbing Denise McGregor, you just saw him standing over her body. Is that correct?"

Cathy nods a little too hard, pleased that this is something she can agree with. "Right. He was just sort of standing there, looking at me. Not moving much."

"I would think something like that must have been very scary, particularly at that time of night."

Another vigorous nod. "Yes, it was."

"Did you run away?"

"Well, no . . . not right then . . . at first I didn't know it was a body he was standing over. It was dark."

"Dark?"

She quickly tries to correct what she realizes was a bad move. "Not so dark that I couldn't see."

I nod. "I understand. It was the kind of dark where you could see a face but not a body. That kind of dark."

"Well . . ."

"And then the defendant looked at you. Is that right?"

"Right. And he looked weird. Out of it."

"Maybe drunk?"

"Right. Yes."

"And what was he doing with the knife?"

"I didn't see a knife," she says.

I look at the jurors, to confirm that they find this as confusing as I do. They don't, but they will.

"Help me out here. In the kind of dark where one can see faces but not bodies, do knives show up?"

Wallace stands. "Objection, Your Honor. This is badgering."

"Sustained. Rephrase the question."

"Yes, Your Honor." I turn back to Cathy. "So you didn't see a knife?"

"I've said that all along. I didn't see a knife. I'm not saying it wasn't there, I just didn't see it."

"No doubt he had run three blocks, placed it in the trash with his fingerprints and blood still on it, and returned in time to be there for your one o'clock walk."

This was aimed at Wallace, but Cathy feels the need to defend herself.

"I know what I saw." She points to Willie. "I saw him."

I shake my head sadly. "No, Ms. Pearl, I'm afraid you have no idea what you saw."

"Objection."

"Sustained. Watch it, Mr. Carpenter."

"Yes, Your Honor," I say, "I will." So I rephrase: "Now, Ms. Pearl, since it was light enough to see the defendant's face, and since he looked right at you, is it fair to say he could see your face?"

"Sure . . . I guess."

"But he didn't try to hurt you? To do to you what you believe he did to Denise McGregor?"

"No, he just ran away."

"Yet he should have realized that you could identify him, isn't that right?"

"I guess . . ."

"He would have known you could someday be an eyewitness, just like you are now?"

"I suppose so."

"Maybe he had nothing to hide," I say. "No further questions."

Wallace gets up to rehabilitate her. "Ms. Pearl, when was the next time you saw the defendant after that night?"

"The next morning, at the police station. He was in the lineup. I picked him out right away."

"With other men?"

Cathy nods. "A bunch of them."

"And you had no doubt he was the man you saw in the alley the previous night?"

"No doubt. He was the one. I was positive then, and I'm just as positive now."

Cathy leaves the stand. I definitely did not do enough to damage her. She seemed credible and has no reason to lie. If I were on the jury, I would believe her. And if I believed her, I would vote to convict Willie Miller of murder in the first degree.

I barely have time to reflect on how depressing the situation is when it gets considerably worse. Wallace tells Hatchet, "Your Honor, the state calls Randy Sacich."

This is not good news; I've never heard of Randy Sacich, and witnesses that I've never heard of are the absolute worst.

"Your Honor," I protest, "there is no such person on the state's witness list."

Wallace nods. "We regret that, Your Honor, but Mr. Sacich only came to our attention late yesterday. Our people were questioning him this morning to confirm that he is a reliable witness."

"Your Honor," I reply, "I'm not sure our 'people' would come to the same conclusion as Mr. Wallace's 'people.' In any event, there should not be surprise witnesses before these people." I point at the jury to show who I am referring to.

Hatchet sends the jury out of the room, and Wallace and I kick it around some more. Hatchet buys his position, and Sacich is allowed in. As the jury comes back into the room, I speak to Willie.

"Do you know who this guy is?"

"Nope."

With the jury seated, Randy Sacich is brought in, and Willie stiffens in surprise. He leans in to me.

"He's the guy in the cell next to me."

"Did you tell him anything incriminating?"

"What's that?"

"Bad. Did you tell him anything bad?"

Willie is wounded. "How many times I got to tell you, man? I got nothing bad to say."

Wallace apparently believes otherwise. He takes Sacich through his connection to this case, which is basically one of geography.

"I'm in the cell next to his."

Wallace continues, "And from this vantage point, are you two able to talk to each other?"

"Sure," Sacich says. "Right through the bars." He says this matter-of-factly, as though they live in suburbia and stop by to borrow cups of sugar.

"Did Mr. Miller ever mention the crime for which he is currently imprisoned?" Wallace asks.

Sacich nods agreeably. "Sure, he talked about it all the time. He didn't talk about nothing else."

"Did he ever speak to the legitimacy of the charges?"

"Huh?"

Wallace rephrases. "Did he ever say whether or not he had done it?"

Randy responds softly, almost hard to hear. "Yeah, a bunch of times. He said he did."

"Please speak up so that the jury can hear you, Mr. Sacich."

As rehearsed, Sacich turns to the jury. "He said he sliced her up and watched her guts pour out."

The jury recoils in horror from this, and there is an audible rumble in the courtroom. Hatchet bangs his gavel and demands quiet. He gets it.

Wallace finishes with his questioning and Hatchet calls us to the bench. Out of earshot of the jury, he gives me the option of adjourning for the day and starting cross-examination tomorrow, or going ahead right now.

It's a difficult choice. If I delay, the jury sits with this in-controverted bombshell all night. If I go now, I do so without any background information on Sacich and his story. I will be breaking the cardinal sin—asking questions I do not know the answers to.

I consult briefly with Kevin, and he agrees with my assessment. We've got to go ahead now.

"Mr. Sacich, how did you come to live in the same neighborhood as Mr. Miller?"

"What do you mean?"

"Well, I'm not asking who your real estate agent was, or how big a mortgage you took out on the cell."

"Objection."

"Sustained. Mr. Carpenter, less sarcasm and clearer questions would be appreciated."

"Yes, Your Honor. Mr. Sacich, why are you in jail? What crime were you convicted of?"

Wallace objects as to relevance, and I tell Hatchet that since I had no time to depose this witness, I really need a little lee-way. Besides, the offense he has been convicted of might well go to credibility.

Hatchet overrules the objection and instructs Sacich to answer.

"Rape."

I nod. "Rape. I see. Who did you rape?"

Sacich's eyes dart around the room; he thought he was here to talk about Willie, and now he's being asked to confess to rape under oath.

"I didn't say I did it."

"Did you do it?" There's no downside to this question. If he says no, he looks like a liar. Yes, and he's a rapist. It's like the old "Do you think I'm fit to live with pigs?"

"No," is his answer.

I walk over to the jury box. "Did a jury, sitting in a jury box like these people, vote to convict you?"

"Yeah."

"You wouldn't lie about whether you actually committed

the rape, would you? Because if you did, then how could this jury believe anything you say about this case?"

"I'm not lying."

"So the jury was wrong?"

"Objection. Asked and answered."

"Overruled. You may answer."

"Yeah. The jury was wrong."

"Now, as to what Willie Miller may or may not have told you—"

He interrupts. "He told me he did it."

"Did anyone else hear him make the confession?"

"I don't know. You'd have to ask them." He's getting more and more belligerent.

"But when you heard it, when he said it to you, were the two of you alone, or was there anyone else around?"

"We were alone."

"How long have you been friends with Willie Miller?"

"We just met . . . we sit there all day and we talk some."

"Do most people consider you a good listener? Do they have a tendency to confide in you?"

He nods; this is something he can agree with. "I guess so. Sure. I'm a pretty good listener."

"Do you have any experience in the ministry?" This draws a laugh from the gallery and jury, and an objection from Wallace.

"Your Honor, this is ludicrous."

"Sustained."

"Did anyone promise you anything at all in return for your testimony today?"

"No."

"No talk of a lighter sentence, or of the authorities treating you more favorably in the future?"

Sacich looks toward Wallace, worried about what he is supposed to say. I jump on this. "Do you want to consult with Mr. Wallace? We can take a few moments, and you can get further coaching if that will help you."

"Objection! This witness has not been coached, and I resent the implication that he has."

"Sustained."

"Mr. Sacich," I continue, "what did the authorities say would result from your testimony today?"

"They told me it would look good on my record."

"Who reviews that record?"

"The parole board," he says grudgingly.

It's time to wrap this up. "Okay, Mr. Sacich," I say, "let's forget about logic and your lack of credibility for a moment, and let's assume this happened the way you said, that Willie Miller told you he had done this crime. Do you believe everything you hear in prison?"

"Depends," he allows.

"Do you think people ever lie, maybe to make themselves look tougher in the eyes of other inmates, distinguished innocent citizens like yourself? Or do you think that everyone in maximum security prisons is scrupulously honest?"

"Look, I just know what he told me, and he didn't seem to be lying."

I shake my head sadly. "I'm surprised, Mr. Sacich, because you of all people should know lying when you hear it."

I dismiss Sacich, and Wallace has only a few follow-up questions for him. Kevin's slight nod to me indicates that he believes we have effectively neutralized Sacich's testimony, and I agree.

Wallace calls Diana Martínez, another name I am not familiar with. I am about to stand and object, when Kevin points to her name on the list. It says that she works at Cranford Labs, a company that does work in DNA and more conventional blood testing. We never bothered to interview her because we had planned our strategy in this area, which was to argue about the collection techniques and possible contamination of the samples, rather than about the science itself.

I'm surprised that Wallace is calling Martínez at this point in the case, but I'm not worried about it. That changes the moment she walks into the room and I see Willie Miller's face. All he says, very softly, is "Ooohhh, shit."

All I can do is sit there and brace myself for what is sure to be a disaster, and it is just that. Martínez is a twenty-six-year-old Hispanic woman, whose connection to the case has nothing whatsoever to do with the laboratory at which she works. That is a coincidence, and one which Wallace knew he could rely on to minimize the likelihood of our checking her out in advance.

Wallace leads her through her story, which takes place on a June night nine years ago, almost three years before the McGregor murder. Speaking with a heavy Spanish accent, she relates meeting Willie Miller at a bar. He was drinking heavily, but she agreed to go outside with him. He walked her into an alley behind the bar, where he became verbally abusive. When she tried to leave and reenter the bar, he punched and kicked her.

"I screamed. I begged him to stop, but it was like he couldn't even hear me. I thought he was going to kill me."

"What happened next?" asks Wallace.

"His friends came out and pulled him off of me."

"Was that easy for them to do?"

"No, it took four people. He was completely out of control. Kicking and screaming profanities."

"Did you speak to any of them afterward?"

She nods. "Yes, they said he had done this before, that he had a drinking problem he couldn't control."

Wallace draws out of her the fact that she was treated at a hospital for her injuries, and produces the emergency room record to substantiate her account. He then turns her over to me to cross-examine. I have no idea what the hell to ask her.

"Ms. Martínez, did you report this alleged incident to the police?" I ask.

"No, I was not a citizen then, and—"

"You were here illegally?"

"Yes, but now I am an American. I became a citizen two years ago," she says proudly. Great, next I'll get her to show the flag she's knitted to hang over the courthouse.

She tells the court that she was afraid to report the incident, because she did not want to risk deportation. And she didn't see any coverage of the first trial, because she was in another city living with her sister. It was only when she saw the current media blitz that she recognized Willie and came forward, which she considered her duty as a citizen of America, the country she loves, the land of the free and the home of the brave.

I end my cross, before I do any more damage to my client's case. I do this even though I would very much like to kill my client for not telling me anything about this.

Kevin, Laurie, and I arrange to meet with Willie in an anteroom after the court session, and we sit there talking, waiting for his arrival. Kevin is distraught that he blew it by not following up on Martínez's name, but I don't blame him. I blame myself.

"I didn't lay a glove on her."

"How could you?" Kevin asks.

I ignore that; it doesn't fit in with my self-flagellation. "I'm a lawyer defending somebody on trial for his life. I'm supposed to be prepared."

Laurie tries to change the subject to the defense's case, which is coming up rapidly. She asks who my first witnesses are going to be.

"Witnesses?" I ask. "You mean I'm supposed to have witnesses that can help my client?"

"Andy—"

I cut her off. "I must have been out the day they went over that in law school. Because I don't have a goddamn thing, and—"

I could go on like this for hours, but I'm interrupted by Willie being led into the room. Thank goodness, the one person I'd rather beat up than myself.

Willie, in an uncharacteristically contrite manner, tells us that the story Diana Martínez told is true. He had a drinking problem for over three years, but he became sober at least six months before Denise McGregor was killed.

"You told us you never had a problem with alcohol before," I say.

"I was embarrassed, okay?"

This man who has been on death row for murder for most of the past decade was embarrassed to reveal that he had a drinking problem, which he subsequently conquered. The mind boggles.

"Are there any more little incidents out there like this that you're too embarrassed to talk about? Were you involved with the Kennedy assassination? Or maybe the Lindbergh kidnapping?"

"Come on, man. There's nothing else."

"How did you become sober?"

"I joined a program. It wasn't easy, man, but I did it," he says with some restored pride. He gives us the name of someone in management at the program, and then we let the guard take him away.

Before he leaves, he says, "I'm sorry if I screwed things up."

My anger has been defused, and I tell him that it's okay, that we'll deal with it, even though we won't.

Laurie, Kevin, and I go back to my office for our evening meeting. I tell Laurie I want her to keep after Betty Anthony. I still have this notion that the answer to everything lies in that photograph, and the answer to that photograph lies with Betty Anthony.

We kick around our plans for the defense's case, and when we're done Kevin is the first to leave. Laurie lingers behind, and we get to talking. I ask her a question that I shouldn't, but which I am psychologically unable to avoid asking.

"How are things with what's-his-name?"

"You mean Bobby Radburn?"

I nod. "That's him. The guy who couldn't throw a baseball through a pane of glass."

"He's a creep," she says. "It's a common ailment among men."

I should be glad to hear this, and I am, but I also feel bad that she has obviously been hurt and disappointed.

"Listen, Laurie . . . there's something I need to tell you." I say this without having a clear idea what it is that I need to tell her.

"Don't." She lets me off the hook.

Before I can get back on the hook, there is a knock on the door. Since this is the same office I was nearly killed in by an intruder, I call out to find out who it is. The response is from Nicole and her father, who had dinner nearby and stopped by to see if I was in the office so he could say hello. I would almost prefer it had been the intruder again.

Nicole and Philip are very friendly, and greet Laurie warmly. Nicole marvels at how many hours we are putting in on the case, but I respond that we unfortunately seem to be running in place and not getting anywhere.

Philip says, "It may not be your fault. Your client just might be guilty this time."

"That makes me feel much better," I say.

Nicole and Philip wait while Laurie and I discuss a few more aspects of the case, including the photograph. I tell Laurie that I am prepared when court reconvenes on Monday to go to Hatchet for permission to depose both Markham and Brownfield about it. It will be a fishing expedition, but I think there's a good chance he'll let me do it.

Laurie, obviously uncomfortable with this little family reunion, says her goodbyes. I drive Nicole home, knowing that I'm with the wrong woman. Someday that piece of information may not stay buried, and it might even come out of my mouth.

• • • • •

SATURDAY IS MY DAY OF REST DURING A

trial. I try and wipe the case from my mind, at least for most of the day, and do something relaxing. There is time to intensify the preparation on Sunday, and I find that if I take Saturday off, or mostly off, I am to a degree rejuvenated.

Today is a particularly perfect Saturday, since the relaxation God has sent me a Knicks playoff game on television. The Knicks are playing the Pacers in the Garden, with the best of seven series tied at two games apiece. I don't bet on Knicks playoff games, because I don't need a rooting interest, and because I could never bet against the Knicks anyway.

Tara and I sit on the couch, potato chips, peanuts, pretzels, soda, water, and dog biscuits all within arm's and paw's reach. At least I start the game on the couch; by late in the first quarter I am pacing the room and screaming at the television. Tara is calmer and more restrained, only barking when the refs make a particularly bad call.

The Knicks go up by eleven but, as is their tendency, seem to lose their concentration and let Indiana back into the game. With three seconds to go and the Knicks down by two, Latrell Sprewell elevates eight feet in the air off the dribble and nails a three. Jalen Rose then draws rim from halfcourt on a desperation shot at the buzzer. The Knicks have won, and I have gone almost three hours without once thinking about real life.

I'm trying to decide who to bet on in the upcoming Lakers-Blazers game when Nicole comes into the room. I have to do a double take to believe what I see; she is carrying a picnic basket.

"Let's go," she says.

"Where are we going?"

"To Harper's Point."

"Are you serious?"

She nods. "Absolutely. You were just going to watch another game anyway, so you don't have to work. And this will give us a chance to be alone and get away from this case. That's something we haven't done in a long time, Andy."

Guilt rears its ugly head and I agree. I don't bring Tara with me, since I have read reports of rattlesnakes in the area, and I don't want a curious Tara going where she shouldn't and getting bit.

Harper's Point is about twenty minutes west of here, in a small range of mountains. Nicole and I have been here frequently in happier times, and it is an extraordinarily beautiful place. There is a small waterfall and a rapidly running stream, as well as a number of lushly landscaped areas cleared out perfectly for picnics.

When we reach the area, we head for our favorite place. We sit on some rocks, right alongside a stream, with a view of the waterfall. I have forgotten how peaceful it can be here.

"We have a lot of memories here," Nicole says.

"We sure do. I think I reached my sexual peak on these rocks."

She laughs. "And it's been downhill ever since."

I try to deny it, but she's probably right. We lie back, taking in the sun and the incredibly soothing sound of the waterfall. What Nicole doesn't know is that I am lying here trying to decide if this is the moment to tell her that we do not have a future together. I don't want to have that conversation before I am really sure, because once we have it there will be no turning back.

Suddenly, despite having decided that this is not the right time, my mouth starts to speak. "Nicole, we need to talk."

She tenses up. "Don't, Andy. No one ever says 'we need to talk' when they're going to talk about something good."

I can't pull back now. "Nicole . . . everybody always says marriages don't work because people grow in different directions. But I don't think that's the case at all."

She is now just waiting to see what I'm getting at, though I think she already knows.

I continue. "I think we were always very different. Sure we've grown, but I think those same differences have always been there. I think that as we get older we notice them more. We're less willing to paper over them."

"What are you saying, Andy?"

I pause for a moment, because I'm having trouble breathing. I remember there being more air at Harper's Point. "I'm saying that it's over, Nicole."

Nicole starts to unpack the lunch, as if behaving normally will negate the conversation. "Andy, don't do this. Please. You're making a mistake."

I feel terribly sorry for her, and for me, but I wouldn't be doing anybody a favor by backing off now.

"No. I'm not."

She's still emptying the picnic basket, and she drops a fork on the ground.

I lean over to pick it up, and as I do I hear a strange sound. For a moment, I think that Nicole must have dropped something else, and it is the sound of that other item hitting the ground. I look around, but there is nothing there.

I sit back up and notice that Nicole has a strange look on her face. And then I see an expanding dark red spot on her shoulder, coming from what looks like an open wound.

"Nicole?"

"Andy, I . . ."

It is not until she falls forward into my lap that I truly register what has happened. Nicole has been shot. My mind goes from wild panic to crystal clear focus in an instant, and I realize that I don't know where the shooter is, and that he certainly can shoot again.

I pull Nicole down behind the rocks, hoping that they will shield us, but I can't be sure of that, since I don't know where the assailant is shooting from. I take a look at Nicole and her eyes are rolling back in her head, as if she is losing consciousness. I have no first-aid experience whatsoever, but I have this vague feeling she could be going into shock, and I know that I have to get her help quickly. The question is how.

I peer out from behind the rock and another shot rings out, ricocheting inches from my head. It is clear that we cannot make it to the car, and just as clear that we can't stay here and hope to survive. It flashes through my mind that this is the time in the old Westerns that the hero turns to someone and says, "Cover me."

I position Nicole so that she is anchored securely and protected by the rocks. I then move along the rocks, keeping them between me and the shooter. When I think I am out of his possible line of fire, I get into the stream. I know from past experience that the water must be very cold, but I don't even feel it.

I let myself be carried along by the current, which is very difficult as the water becomes more turbulent as it goes downstream. About a hundred and fifty yards away, I grab on to a branch and pull myself up to the bank.

I work my way inland, planning to go up the hill and come down behind the gunman. I'm going to have to surprise and disarm him. This is not exactly my specialty, but I have a curious lack of fear. Maybe I'm too scared to be afraid.

As I head to where I estimate him to be, I hear a car engine start. I move quickly toward the sound, and I reach a clearing just as the car is pulling away. It is a late-model BMW, and I am able to see the license plate, CRS-432. It etches itself indelibly in my mind.

I rush back down to the stream where Nicole is still lying. I pick her motionless body up and put it over my shoulder, carrying her to the car. I lie her down in the back seat and quickly apply a cloth to her shoulder, though the bleeding has for the most part stopped. I don't want to let myself think about the possible implications of that, and I speed to a nearby hospital, calling them from my cell phone so they will be prepared for our arrival.

We arrive at the hospital in five minutes that seem like five hours. They are indeed waiting for us, and perform with incredible efficiency from the moment we arrive. The paramedics immediately have Nicole on a stretcher and bring her inside, with one of them having the consideration to tell me that yes, she is still alive.

I am led to a waiting room, where I spend the next two hours totally in the dark about Nicole's condition. I call Philip and leave word in his office as to where I am and what has happened. They tell me he is in Washington, but they reach him and he is going to fly back immediately.

Finally, a young woman comes out and introduces herself as Dr. Summers. She wastes no time.

"Your wife is going to pull through. The bullet did not strike any vital organs."

It takes a moment for these words to register, so that I can then ask other questions. Dr. Summers tells me that Nicole has lost a significant amount of blood, and they are in the process of finishing a transfusion. Her collarbone is shattered, but it will heal over time.

"When can I see her?"

"I would say in about an hour."

I thank her and sit back down. The police arrive, and I tell a detective what I know. The only thing I leave out is the most significant fact, the license plate number. Right now I'm not trusting anyone, and I'm going to play my cards close to the vest.

Moments after the police leave, Laurie arrives, though I have no idea how she has heard about what happened. She sees me, comes over and hugs me.

"Andy, God, I'm sorry. How is she?"

I tell her what the doctor has told me, and Laurie asks if I have any idea who was behind this.

"No," I say, "but I know who they were after. Me."

Suddenly, the pent-up anger and frustration overwhelms me, and I punch a hole in the wall. Well, a dent in the wall.

"Goddammit! Nicole told me to drop it, and somebody fired a bullet into her body when I wouldn't."

Laurie puts her hand on my shoulder, but there is no consoling me. This is the closest I have ever come to being out of control, and I have to fight to keep what little composure I have left.

"Andy . . ."

"Laurie, just before this happened, I told Nicole that things were not going to work out for us. That my heart wasn't in it anymore."

"Oh, God . . ."

"And now, because of me . . . she's lying in there with somebody else's blood being pumped into her to keep her alive."

Laurie stays with me until the doctors say that I can see Nicole. Before she leaves, I remember to tell her the license plate number of the car that I saw on the scene, and she promises to check it out.

When I walk into Nicole's room, I am jolted by the sight of her. She lies, pale and weak, connected to machines by tubes. Her eyes are open, but she seems groggy.

I try to be upbeat. "Nicole, how are you feeling?"

She looks in my direction, and I watch as her eyes try to focus. She finally realizes that it is me, and she starts to cry softly.

"Andy . . . oh, Andy."

I move toward her and hold her, trying my best not to interfere with any of the tubes.

"Calm down . . . take it easy, now. You need your rest. The doctor said you're going to be fine, as long as you take it easy."

"It hurts so much, Andy."

"I know. I know it does."

"Where's my father?"

"He'll be here soon. He was in Washington, but he's on the shuttle. He's very worried about you."

She nods softly, obviously very tired.

"Nicole, I'm sorry. You have no idea *how* sorry. You don't belong in this . . . you don't deserve this." But she is already asleep, and she can't hear me. We haven't been able to hear each other for a very, very long time.

Philip arrives about an hour later and completely takes over. He arranges for Nicole to be transferred to a more prestigious hospital near his home, and is already having his personal physician consult with the doctors who have taken care of Nicole.

Philip has very little to say to me, and I can't say that I blame him. He's warned me that something terrible could happen if I didn't back off, and he's been proven right.

• • • • •

OUR DEFENSE BEGINS ON MONDAY MORNING, AND our first witness is Lou Campanelli, the leader of a local drug and alcohol rehabilitation program. Kevin has interviewed him over the weekend, and has reported to me that we have some gains to make by putting him on. Kevin also has come up with a way that we can use Lou to help our theory that Willie was framed.

A lot of people talk a good game about helping people, but Lou Campanelli has devoted his life to it. He is sixty-four years old, and has been helping people deal with their addictions for the past forty-two of them. There aren't enough Lou Campanellis in the world.

After I take him through his background and have him describe the type of program he runs, I ask him if Willie was a member of that program.

Lou nods. "He was an outstanding member. Totally committed to remaining sober."

"So were you surprised to discover that he was found drunk the night of the murder?"

"I was quite surprised. It's always a possibility, of course, every day can be a struggle. But yes, in Willie's case I was surprised and disappointed."

"What about drugs?" I ask. "To the best of your knowledge, did Willie ever use drugs?"

Lou shakes his head firmly and emphatically. "No way. Willie lost a sister to drugs. He wasn't just against them for himself; he wouldn't tolerate anybody else using them either. It just isn't possible."

I nod. "What would you say if I told you that there has been testimony about drug needle marks in Willie Miller's arms?"

"I'd say somebody's lying."

I go over to the defense table, and Kevin hands me a folder.

"Your Honor, I would like to introduce this as defense exhibit number four. It is the results of the blood test taken at the time, which shows no drugs in Mr. Miller's blood whatsoever."

I walk back toward Lou, whose face shows something between a grin and a sneer. "I told you."

I can't help but smile. "Yes, you did, Mr. Campanelli. Now tell me . . . as an expert on alcoholism . . . how does one go about getting drunk?"

"What do you mean? By drinking alcohol."

"Does the alcohol get into the drinker's bloodstream?"

"Yes."

"Is drinking the only way to do it?"

"Far as I know," he says.

"Suppose," I ask, "suppose I were to inject a large amount of alcohol into your arm with a syringe. Would that do the trick? Could you become drunk that way?"

Wallace realizes where I'm going. "Objection. Pure speculation."

"Overruled. Witness will answer the question."

Lou shrugs. "I guess it would. Sure."

"Objection! Your Honor, the witness is not qualified as an expert in this area."

Hatchet overrules again and Wallace asks for a conference out of earshot of the jury. We go back to chambers, where he again makes the case that I am advancing wild theories that Hatchet should protect the jury's delicate ears from having to hear. Hatchet refuses to do so, and we head right back into the court.

As I stand to continue my direct examination of Campanelli, I notice Laurie coming in the back door and sitting at the defense table.

"Mr. Campanelli," I resume, "could such a large amount of alcohol be injected into a person's bloodstream that the person could be rendered totally drunk? Smashed?"

"Sure."

"So that he couldn't remember anything afterward? Including the injections?"

"I guess it would depend on the person, but . . . why not?"

I smile. "I don't know why not, Mr. Campanelli. I don't know why not at all."

I go back to the defense table as Wallace starts his cross-examination. I hear him getting Campanelli to speak about how common it is for program members to fall off the wagon and go on binges.

I lean over to talk to Laurie. "Any news on the license plate?"

She nods. "Yes, but you're not going to like it. It's a registered plate, top government security clearance. There is no way to find out who has it."

This is a stunning piece of news. The goddamn government is trying to kill me?

Campanelli leaves the stand, and Hatchet announces that one of the jurors has a medical situation that needs attention, canceling court for the afternoon. Considering the state of my case, I hope it's a twenty-four-week virus.

Nicole, amazingly, has been cleared to leave the hospital, mainly because Philip is setting up a special facility for her in his home, complete with round-the-clock nurses and a doctor who will check on her twice a day.

Actually, I find out about Nicole's departure from the hospital inadvertently. I happen to call her while she is in the process of leaving. I have the feeling that right now I am not wanted or needed by either her or her father. In Philip's eyes I have committed the cardinal sin of exposing his daughter to serious danger, even after I was warned about the possibility of that danger. To compound the offense, I have also rejected her. His accusations are fair; I am guilty as charged.

Laurie and I go to Charlie's bar to discuss the latest developments. I don't have many options for the defense; my strategy has been to cast doubt on the prosecution's witnesses, to raise the possibility of a frame-up.

The simple fact is that, while I've had some success, it hasn't been enough. Absent a major development, Willie Miller is going to be convicted. And if there's a major development coming, it's news to me.

Laurie asks, "Are you going to put Willie on the stand?"

"How can I? All he'll say is he has no idea what happened. Wallace will have him for lunch."

As has been my custom during my slide into frustration dementia, I take out the photograph from my father's house and put it on the table. I know every square millimeter of it by heart, but I keep looking at it, hoping that it will jog something in my mind. It never does; the sad truth is I'm no closer to figuring it out than the day I first saw it.

Of course, the list of things that I'm not close to figuring out is as long as my arm. Right near the top is why the person who shot at me and hit Nicole was driving a government vehicle, and a classified one at that.

And then one of those moments happen that are impossible to predict, but have the power to change everything. As we are talking about the license plate, my gaze wanders back to my father's picture, still on the table. Between my eyes and the picture is Laurie's beer bottle. The glass has the effect of magnifying the picture, and ringing a bell inside my head.

"You know something," I say. "I'm a genius."

"You've certainly been hiding it well," Laurie answers.

"Let's go." I put money down to cover the check and head for the door. Laurie has to hurry to keep up behind me. She calls out to me as I head for the parking lot.

"Where are we going?"

"I'll tell you on the way."

Vince Sanders is in his office at the newspaper when we

barge in. I tell him that we need his help urgently, but I'm not sure he hears me because he can't stop staring at Laurie. He probably thinks she is one of the twins I promised him.

Finally, he acknowledges my presence. "How did you know I'd be here this late?"

"Where would you be? On a date?"

Vince asks Laurie, "Is he always this big a pain in the ass?"

"I can only speak for the last three years," Laurie says.

Vince shrugs. "Okay, what can I do for you?"

I take out the picture and put it on the table.

Vince sighs. "I already told you, the only guy I recognize is Mike Anthony."

I shake my head. "I don't care about the people. I care about the license plate."

All this time I have been focusing on the people in the picture, not on the cars. Now I point to the license plate on one of the cars, the one that is facing the camera. It is certainly too small to be read by the human eye, but I can tell that the letters and numbers are there.

"Can you have this blown up so we can read it?"

He looks at it, squinting as he does. "We can try."

He stands up, grabs the picture, and takes it out of the room, coming back after only a few minutes.

"We'll know in five minutes," he says.

He's right, although the five minutes feel like five weeks. Finally, his phone rings and all he says is "Yeah?" then hangs up.

He turns to Laurie and me. "Follow me."

Vince takes us down the hall and into a room filled with computers. He introduces us to Chris Townshend, a twenty-four-year-old who Vince describes as "the best there is." He doesn't say at what, and I'm not about to ask. There is only one answer I want, and if I'm really, really lucky, it's about to come on the computer screen.

Chris takes us over to the largest screen in the room. He works a console full of buttons and gadgets like a maestro. Suddenly he pauses, presses a button, and the photograph appears, still far too small to make out the license plate. He starts to zoom in on the plate, each time making it larger and larger. I can feel the excitement building; this is going to work.

After a few more clicks, Chris says, "That's as close as I can get without it becoming too diffuse." We all peer in to try and read it; it's not easy.

"J . . . B . . ." I say.

Laurie points at the letter I have identified as a B. "That's an R," she says. "Let me do this, I'm younger than you."

"It's okay with me," Vince says. "I'm blind as a bat."

Laurie keeps reading, and I'm writing it down as she does. "J . . . R . . . C . . . 6 . . . 9 . . . 3."

"The last number is a 2," Chris says.

I say to Laurie, "He's younger than you."

Laurie stares a quick dagger at me, but it doesn't concern me. "What state is it?" I ask.

Chris responds: "It looks like New Jersey."

I put the piece of paper in my pocket, and Laurie and I start heading for the door.

"You got what you need?" Vince asks.

"I sure as hell hope so," I answer.

• • • • •

A LICENSE PLATE FROM THIRTY-FIVE YEARS AGO represents the best clue we have had into the meaning of the photograph. This is in itself a commentary on how little we've accomplished. For instance, the license could well turn out to have been issued in my father's name, which is to say it would be of no use to us.

The next task, of course, is to find out who the plate belonged to. This is not going to be easy, and there is only one person I know who can accomplish it quickly and with the discretion required. Unfortunately, it is the person I attacked on the witness stand a few days ago, Pete Stanton.

I know where Pete lives, so Laurie and I drive out there. It's about forty-five minutes away, in a little town called Cranford.

"I thought cops were supposed to live in town," I mutter, unhappy with the length of the drive, and dreading Pete's reaction to my arrival.

"You might not want to complain about it to him," Laurie suggests to me. "He's not going to be that anxious to do you a favor in the first place."

We are about five minutes away, off the highway, when we pass a sign on the road. It directs the driver to make a right turn to get to the Preakness Country Club.

"That's Markham's club," I say. "We should sneak in and put shaving cream in his golf shoes."

Laurie doesn't think that's a very mature idea, so we continue on to Pete's house, a modest colonial in a quiet, unassuming neighborhood. I would love to send Laurie in alone, but my male ego won't let me do it, so I walk with her up the steps and nervously ring the bell.

After a few moments, Pete comes to the door. He opens it and sees me standing there.

"Oh, Christ," he says.

My plan is to immediately apologize for being so tough with him on the stand. I'm going to talk about the fact that I was just doing my job, unpleasant as it sometimes is. I'll beg for his forgiveness, tell him how important his friendship is to me, and hope that bygones can be bygones.

Unfortunately, my plan goes up in smoke when I see that he is wearing a ridiculous red bathrobe, so comical that I am physically and emotionally unable to avoid mocking it.

"Nice outfit, Pete. Does the whole team have them?" I ask.

For a brief moment he looks as if he is going to kill me, but I think he decides it's not worth doing all the paperwork that would be involved afterward. Instead, he starts to close the door.

I push back against it, holding it open. "Wait a minute! We need your help!"

"Forget it." We're actually pushing against the door from opposite sides in a weird reverse tug-of-war, and I am not coming out on top.

"Come on, I'm sorry!"

I think he can tell that it was not the most sincere of apologies, because he keeps closing the door.

I yell to Laurie, "Don't just stand there!"

After a brief moment that seems like an hour, she shrugs and says, "I need your help, Pete."

Pete immediately relaxes and opens the door. He speaks only to Laurie. "Why didn't you say so? What's up?"

I jump in. "We have to run down an old license plate."

Pete ignores me and again speaks to Laurie. "What's up?"

"We have to run down an old license plate," Laurie says.

This is starting to annoy me—I mean, all I did in court was my job. "Hey, what am I, invisible?"

"You're lucky you're not dead," Pete snarls. "You turned me into a goddamned idiot on the stand."

"You were already a goddamned idiot. I just brought it out into the open."

This time I'm pretty sure that if he has a gun in that cute red bathrobe he will shoot me. Laurie tells me to go wait in the car, which I think is a wise idea.

From the time I get in the car, it only takes a minute or so. Laurie comes back and gets in the passenger seat.

"Let's go," she says.

"What happened?"

"He's going to call it in. We should have it tomorrow."

"See?" I say. "I told you I could handle him."

I drop Laurie off at her apartment and then head home. Pete's going to get us the information, and then we'll either have something or we'll have nothing. I have rarely felt less in control.

The next morning I ask for a meeting in Hatchet's chambers with him and Wallace. They have heard about Nicole getting shot, and I lay out for them the threats we had received and the attack in my office. I make the case that someone is actively trying to prevent justice from being carried out, and I ask that I be allowed to depose Victor Markham and Brownfield about the photograph.

Wallace seems genuinely sympathetic to my situation, but is obligated to make the point that no significant legal link has been made between the photograph and the Miller trial. He is technically correct, and Hatchet is also technically correct in denying my request. Which he does.

Our first witness this morning is going to be Edward Markham, on whom I am planning to take out my frustrations. Laurie has joined Kevin and me at the defense table for the day's festivities.

As I glance around the courtroom, I see that Victor is there to provide sonny boy moral support. He's going to need it.

Just as Hatchet is taking his seat behind the bench, the door in the back of the courtroom opens and Pete appears. He walks toward me as Hatchet is instructing me to call my first witness.

Pete hands me a small piece of paper and says, "I figured I should deliver this one personally."

I look at the paper and say, "Holy shit."

Laurie nudges me. "What is it?"

I hand her the paper; her whispered reaction is more biblical than mine. She says, "Jesus Christ." She passes the paper down to Kevin, but I can't hear what he mutters.

Hatchet sees all this. "Are we going to pass notes in class today or might we call a witness?"

I stand up. "Your Honor, we call Edward Markham, but a significant development has taken place, and we would request a brief recess prior to his testimony."

"How brief?"

"The balance of the morning, Your Honor. We would be prepared to question the witness right after the lunch break."

Hatchet asks Wallace and me to approach. We do, and I tell them that this can be a crucial breakthrough, and that I need the morning to follow through on it. It can change the entire case.

I am shocked when Wallace doesn't object. He knows that his position will not be harmed by waiting a few hours, and he trusts me that this is in fact an important development. What he is doing is putting justice ahead of victory; my father would have been damn proud of him.

Hatchet goes along with it, and I head back to the defense table. I tell Kevin that if I'm not back in time, he is to question Edward for as long as it takes, just making sure that he does not leave the stand before I get there. I don't even wait for an answer; I'm out of the building and on the way to my car.

My trip out to Betty Anthony's is a nerve-racking one. Pete's information has the promise of cracking this case wide open and letting the long hidden secrets pour out, but it will be of no value if I can't get Betty Anthony on my side. And so far I have had no success at doing that.

I try her apartment first, hoping that she is not at work. When I arrive and prepare to ring the bell, I hear the strains of Frank Sinatra singing Cole Porter, coming from inside the apartment. She's home.

Betty comes to the door, and her expression when she sees that it's me is a combination of exasperation and fear. She's fended me off until now, but she's afraid that I'll come at her from an angle that will shake up her world. Which is exactly what I'm about to do.

"Hello, Betty."

"Mr. Carpenter, I really must ask you to stop bothering me like this. It's not—"

"I know about Julie McGregor."

The effect is immediate, and it is all in her eyes. First there is the flash of fear, as she starts to process the words she hoped never to hear. Then comes the realization that there is no defense to those words, that resistance is futile. Then her body catches up to her eyes, and she sags noticeably, the fight taken out of her.

Watching her reaction is exhilarating and terribly, terribly sad.

She doesn't say a word, just opens the door wider for me to enter. The apartment is exactly what I would have expected . . . small, inexpensively furnished, but meticulously kept. There are a number of religious artifacts around, as well as pictures of family members, including many of Mike.

Betty starts to straighten the place up, dusting areas without dust and moving things which do not need to be moved. I suppose it is her way of trying to bring order into what is soon to be a chaotic situation.

"Would you like some coffee?" she asks.

"Yes, thank you."

She is trying to find something to do. We both know that she is going to speak to me, but I'm helping her put it off at least for a few more minutes.

She makes the coffee and brings it to me. Finally, she says, "How much do you know?"

"Enough to tell the world the story. Not enough to prove it."

She nods. "He was never the same after that night. He thought it would get better, but it got worse as the years went by."

"Did you know him then?"

"Yes. We were engaged. But he didn't tell me the full story about what happened until years later."

A pause, as she struggles with her own guilt. "But I couldn't help him with it."

"Down deep he had to know it would come out," I say. "He couldn't keep it inside any longer. And neither can you. Not anymore."

She sighs. "I know."

"Tell me about that night."

She takes a deep breath and lets it out. "They were in Manhattan for a dinner, some kind of awards event for the best students from around the country. A future leaders thing, or something. Most of them never met each other before that night."

I start to ask her if she knows their names, but I decide I'm not going to interrupt. The story is going to come pouring out of her, and I'm not going to do anything to influence or derail it.

She goes on. "A group of them began drinking at the banquet, and then went to a bar on the Upper West Side. All they were interested in was alcohol and women, but it was late on a slow Tuesday night, so they were having much more luck with the alcohol.

"The bar was about to close, and nothing much was happening, so they accepted the offer of one of their group to go to his house, where they could keep drinking and swim in his pool.

"On the way out into Jersey, they called out to other drivers, yelling jokes and having fun. A few people yelled back, but most just ignored them.

"Five minutes from the house, a young woman that seemed to match their fun-loving attitude pulled up next to them at a traffic light. The fact that she was young and great-looking made the situation almost too good to be true, and they asked her to follow them to the house for a swim, never really expecting that she would.

"But she did follow them, and pulled her car in the driveway behind theirs."

I already knew that, because her car would later that night be in a photograph, and many years later her license plate would be computer-enhanced and read. Lieutenant Pete Stanton would check that plate number and learn her identity.

The young woman's name was Julie McGregor. Wife of Wally. Mother of Denise.

I finally interrupt Betty to ask her if she knows the identity of the other men with Mike that night.

She shakes her head. "No, Mike would never tell me. I only knew one of them; he was the friend that Mike came to New York with."

Then she hesitates, as if unsure whether to continue. But she understands there is no turning back now. "There is something else you should know."

"What's that?"

She's in terrible pain. "That poor young woman. The reporter that was killed."

"Denise McGregor," I say.

She nods. "Yes. She was here, tracing what happened. She was piecing it together. I felt so badly for her."

"How long was this before she was murdered?"

"I think a few months. I didn't find out about her death until much, much later."

"Had she learned who was there that night?" I ask.

"She only knew about the same two people that I did . . . Mike and Victor Markham."

• • • • •

IT'S ELEVEN-THIRTY BEFORE I LEAVE BETTY
Anthony's. Court is going to reconvene at two, but I have someplace where I must stop first, even if it means being late. It's
not a newsstand, and it's not some superstition that has to be
indulged.

I have to go talk to my father.

I get to the cemetery, not swarming with people as it was
the last time I was here, only a few visitors paying their re-
spects to those they loved. I find my father's grave, and take a
few moments to get my emotions in check.

"Dad, I have something to do today . . . I don't know how
it's going to come out."

I am overcome by a feeling of closeness to him; I have
never really believed in an afterlife, yet I know in the depths
of my being that he can hear me.

"I know about the money . . . and Victor . . . and Mike Anthony . . . and now I know what happened that night. But I
don't know about you. Were you a part of it, or did you just
know about it? Why did you take the money, if you'd never let
yourself touch it?

"Dad, I know who you are, nothing can ever change that.
But please understand, I need to know what you did."

A woman walks by, and she speaks to me, hesitatingly.

"Excuse me," she says. "Were you talking to me?"

Not wanting to look like a complete lunatic, I say, "Yes. I asked you what time it was."

She looks at her watch. "One o'clock."

"Thank you," I say. And then I turn back to my father. "It's time to move on."

I race back to the courthouse and arrive a little after two. When I enter the courtroom, Kevin is questioning Edward Markham. Obviously Hatchet had not granted him a further delay.

I stay in the back of the room for a while, watching Kevin and deciding exactly how I am going to handle things. Kevin really has nothing to ask Edward; I have not given him any instructions on what I want to accomplish. He is vamping for time, taking Edward through what is basically a rehash of his direct testimony for Wallace.

"So after you found her, what did you do?" asks Kevin.

"As I said previously, I called the police first. I wanted them to get an ambulance there right away, just in case there was any hope. Then I called my father."

"He was at home?"

Wallace objects, stating the obvious, that all these questions have been previously asked and answered. Hatchet overrules the objection, but his patience is wearing a little thin.

"No, it was Friday night," says Edward. "He's always at the club on Friday nights."

Kevin prepares to ask another question he already knows the answer to, when he turns and sees me coming toward him. The look of relief on his face is palpable.

"No further questions, Your Honor," I say.

"Well, Mr. Carpenter," says Hatchet. "So glad you could join us."

"Thank you, Your Honor, nice to be here."

"Would you like to call another witness, or do you have any more errands to run?"

"If it pleases the court, the defense would like to call Victor Markham."

Victor does not seem surprised to hear his name called, nor

does he seem in any way worried. He's quite willing to take the time from his busy schedule to help further the cause of justice. The bigger they are, the nicer they are.

I approach Victor with a nonthreatening smile on my face, and speak softly. "Mr. Markham," I begin, "did I have occasion to question you under oath in the office of your attorney a couple of weeks ago?"

"You did."

"Would you like to have a transcript of that interview so that you can refer to it?"

"That won't be necessary. I just told you the truth about what I know. That hasn't changed any."

"Do you remember my asking if you knew what story Denise McGregor was working on in the days just before her death?"

"Yes."

"And what did you say?"

"I told you I had no idea."

"But you did know her?" I ask.

"I really only knew her casually. She seemed very nice. The important thing to me was that my son liked her. And he certainly did."

"And she liked him?"

"She seemed to." He answers quickly, so that Wallace gets to his feet but does not have time to object that Victor could not possibly know what Denise's feelings were.

Hatchet instructs Victor to wait a beat before answering, to give Wallace time to object if he chooses to do so.

"Is it possible that she didn't like him at all, but went out with him for the purpose of finding out information?"

"I can't imagine why she would do that."

"Perhaps that information would be of help to her in the story she was working on?"

"I'm certainly not aware of any such thing. I don't believe Edward would have had any information that would be useful to a reporter. You might have asked him that when you had him on the stand."

Victor is good; he must be worried about where this is going, but he doesn't display any sign of it.

I nod. "Maybe I'll be able to help you with that. When your son called you that night, to tell you that Denise McGregor had been murdered and that he had discovered the body, did he seem upset?"

"Obviously."

"And you shared his distress? You were upset at the news as well?"

He shakes his head slightly, conveying to the jury his frustration with such obvious questions. "Of course I was. A young woman had been murdered."

"What were you doing at the time?"

"I was in the lobby of my club, chatting with some friends."

"Which friends?"

A frown. "I'm afraid I really don't remember. This all took place a number of years ago, Mr. Carpenter, and I'm sure the conversations were casual. Besides, I am blessed with a great many friends. We were relaxing at our club on a Friday night."

I smile my understanding. "But might the conversations have been about golf, the weather, that kind of thing?"

He returns the smile; we're getting to be good buddies. "Most likely about golf."

"So you're in the lobby, probably talking about golf, and this call comes in. Who called you to the phone?"

"I don't remember. I assume the concierge."

"Your club has a concierge? Wow."

"Objection. Relevance."

"Sustained. Mr. Carpenter, move this along."

"Yes, Your Honor. So you got the call, Edward tells you he found his girlfriend's body in an alley, and boy, were you upset. Did you rush to your car?"

"Yes. Immediately."

"By the way, where do people keep cars at fancy clubs like that?"

"What do you mean?" he asks.

"Are they parked out in front? Do you park far away and take a tram to the main building?"

"There is valet parking."

"Of course, valet parking." I slap myself in the head, as if to say, "How could I be such a stupid peasant." The jury laughs.

"So you get this news and you rush out, and you say, 'Valet parking person, get me my car, and pronto.' "

I pause a moment. "Do rich people say 'pronto'?"

Wallace objects again, effectively getting on my nerves. "Your Honor," he says, "I fail to see the relevance of this."

"Your Honor," I respond with some anger, "I have a certain momentum going here, which is being interrupted by Mr. Wallace's constantly claiming that he doesn't see the relevance in what I am saying. Therefore, I would request two things. One, that the court instruct Mr. Wallace to stop interrupting; and two, that you force him to take a night course in relevance detection techniques."

Wallace is angry. "Your Honor, that is the most—"

Hatchet's gavel cuts him off. "That's enough, both of you. Mr. Wallace, I'm going to overrule your objection. Mr. Carpenter, I'm also having trouble figuring out where you are going with this, and I have no intention of going to night school. So get to it."

I promise that I will and turn back to Victor. His attitude has become more hostile, sensing that the jury will agree I am wasting all of their collective time.

"So after you got your car, did you head for the bar where the murder took place?"

"Yes."

"Is it a bar you frequented yourself, that you were familiar with, or did Edward tell you where it was?"

"He told me. It was not hard to find."

"Did you drive quickly?"

He nods. "Very. I was quite upset."

"I know. You've told us that. How far would you say it is from your club to the bar?"

He shrugs. "I don't know. Maybe twenty miles."

"Actually, it is twenty-nine point seven miles. I drove it. I made it in forty-seven minutes, but I wasn't rushing because I wasn't as terribly upset as you were. How long would you say that it took you?"

"I don't know, but I'm sure it was faster than that."

"How fast?" I press him.

"I don't know; I had no reason to time the trip. But I was driving quickly."

"Because you were so upset."

"Yes."

"Do you think you could have made it in forty minutes?"

"Maybe . . . I can't be sure."

I walk toward him, firing questions almost before he finishes his answers.

"Thirty-five? Thirty?"

He is getting flustered. "I told you, I can't—"

"Twenty-five? Twenty? Fifteen? Do you think you could have made it in fifteen minutes?"

"Of course not," he says.

"Because according to the police records and tape recordings, the police were at the scene fourteen minutes after Edward's call, and you were already there."

"So?"

"So Edward testified that he called them first."

Victor can't conceal the worry permeating his brain. "That's impossible. He must be mistaken about the order in which he made the phone calls. It was a very stressful time. A woman had been murdered."

"He told this jury that he called the police first. He was quite definitive about it."

"Well, he was mistaken. People make mistakes."

"Yes, they do," I say, "and then they'll do whatever is necessary to cover them up."

"You're making things up, trying to make something out of nothing. To make my son and me look bad, as if we're lying . . ."

"You are lying."

"I am telling you the truth."

"Mr. Markham, why did you rape Ms. McGregor?"

Wallace jumps up as if he had been in an ejector seat. "Objection, Your Honor, this is crazy! There is absolutely no evidence that Denise McGregor had sex of any kind that night, consensual or otherwise. To accuse Mr. Markham like this is unconscionable."

Hatchet peers at me sternly. "Mr. Carpenter, if you have any evidence whatsoever to indicate that the victim had sexual relations the night of her death, I suggest you bring it forth now."

"Oh, sorry," I say, "I wasn't talking about that night . . . I was talking about a different night. And I wasn't talking about Denise McGregor, I was talking about her mother."

The courtroom explodes in slow motion, but Victor Markham alone does not seem excited or agitated by what has been said. His eyes are glued to the back of the courtroom as the door opens, and Betty Anthony comes striding in, immediately lending dignity to the proceedings with her presence. He seems to sag; his dread of the last few minutes has become his certainty.

He knows that I know.

I want to savor the moment, I want him to twist in the wind up there as long as possible. I want him to sit and deal with the fact that justice is about to be realized for Denise and Julie McGregor. So I wait a few moments before continuing, until Hatchet orders me to.

Finally, I say to Markham, "It was thirty-five years ago, but you remember it as if it were yesterday."

Markham denies everything, and I let him off the stand, subject to recall. I call Betty Anthony as the next defense witness. Wallace objects, accurately claiming that Betty is not on the witness list that we provided for the prosecution.

I ask for a meeting outside the presence of the jury, and Wallace and I head for Hatchet's chambers. I state that Betty had not come forward with information until just this morning, and I lay out in detail exactly what she is going to say.

To his everlasting credit, Wallace withdraws his objection, and Hatchet allows Betty to testify. I believe he would have ruled so anyway, but Wallace takes it upon himself to ensure that he does. Wallace is that rarest of prosecutors, of lawyers, one who believes that finding out the truth is more important than winning. When the truth comes out, everyone wins.

Betty Anthony takes the stand to tell the story that she swore she would never tell, to reveal the weaknesses in her husband that she would never reveal, to right the wrong that she had concluded she would never right.

I take her through a brief discussion about who she is, where she works, and who she had been married to, just enough to establish her as a good and decent, hardworking woman, who certainly would be credible to a jury. Then I lead her to that night, and how Julie met and followed the group back to the house. She is telling the secret that her husband kept for his entire adult life, a secret which caused him to end that life.

"Mike said she wanted to swim, and to drink, and maybe to tease," Betty said. "But that wasn't what they wanted. They wanted to have sex with her. It would cap off an incredible evening in the big city, one they could tell their friends about for months to come."

She starts to falter, so I'm forced to prod her. "But it didn't happen that way, did it?" It's a leading question, but Wallace doesn't object.

She shakes her head sadly. "No. They became too forward for her, groping her, and she wasn't too drunk to put a stop to it. She got angry at them, then got out of the pool and started to walk to her car. But I guess the alcohol had increased their courage and decreased their intelligence, so they chased after her and pulled her back. They weren't going to let her spoil their night, not after it had gone that far."

Betty takes a deep breath, drawing in the strength to continue. "She lashed out, kicking and screaming and scratching two of them. This got them angry, and they attacked her. She screamed and fought, but they were too powerful for her, too far out of control."

Betty is verbally staggering, having trouble keeping her own emotions in check. "Tell the rest," I say very gently. "It's time for the truth to come out."

She nods. "They gang-raped her, taking turns holding her

down, paying no attention to her screams. Finally she broke away and ran, but in her panic she slipped and fell on the wet surface near the pool, smashing her head into a cement table. She was unconscious and bleeding, and they didn't know if she was alive or dead. Then one of them . . ."

"Go on, Betty . . ." I say.

"One of them . . . I don't know who, pushed her into the pool with his foot. She went under the water and stayed there."

The jury and everyone else within the sound of Betty Anthony's voice is spellbound by her story. Even Hatchet seems mesmerized by her as she weaves the tale she has protected for so long.

I look in the gallery and see that Victor has left the courtroom; that's okay, he'll read all about it tomorrow. All that is left now is for me to wrap up Betty's testimony.

"Mrs. Anthony, did you ever have occasion to meet Denise McGregor, the woman whose murder has caused all of us to be here today?"

"Yes. She came to see me."

"Why did she do that?"

"She told me that she was a reporter, doing a story about a murder that she believed was committed many years earlier. She told me that the victim was her mother."

"Go on, please."

"She knew quite a bit about it, about my husband's involvement, and about one other man who was part of the group."

"Did she say who that was?"

"She did . . . Victor Markham. I already knew that."

A rumble goes through the courtroom, which Hatchet quiets with his gavel.

"Thank you, Mrs. Anthony," I say. "Your witness."

Wallace dreads this cross-examination, but must go through with it. He gets Betty to admit that she has kept this information a secret all these years, implying that this means what she has to say is somehow suspect. He also brings out that she has no physical evidence of the crime, only the word of her late husband. He does a very professional job in a very difficult situation.

On redirect, I introduce my father's photograph as evidence. It tends to corroborate her testimony by placing the conspirators together with Julie's car. Clearly, though, it does not show any conclusive proof of their guilt.

When I go back to the defense table, Willie leans over to ask if we've already won. He thinks they're going to come over and cut his handcuffs off, and he can go home. I tell him we're a long way from that, and I arrange to meet at seven with Kevin and Laurie at my house.

· · · · ·

THE GUEST HOUSE ON PHILIP'S PROPERTY
has been converted into a small hospital. Nicole has a hospital
bed, modern medical machines, a full staff of nurses, and a
doctor who does regular rounds. It is an amazing transforma-
tion.

Philip is out at a political dinner, a small blessing for which
I am grateful. I had called ahead and asked Nicole if I could
come over, and she didn't say that I shouldn't. It is not a visit
that I am relishing, for obvious reasons, but one that I know I
must make.

I tell one of her nurses who I am, and she informs Nicole,
who comes right out. She is doing remarkably well, and is
wrapped in bandages around her upper body, so as to help her
broken collarbone heal. But she is up and around, albeit gingerly,
and though she looks pale, it is hard to believe that it's only a
few days since she was lying unconscious behind those rocks.

The tension between us is obvious. No sooner do we say
hello to each other than I feel a need to change the subject. I
look around the house. "I forgot how amazing this place is."

She smiles. "My father wanted us to live here, remember?
He built the house for me even before I was born."

"Looking back, I can't remember how I had the courage to
tell him we wouldn't."

She laughs. "You made me tell him."

"Even then I was a man among men."

"You stand up to him better than most."

I nod; that's probably true. "How are you feeling?"

"Pretty well. I mean, I don't get shot that often, but I think I'm recovering rather quickly."

"I'll never forgive myself for letting this happen to you," I say.

She chooses not to respond to that, and changes the subject. "I saw what happened with Victor Markham on the news tonight. Does it mean you're going to win?"

"Not necessarily, but it certainly helps. Closing arguments are tomorrow."

She nods. "Have you had your dinner? Would you like something to eat?"

I shake my head no. "Nicole, I'm not sure we finished what we needed to say."

She tenses up. "Don't, Andy. I didn't need to say anything, and you said a lot more than I wanted to hear."

"I'm sorry . . . it's not how I wanted it to end."

She smiles a slight, ironic smile. "See? We do have something in common."

I start to tell her again how sorry I am, but she can't listen anymore. She just shakes her head, turns, and goes back to her room. I let myself out of her house and I head back to mine.

Tara is waiting for me at home, tail wagging, to congratulate me on a good day in court. Laurie arrives and shares Tara's enthusiasm, which is tempered by the dose of realism which Kevin soon provides, and with which I concur.

The fact is that Willie Miller remains in a very precarious situation. Nothing has been proven against Victor Markham, and it is unfortunately not up to our jury to ponder or even consider his guilt or innocence. They are empaneled to judge only Willie, and the evidence against him remains overwhelming. Whatever might or might not have happened on that night all those years ago, it does not mean that Willie Miller is innocent of the Denise McGregor murder.

Laurie and I are going over my closing argument, which

will follow Wallace's tomorrow. Our thrust will be two-pronged: We will contend that Willie was framed, and we will serve up Victor Markham as the person who framed him. I believe it is a winning strategy, but I've been wrong before.

Pete Stanton calls, asking if we can meet before court tomorrow. He's received a report regarding the Betty Anthony testimony, and he wants to begin an investigation of Victor Markham immediately. We agree to meet for a quick cup of coffee.

Kevin and Laurie leave by ten o'clock, a comparatively early night for this trial. I sleep well tonight; the only time I wake up is when Tara's tail hits me in the face. I reach out and scratch her stomach, and the next thing I know, it's morning.

Pete is pumped to go after Victor Markham, and the prospect of doing so has apparently caused him to at least temporarily forget how much he hates me for attacking him on the stand. During breakfast, I take him through the entire story of the photograph and the money in my father's estate, right up to the present moment. He feels he can build a case against Victor, but we both know it won't be in time to help Willie with the jury.

The press this morning has been filled with news of the trial; Victor Markham's potential downfall has changed it from a big story to a mega story. I'm being cautiously praised by the same pundits who've been calling me overmatched, but they still feel we have an uphill battle ahead of us.

The crowds outside the courthouse are much larger the next morning, and there are far more media present. When Wallace stands to deliver his closing argument before a packed gallery, the courtroom feels considerably more tense than it has at any time during the trial.

"Ladies and gentlemen of the jury, you're in the home stretch now. I'm going to make a few remarks, and then Mr. Carpenter will do the same. Following that will come the most important moment of this trial, when Judge Henderson instructs you about your responsibilities under the law. He will tell you a great deal, but the most important thing he will say is that you must follow the evidence.

"So I am here to ask that you not take your eyes off of that evidence, through our statements and through your deliberations. Mr. Carpenter will talk of an alleged murder that took place over thirty-five years ago, a murder for which no body has ever been found. He will also talk of an alleged conspiracy, revealed only through hearsay testimony, and conveniently withheld for all these years, right up until the eve of your deliberations.

"He will try to substitute another villain, Victor Markham, for the one he represents, Willie Miller. But it was not Victor Markham's blood and skin under the fingernails of Denise McGregor. It was not Victor Markham that was seen standing over the victim by a very credible eyewitness. It was not Victor Markham whose fingerprints were all over the murder weapon. And it is not Victor Markham who has a history of attacking women when under the influence of alcohol.

"The only person all that evidence points to is Willie Miller, and that is who you are here to judge. I ask that you find him guilty as charged."

Wallace offers me a slight nod and the trace of a smile as he sits down. I know that he's feeling justifiably pleased that he's done a fine job, and thoroughly relieved that his job is over. It's now my turn, and it seems like every eye in the courtroom simultaneously shifts to me.

When I took on this case, I convinced myself there was a chance Willie was innocent. I need to do that to perform at a peak level. But back then I only believed in the possibility of his innocence, and I have now reached a certainty of it. It puts far more pressure on me to win, and it is that pressure that threatens to suffocate me as I stand to give my closing argument.

Just before I begin, I glance toward the back of the gallery and see Wally McGregor, in court for the first time, sitting up straight and waiting for justice for his family. This one's for you, Wally.

"Ladies and gentlemen, I believe that Victor Markham was one of a group of men who raped and murdered Julie McGregor many years ago. But on one point I agree with Mr. Wallace:

You are not here to decide that case. And that murder, horrible though it may be, is your concern for one reason and one reason only. It became the motive for Victor Markham to murder Julie's daughter, Denise McGregor, who had learned and was about to reveal the truth.

"He took the life of a mother, then waited almost thirty years to wipe out her offspring.

"But you cannot make him pay the price for either of those deaths. That is for another jury to do, and believe me, I will not rest until they have done just that. What you can do is make sure that Victor Markham does not claim still another victim— my client, Willie Miller.

"There is a great deal of evidence against Willie Miller, and Mr. Wallace did an outstanding job presenting it. But every single shred of it can be explained consistent with Victor Markham using his awesome power to frame him for the murder.

"Mr. Wallace talked about what Judge Henderson will tell you. But he left out the most important part. The judge will say that in order to convict, you must consider Willie Miller guilty beyond a reasonable doubt. I would respectfully suggest that you are up to your ears in reasonable doubt."

I walk over to Willie and put my hands on his shoulders.

"This man has spent the last seven years of his life on death row for a crime he did not commit. All of us can only imagine the horror of that, but he has lived it.

"It is not your fault, you had nothing to do with it, and you cannot erase it. But there is something you can do: You can end it. You can give him back his dignity, and his self-respect, and his freedom.

"Ladies and gentlemen, you can go into that jury room, and you can do something absolutely wonderful. You can give Willie Miller his life back."

I go back to the defense table, to the whispered congratulations of Laurie and Kevin, and the gratitude of Willie. I'm filled with a fear that I did not do or say enough to make the jury understand, and I want to get back up there and scream at them, to make them see the truth according to Andy Carpenter.

Hatchet gives the jury his instructions. My feeling is that he puts too much emphasis on the jury not considering the guilt or innocence of Victor Markham, but basically I think it's fair.

Actually, I'm pleased with Hatchet's performance throughout; I don't think he showed a preference to one side or the other. All in all, I'm glad he turned down the change of venue request.

Hatchet sends the jury off, and this case is officially out of my control. Before they take Willie away, he asks me what I think, and I tell him what I tell all my clients at this stage.

"I don't think, I wait."

• • • • •

THE PRESSURE OF WAITING FOR a jury to finish its deliberations is unlike anything else I have ever experienced. The only thing I could liken it to, and fortunately I'm just guessing, is waiting for a biopsy report to come back, after being told that the report will either signal terminal illness or good health. At that point matters are completely out of the hands of the patient and the doctor. Lawyers experience the same impotence while waiting for a verdict.

Every eccentricity, every idiosyncrasy, every superstition I possess comes out during this waiting period. For instance, I tell myself that if the jury gives us an even chance, we will win. Therefore, I do everything by even numbers. I'll only get out of bed in the morning when the digital clock shows an even number, I'll pump an even number of gallons of gas into my car, I'll only watch even-numbered channels on television, etc., etc.

Additionally, I'll also tell myself that our cause is in the right, which I react to by doing everything right-handed, by making three right turns rather than one left, and so on. There is no doubt about it—while waiting for a verdict, I become a crazed lunatic.

Fortunately for the rest of the world, I also become a hermit. I absolutely prohibit anyone involved with the defense from contacting me unless it is an absolute emergency. I want to be alone with Tara and my thoughts, and I want to do everything I can to try and keep those thoughts away from the case and the courtroom.

The Miller deliberations enter their third day with no word from the jury. They have not asked to have any testimony read back to them; nor have they asked to examine evidence. If they had done either of these things, Hatchet would have had to notify the attorneys, and we've had no such notification.

By accident, I hear a television commentator, a "former prosecutor," say that the lengthy deliberation is a bad sign for the defense, but I turn it off before I can hear why.

I take Tara to the park to throw a ball, bringing my cell phone along in case the court clerk needs to reach me. We play catch for only about fifteen minutes; Tara seems to be slowing down as she gets older. If there is a God, how come golden retrievers only live until their early teens?

We stop at a café on the way home, where we take an outdoor table. I have iced coffee and an apple turnover; Tara has a bagel and a dish of water. We're just finishing up when the phone rings, and my stomach springs four feet into the air.

"Hello?"

"Mr. Carpenter?"

I have an overwhelming urge to tell the clerk she has the wrong number, but I don't. "That's me."

"Judge Henderson would like you in court at two P.M. The jury has returned a verdict."

There it is. It's over, but I don't yet know the ending. The only feeling more powerless than waiting while a jury is making its decision is waiting *after* they've made that decision. Now the result is even out of *their* control.

I take Tara home, shower and change, then head back to court. I arrive at one-forty-five and wade through the crush of reporters and cameramen calling out to me, all their questions blending together.

They want to know what I think, when in fact there is at this moment nothing on earth less important than what I think. The die has been cast; this is like taping a playoff game and then watching it afterward without knowing the final score. There's no sense rooting, or hoping, or guessing, or thinking. It's already over, one way or the other. The boat, as they say, has sailed.

I nod to Kevin and Laurie, who are already at the defense table when I come in. Richard Wallace comes over to shake my hand and wish me well, and to congratulate me on a job well done. I return the compliment sincerely.

When Willie is brought in, I can see the tension in his eyes, in his facial muscles, in his body language. If doctors say that normal, everyday stress can take years off one's life, what effect must this be having on Willie? Has he already received a death sentence of a different type?

Willie just nods at us and takes his seat. He's smart enough not to ask me what I think; he's just going to wait with the rest of us.

Hatchet comes in and court is called to order. He doesn't waste any time, asking that the jury be brought in, and moments later there they are, revealing nothing with their impassive expressions.

Hatchet gives the obligatory lecture about demanding decorum in his courtroom once the verdict is read, and he is stern enough that it will probably have an effect. He then turns to the jury.

"Ladies and gentlemen of the jury, have you reached a verdict?"

The foreman stands. "We have, Your Honor."

"Please present it to the bailiff."

The bailiff walks over and receives a verdict sheet from the foreman. He then carries it over to the clerk.

Hatchet says, "Will the defendant please rise."

Willie, Kevin, Laurie, and I stand as one. I can see that my hand is on Willie's shoulder, but I don't remember putting it there.

"The clerk will read the verdict."

The clerk takes the form and looks it over. It seems as if it takes four hours for her to start reading, but it is probably four seconds in real time. Each word she says sucks more air out of the room, until I think I am going to faint.

"We, the jury, in the case of the State of New Jersey versus William Miller, find the defendant, William Miller . . . not guilty of the crime of murder in the first degree."

The gallery explodes in sound, and air comes flooding into the room and my lungs. Willie turns to me, a questioning look on his face, as if for confirmation that he has heard what he thinks he's heard. I have a simultaneous need to scream and to cry, which my inhibitions convert into a smile and a nod.

Willie turns and hugs me, then Laurie, then Kevin, and then we all in turn hug each other. As I mentioned previously, I'm not a big hug fan, but these don't bother me at all. Especially the one with Laurie.

Hatchet gavels for quiet, thanks the jury for their contribution to society and sends them on their way. He then takes the unbelievably un-Hatchet-like, human step of apologizing to Willie for his years of incarceration, hoping that he can rebuild his life despite it. This case, according to Hatchet, points out the flaws of our imperfect system, while at the same time demonstrating its incredible capacity for ultimately getting things right.

Wallace comes over to congratulate me, and he then shakes hands with Kevin, Laurie, and Willie. The bailiff comes to take Willie away, and Willie glances at me with concern and confusion. I assure him that he is only going to complete some paperwork, and then he is going out into the world.

The defense team makes plans to meet Willie tonight at Charlie's for a victory party, and I go home for a quiet celebration with Tara. She and I spend a couple of hours watching television, with the assembled legal pundits anointing me a legal genius. Turns out they're not so dumb after all.

Tara seems unimpressed, so we head out to the park. I use up my fifteen minutes of fame tossing a ball to Tara, and I am actually interrupted three times by other dog owners seeking my autograph, which I sign with a flourish.

I get back home to change for the party, and there is a message on my voice mail from Nicole, congratulating me on the verdict.

On the way to Charlie's, I stop off at the police precinct to talk to Pete about his efforts to go after Victor Markham. He's upbeat about nailing him for the murder of Denise. Betty's testimony provides the motive, and the flaws in Victor's story, such as the time it took to get to the bar, are incriminating.

The police never had reason to investigate Victor before, so it is only now that they are learning things like the fact that there is no record of any phone call that night from Edward to the club. Additionally, and amazingly, the valet people at the club keep detailed records of the times members' cars come in and out, and rather than throw those records away, they consign them to a life in storage. They have been retrieved and are totally in conflict with Victor's story.

Troubling to Pete is his feeling that Victor could not have done this alone, and in fact is not the type to dirty his hands. Edward, who is also legally vulnerable, could not have participated in the actual murder, since he was in the bar the entire time and had no blood on him. Pete believes Victor had help, but he has no leads as to who may have provided that help.

Charlie's is overflowing; word has apparently gotten out that we were coming here. Willie is in his glory, reveling in this first flush of freedom. He's invited Lou Campanelli, and when Laurie and Kevin arrive, the owner of the place puts us in a side room in which we can have some privacy.

Willie, to his credit and to Lou's obvious relief, is downing Virgin Marys right and left. With his other hand, he is waving to and leering at every woman in the place, enjoying his celebrity and obviously hoping to capitalize on it. Marys are the only virgins that Willie is interested in right now.

He holds up his glass to me in a toast.

"Man," Willie says, "you're the most amazing genius of all time."

I modestly wave off the compliment, though the accuracy of it is obvious to even the most casual observer. I go on to tell Willie that he hasn't seen anything yet, that he should wait until he sees me go after Victor Markham on his behalf in a civil suit.

After about an hour at the party, I start to feel overwhelmingly tired. The intense pressure and emotion have taken their toll, and I say my goodbyes. I make plans to meet with Willie about the lawsuit and his life in general, with Kevin about the prospects of getting him out of the Laundromat and into a form of partnership with me, and with Laurie about, well, who knows?

But all of these meetings are going to have to wait until two weeks from tomorrow, because, as they say, I'm outta here.

• • • • •

LOVELADIES IS THE NAME OF A small town on Long Beach Island. Its colorful name has absolutely nothing whatsoever to do with the town as it exists today; it is a wholesome, family community set on the most magnificent, pure white beach in New Jersey.

I've spent a good deal of time there in the past; it's a place where I can unwind and depressurize after the intensity of a trial. For the next two weeks my life will consist of lying on the beach with Tara, walking on the beach with Tara, and reading on the beach with Tara. There is also a seafood place called the Shack, where Tara and I can sit outside and eat terrific shrimp and lobster. To say that I'm looking forward to this time is to expose the inadequacy of language.

But before I can get to that, I've got a promise to keep, and I take a detour out to Wally McGregor's trailer. He's sitting in his rocking chair, as if calmly waiting for my arrival, though I hadn't called ahead. His German shepherd companion looks just as mean as ever, but Tara seems to see something in him that I don't, since she jumps right out of the car and ambles over to him. They commence sniffing each other, which seems to go well enough, since in a few seconds they're lying down next to each other in the sun.

"Hello, Wally," I say. "I saw you in court the day of closing arguments, but afterward I looked for you, and you had gone."

"You seemed pretty busy," he says.

"Have you heard what happened?"

He nods. "Lieutenant Stanton called and told me. He said Markham was the real killer."

"Yes."

"He took my whole family. Doesn't seem right that he lived free all these years. Or that Willie Miller didn't."

"No," I say, "it's certainly not right."

"But better late than never."

"Much better," I agree.

"You did a good thing, and I thank you for it," he says.

"Believe me, I was glad to do it."

I stay another two hours, during which time not another word is mentioned about the murders or the trial. We mostly talk baseball, a subject on which his knowledge is virtually encyclopedic. By the time I leave, Wally McGregor is no longer a man I've helped, nor is he a man I feel sorry for. He is simply a good friend.

Tara and I arrive on Long Beach Island in the early evening, as ready for peace and quiet as I have ever been in my life. The first thing I do, since I know it will hover over me if I don't, is try to understand my father's role in the events that shaped and destroyed so many lives. Unfortunately, I have limited success in doing so. There is no one to tell me if he had direct involvement in Julie McGregor's death and murder, or why he took and then never touched the two million dollars. I can make guesses, some exculpating and some painful, but they seem destined to remain guesses.

I can make a more informed judgment of his involvement in the Willie Miller trial. I believe that he considered Willie to be guilty. He would likely never have known Julie McGregor's name, and therefore would have had no reason to connect Denise's murder to that horrible night all those years before. He may have taken a hands-on role in the prosecution because of his prior friendship with Victor, but he must have believed that Willie was guilty. I suspect that years later he may have started to question that belief, and that is why he asked me to take the case.

I've given a few people permission to call me on my cell phone, while admonishing them to make sure they do so only in an emergency. I'm lying in bed on the tenth day, about nine o'clock in the morning, when the phone rings. It's Pete Stanton calling, with the briefest of messages. "Turn on CNN."

He hangs up without waiting for me to say anything, and I rush to the television and do as I'm told. There is a press conference taking place, featuring the current DA, Richard Wallace's boss. Wallace is at his side as he announces the arrests of Victor and Edward Markham. They have turned themselves in, rather than face the indignity of being brought into the jailhouse in handcuffs, and they are facing arraignment the next morning.

I'm pleased and more than a little gratified, and I suppose my thirst for revenge is at least partially quenched, but I'm also strangely detached from this news. My role in this case is over, and I have no desire to relive or resurrect it. It is in competent hands, as evidenced by the speed with which the investigation has been conducted, and I'd just as soon leave it alone.

So, in terms of the last four days of my stay here at the beach, I wouldn't describe the impact this news has as drastic. Instead of spending all my time walking, sunbathing, and reading, I add a Walkman to the mix, and occasionally listen for radio reports on the Markham situation.

I learn that a conditional bail has been set at two million dollars for both Victor and Edward, an amount which of course Victor is able to raise with ease. He and Edward have been released to electronic house arrest, which means that they must stay in Victor's house, with high-tech ankle bracelets recording their movements and ensuring they cannot flee. Victor in electronic shackles; now that is something I would buy a ticket to see.

Tara and I reluctantly pack up the car and head for home. We make the two-hour drive listening to the Eagles' *Greatest Hits* and *Ragtime*; let no one accuse us of having particularly modern taste in music.

I'm feeling the benefits of the time off, and I'm even experiencing rumblings inside myself of wanting to get back into the fray. It's hard to know what is going to come up next, but surely the notoriety of the Miller case should result in a wide array of clients wanting to hire my services.

I'm about five minutes from my house when I realize that I'm not driving to my house at all. I seem to be semivoluntarily driving to Laurie's, though I certainly haven't called her and told her I was coming. In fact, I haven't spoken to her since I left.

I'm about three blocks from her house when I see her jogging on the side of the road, ahead of me and going in the same direction. She looks phenomenal in shorts and T-shirt, and I drive very slowly behind her all the way to her house, not wanting to spoil this picture.

When she reaches the house, I speed up and pull up in front, pretending that I'm just seeing her for the first time.

She comes over to the car, a little out of breath. "Into stalking, are we?"

"You knew I was there?" I ask.

She nods. "I'm a trained investigator. And I have a slimeball detector that can locate leering, drooling men up to a mile away."

Seeing Laurie is jarring, in a good way. For two weeks I have kept myself in a plastic bubble, not letting real life enter. Now I see Laurie, and I'm incredibly glad that she is a part of that real life. I am stunned by the realization of how much I have missed her.

Laurie leans in and gives me a light kiss on the cheek, then pats Tara's head. "Come on in," she says, and Tara and I do just that.

Laurie gives Tara some dog biscuits that she has in the house for her neighbor's dogs, then showers and changes. Tara then jumps up on the couch to take a nap, and Laurie and I go over to Charlie's for dinner.

We order a couple of burgers and fries, though we have to get separate orders of fries. I want mine very, very crisp, but cooks seem to have a resistance to making them that way. I have come to ordering them "burned beyond recognition, so that their own french fry mothers wouldn't know who they are," but it never seems to help.

We also get bottles of Amstel Light, and toast to Willie's freedom. The discussion then turns to other cases, future clients, other work issues. Laurie does most of the talking, while I do most of the staring.

She finally notices and asks me why it is that I'm staring, and when I don't respond immediately, she figures it out.

"Oh, come on, Andy."

"What?" I innocently inquire.

"You can't expect us to just get back together, as if nothing had happened."

"I can't? No, of course I can't. Can I?"

"No, you can't. I know you went to law school, Andy, but did you ever go to grammar school? Because you're acting like you're there now."

"All I'm suggesting is that we slowly, very slowly, see if we can rebuild the nonbusiness portion of our relationship." I'm crawling now. "Which I screwed up by acting like the idiot that I am."

"That's a little more like it," she says, weakening slightly.

"Also, I can't remember if I've mentioned this previously, but I'm really rich."

"That's much more like it," she says, weakening greatly.

"I'm a multimillionaire, desperately in need of a woman to shower with gifts."

She nods, feeling my pain. "And I'm a woman who believes in second chances," she says.

I lean across the table and kiss her, and she responds. As Jackie Gleason would say, "How sweet it is." Unfortunately, the moment is broken by a guy who comes over with a camera, unusual since Charlie's is not exactly a tourist trap. The guy has seen me on TV in connection with the Miller case, and he asks me to take a picture with him. Laurie agrees to take the picture, and the guy leaves happy. Ah, stardom.

We go back to Laurie's, but I don't think that I'll try anything sexual; it seems like that would be rushing things. Fortunately, Laurie disagrees, and she tries something very sexual. Not only does she try it, but it works. Really well.

It works so well that it leaves me exhausted, but even though we've agreed that I'm staying over, I can't go right to sleep, because Tara has to be walked. We go outside for what I hope will be a short walk, but which I extend because she's enjoying the smells of this new neighborhood so much.

I'm feeling good, make that great, about the turn of events with Laurie, and I sort of relive the day in my mind. It's when I'm thinking about our evening at Charlie's, about the guy wanting the picture, that it hits me, and I take Tara back to Laurie's at a full run.

We rush into the house and I head straight for the bedroom, where Laurie is sound asleep. I try to wake her, which is no easy task. When I exhaust a woman, I exhaust a woman.

I finally get her coherent enough to respond. "What the hell do you want?"

"Laurie, it's about the picture."

I think the intense tone of my voice pulls her out of her sleep. "What picture?"

"My father's picture, the one of the four men."

"What about it?" she asks.

"There's somebody not in it."

"Who?"

"The person that took it," I say.

• • • • •

I'M CARRYING A PAPER BAG AND
waiting outside Vince Sanders's office when he arrives at nine-
thirty in the morning. He had left a surprisingly warm message
on my answering machine while I was away, congratulating
and thanking me for my work in finding Denise's real killer.

"Oh, shit," he says when he sees me. "What the hell are you
doing here?" Obviously he doesn't retain warmth real well.

"I need your help," I say.

"Forget it. I'm too busy."

I hold up the bag. "I brought you a dozen, fish-free jelly
donuts."

He looks at the bag, then opens the door and motions me
in. "Make my home your home."

We enter and he proceeds to eat three donuts and drink
two cups of coffee in about a minute and a half. The time is
not completely unenlightening, however. He explains to me
that the way to prevent jelly from dripping out of a donut is to
bite into the hole on the side through which the jelly had been
inserted. Brilliant, but not what I came here to learn.

Vince can tell that I'm anxious to get down to business, so
he pauses midway through the fourth donut to ask me what I
need.

"I want to go through copies of your newspaper for the

week of June fourteenth, nineteen sixty-five. I assume you have it on microfilm."

"Microfilm?" He laughs. "Nowadays that would be like having it on parchment. It's all computerized."

I nod. "All the better."

"What are you looking for?"

"The night Julie McGregor was killed, my father, Markham, Brownfield, and Mike Anthony were at some kind of future leaders conference in Manhattan. I want to know who else was there."

He looks doubtful. "So what are you doing here? In case you forgot, this is a Jersey paper. We wouldn't have covered it."

"I'm betting you did."

Within five minutes, Vince and I are going through the old papers. He finds the article almost immediately, and instantly understands why I am sitting in his office.

"Jesus Christ," he says.

I jump out of my chair and go over to his computer screen. The article is there, and the headline jumps out:

PHILIP GANT NAMED A FUTURE LEADER OF AMERICA

I can't say this is exactly what I expected, but it does give me an even healthier respect for my own hunches. The potential implications of this are stunning, and my mouth opens in amazement. It is the only mouth in the room that isn't filled with jelly donut.

Vince looks to me for confirmation. "Gant was a part of this?"

I shrug. "I can't be sure."

"But you think he might be?" Vince is a reporter, and he's sensing a beauty of a story.

I nod. "I think he might be."

Vince takes a final swallow; he wants to be able to clearly enunciate this point. "If he is, I get the story first. We clear on that?"

"Crystal," I say.

I meet up with Laurie back at the office. She's been tracking this on her own, and I'm not surprised to hear that she's gotten even further than I have. Not only has she confirmed that Philip was there that night, but she has the entire list of that year's future leaders.

A quick check shows that it includes young men and women from all over the country, and that in fact Philip was the only one besides my father living in New Jersey. I know for a fact that my father's house did not have a swimming pool, so it may well be that Philip's house is the one at which Julie McGregor was killed. The question is how to prove it.

Laurie logically points out that a crime this old is not going to be solved by physical evidence, and requires a witness. Victor has steadfastly refused to implicate anyone else, and for that reason Brownfield is not in custody. But with Victor facing murder one for Denise's murder, he seems the one most likely to crack.

We make two decisions, not necessarily in order of importance. One, we're going to include Pete Stanton in our deliberations, and two, I'm going to spend tonight at Laurie's. Therefore, we pick Tara up, take her for a brief walk, and then bring her to the precinct with us. Maybe I can introduce her to a male from the K-9 squad.

Pete's not there when we arrive, but he shows up a few minutes later. He is of course surprised to see Laurie, myself, and especially Tara sitting there.

"What the hell is this? A family picnic?" He points to Tara. "Is he house-trained?"

"She," I say. "Her name is Tara, and you would shit on the floor before she would."

"Okay," he shrugs, "what do you guys want?"

I proceed to tell him, and he listens to the story without interrupting. When I'm finished, he thinks for a few more moments before responding. "You know Gant well. You think he could be involved?"

"I think he's a pretentious, controlling asshole, but I've never thought of him as a murderer."

"That wasn't my question."

I nod. "I think he was there that night. I think he'd do any-thing to protect his position. Yes, I think he was involved."

Pete cuts right to the meat. "You're going to need Markham to give him up."

"Do you think he would?" Laurie asks.

Pete shrugs. "Hasn't so far."

"Can you get me in there?" I ask.

Pete laughs. "He'd be real happy to see you. You guys are good buddies."

"Just get me in."

Pete nods. "Okay. But only with Wallace on board. You want me to talk to him?"

I tell Pete that I'll talk to Wallace, and I call him. He's more skeptical than Pete, perhaps because he's not feeling the force of my face-to-face charm. Wallace's boss has to get elected every two years, which makes him sensitive to life's political realities. He sounds sorry he even answered the phone.

"Andy, I'm not even talking about whether or not Gant is guilty, or whether we could make it stick even if Markham gave him up. I'm saying that making the decision to go after Gant is a huge one. The kind we'd both better be right on."

"I agree, but we're not making that decision now. Right now we're just talking to Markham."

He finally agrees, which I knew he would. Wallace is not the type to sweep things under the rug, no matter how politi-cally powerful those things might be.

Pete makes a phone call to get us in to see Markham at his house. I drop Laurie and Tara off, then pick up Wallace. We drive out in my car.

We arrive at Markham's and the patrolman at the gate lets us through. The justice system has determined that electronic ankle bracelets are not enough to keep Victor and son con-fined, and that armed guards are necessary to prevent their possible flight. I concur.

The house is on a par with Philip's, which is to say it is magnificent. I reflect to myself that this scene of Victor's incar-ceration, albeit temporary, is rather different from Willie's resi-dence for the past seven years.

them. If true, it would also explain how the various attacks and threats were accomplished over the past weeks.

A proffer of this type is a document written by the plea bargainer, detailing what his testimony will be if an agreement can be reached. The law states that if the parties fail to agree, the prosecution cannot benefit from the proffer in any way. It thus becomes a confession and testimony that never legally existed. The purpose is to allow the prosecution to know exactly what testimony it is bargaining for, so that if the accused subsequently reneges and testifies differently, his reduced sentence is reinstated in full.

Wallace already knows what his boss will go for regarding Edward's sentence, and this proposal fits within those guidelines. He conveys to Sandy that the state agrees; all that remains is for Hatchet to put his rubber stamp on it. Wallace offers me the right to sit in on that meeting in Hatchet's chambers, which I am very grateful for.

Even though I won't have a significant role in the meeting, I still want to be prepared, so I bring home some books to study up on the relevant law. When I get home, there is a message on the answering machine from Nicole. She sounds tentative, a little nervous, but basically just wants to know how I am doing. I don't call her back; I can't tell her what's going on with her father, and it seems too dishonest to have a conversation without bringing it up.

The next morning at nine o'clock Wallace, Sandy, and I are ushered into Hatchet's chambers. His eyes focus on me. "What are you doing here?"

"I'm a friend of the court," I answer cheerfully.

"Since when?"

The meeting goes without a hitch. Hatchet has to be surprised when Philip's name is mentioned, but he doesn't show it. He asks the correct, perfunctory questions of Wallace and Sandy, and they provide the proper answers. At the conclusion, he signs off on the plea bargain. Nothing to it, but when the results of this meeting are made public there will be a political firestorm unlike any since the Clinton impeachment.

When we leave the chambers, there is little said between

the three of us. We all know the implications of what we are doing, and we're going to go about our business professionally. Sandy goes to Victor's to get him and Edward to sign off on the final agreement, Wallace goes to prep his boss for an afternoon press conference announcing the news, and I go home to watch what promises to be an amazing night of television.

• • • • •

THE PHONE CALL FROM SANDY MICHELSON

comes at three o'clock. In a fairly steady voice he says that he's calling to inform me that his client, Victor Markham, is dead. After signing the proffer and watching Sandy leave with it, he went into his bathroom and took enough powerful pain medication to kill himself three times over.

Sandy speculates that despite his careful explanations, Victor may well have believed that simply the act of signing the proffer meant Edward's deal was secure. He also believes that Victor's ego would not let him face the public humiliation that his confession would bring.

I'm not really interested in dwelling on the tragedy that is Victor Markham. The fact is that as evidence the proffer is useless, inadmissible hearsay in a court of law. With the lack of physical evidence that exists, Philip is off the hook before he even knew he was on it.

My frustration is complete. Laurie comes over to commiserate, but I really don't want anybody around me right now. I want to be alone to wallow in my misery. I don't tell her that, because even in this frustrated state, I retain my wimpy tendencies.

Laurie is of the opinion that we shouldn't give up, that there still has to be a way to tie Philip to this. I know better and I tell her so, but she keeps throwing out ideas, which I keep shooting down.

She asks me to take out the photograph, which I reluctantly do. Between the two of us, we've probably looked at it five hundred times, but now she looks at it carefully, as if she's never seen it before. It's an investigative technique she uses, which she has often told me about. She is able to will herself to take a fresh approach to evidence.

This time it doesn't seem to get her anywhere. She looks at it for almost five minutes, then turns to me. "Are you sure there's nothing in the background that identifies this as Philip's house?"

"I'm sure," I say.

She tries to hand me the picture. "Look again."

I don't want to; I never want to see that stupid picture again. "Come on, Laurie . . ." I whine.

"Please, Andy, I hate seeing you like this."

"It'll get worse before it gets better."

She keeps insisting, so I sigh and take the picture and look at it. My assessment is it hasn't changed much, and I tell her so.

"So you can't tell that's Philip's house?" she asks.

I look still again. "Nope. In fact I've never seen those trees. He must have cut them down."

Now she looks again. "Why would he cut down beautiful trees like that?"

So I look again, a fresh look like Laurie taught me. And all of a sudden, I know exactly why Philip Gant would cut down beautiful trees like that.

• • • • •

I ARRIVE AT THE GANT ESTATE

at eleven the next morning, having called ahead to tell Philip I
needed to speak to him. He was cordial and without a hint of
concern in his voice; he seemed to know nothing about
Markham's proffer. I ring the bell and the butler, Frederick, answers.

"Good afternoon, Mr. Carpenter."

"Hello, Frederick. The Senator is expecting me."

Frederick nods. "Yes, sir. He's at the pool."

I nod and move quickly through the house and out to the
back. I head toward the pool, and find Philip sitting in his
bathing suit at an umbrella-shaded table, nursing a drink and
reading a book. He hears me coming and looks up.

"Hello, Andrew."

"Hello, Philip. Am I interrupting anything important?"

"No . . . no . . . not at all. It's very disappointing about you
and Nicole. I very much wanted it to work out."

"And you usually get what you want," I say.

I can see him react to this; it is not something that someone would ordinarily come out and say to him, even though it
is obviously true. He decides to let it pass by treating it good-
naturedly.

He grins. "Yes, I guess I do. I guess I do. Congratulations on your victory in that trial."

"Did you hear about Victor Markham?" I ask.

He nods. "I did. The entire episode is terrible. Just terrible."

"You know," I say, "it's funny. A secret like that is kept for almost forty years, and then it comes out, just like that. Makes you think, doesn't it?"

"About what?" he asks.

"That if you have something to hide, you can never be sure it will stay hidden. There's always that worry, always that chance that a base hasn't been completely covered."

"I suppose that's true." Philip's tone is now a little uncertain, tentative.

"I mean, think about this case. There's still a secret to be revealed. There's still someone who hasn't been accounted for."

"And who might that be?" he asks.

"The guy who took the picture."

The look in his eyes says I've got his attention, so I continue. "Maybe he's the one who gave my father the money. Maybe he's the one whose house it was."

Philip sits there, sipping his drink, unruffled. The son of a bitch. "Andrew," he says, "you don't want to go any further."

But I do, and I will. "Maybe he's the one who was afraid he'd be ruined . . . that his perfectly planned future could be destroyed. Maybe he's the one who killed Julie McGregor to protect himself."

Philip puts down his drink: his way of saying that it's time to get serious. "All right, Andrew, what exactly are you saying?"

"I'm saying that if I were that person, I'd be worried. Because secrets like this are very difficult to keep. And if that person were somebody prominent, somebody hot-shit important, then his whole life could go down the drain, slowly . . . surely . . . totally."

As much as I despise this man, I am almost mesmerized

by him. He is being confronted with the revelation of a secret so terrible that he has murdered to preserve it, yet he seems unfazed and totally in control. It's either a confidence bordering on invincibility, or an Academy Award winning performance.

"Goodbye, Andrew," he says.

But I'm not going anywhere. "I know my father took your money, and that was wrong. But you had saved his life when he fell through the ice, and now he was saving yours. You were his oldest friend, and he let that cloud his judgment. But it doesn't matter anymore, because you know what, Philip? The bad news for you is that I'm not my father."

"That much is true," he says. "You're not even close."

"Victor Markham gave a proffer for a plea bargain, Philip. He said that you were there . . . that you all took Julie McGregor to this house."

For a moment there is a flash of uncertainty in Philip's eyes, but it is immediately replaced by confidence.

"I don't believe that is true. But even if it were, his death renders that useless."

"You know," I say, "Julie McGregor's body was never found."

Philip smiles, serenely confident. "Is that right?"

"If it was me, if I were a pig like yourself, I would have buried the body. And then I would have covered it up . . . like maybe with a guest house. Which was built not long after that night. You didn't build it as a future home for your child, Philip. You built it as a headstone for Julie McGregor."

I see it, a quick look of panic, a steel blade of truth cutting through to the bone. "Andrew . . ."

"Philip, you went to Yale Law, so how about we try a legal riddle? Ready? When is a useless proffer not useless?"

Philip doesn't answer, so I continue. "Give up? It's when you want to use it to get a search warrant."

He knows I have him, but he's not giving up. He smiles, almost sadly. "We can reach an accommodation, Andrew. It was so long ago."

There are some things that I've got to know before this is

over. "Why did you do it, Philip? A guy from your family, good-looking, smart, you could have had a lot of women. Why did you have to have Julie McGregor that night?"

"She was no innocent, Andrew. She wanted to as much as we did; then she pretended to change her mind. Well, the unfortunate fact was we hadn't changed ours."

"So you did what you had to do."

"And we have had to live with it ever since. Not an easy thing, I assure you."

"Yeah, you've really suffered. Where was my father when all this happened?"

"In the house." Philip laughs, as if recounting a funny story from long ago. "He drank too much and he was throwing up." He laughs again, even harder. "He had a weak stomach and it cost me two million dollars."

It is all I can do not to strangle him. "You are a scumbag, Philip. My father lost a piece of himself that night—and he never got it back. And you deserve everything that is going to happen to you."

Philip starts to speak, but when I hear a voice it is not his. "Andy, what are you doing?" It is Nicole, having walked in on us. I'm not sure how much she has heard, but my guess is it's enough.

"I'm sorry, Nicole. It's already done."

"Andy, what will this accomplish? For God's sake, he's my father."

"Your father is a rapist and a murderer."

Before she can respond, Pete, Wallace, and two patrolmen walk from the house to the pool. Frederick walks with them, as if he is escorting them. Wallace goes up to Philip and hands him a piece of paper, which Philip does not take. Wallace puts it on the table.

"This is a search warrant for these premises, Senator. It authorizes us to excavate under the guest house, and it will be lawfully executed this afternoon."

Nicole goes over to Philip and grabs on to his arm. "Daddy . . ." she says, as if he is going to fix this.

He just sits there, nothing to say and nothing to do.

Nicole sits there with him. They'll probably still be there when Julie McGregor's body is dug up. But I won't be here. I want to get as far away from this as I can.

• • • • •

"RICH OR POOR, IT'S GOOD

to have money." That's what my mother used to say, tongue firmly tucked in cheek, when she'd see an ostentatious display of wealth. Of course, she had no idea she was already rich by virtue of my father's hidden fortune, but I'm learning to accept that and deal with it.

I'm having more trouble learning how to be rich.

It's been two months since the end of the Willie Miller trial, and I still haven't touched the money. I make plans to touch it, I come up with strategies to touch it, but so far no actual contact has taken place.

Laurie thinks I need psychiatric help, an opinion that has become more strident since she happened to be at my house when the mail arrived. The thing is, I've taken to ordering catalogues of every conceivable product ever produced; my mailman has vowed to bill me for his hernia operation. A lot of the merchandise is appealing to me, and Tara has her eye on a cashmere dog bed featured in the "Yuppie Puppy" catalogue. But I haven't actually purchased anything from anywhere. There's time for that.

Philip has resigned from the Senate and is in prison awaiting trial. He's in an actual prison, as the justice system in its infinite wisdom decided that, based on the Victor Markham experience, the ankle bracelet idea just might have some flaws. Philip was arrested the moment poor Julie McGregor's remains were unearthed.

I speak to Wally McGregor at least once a week. He took the news about Philip in stride, and we got back to talking baseball. Wally thinks Willie Mays was better than Mickey Mantle, which pleases me, since it means we'll always have something to argue about.

I haven't heard from Nicole since that day at Philip's house, but I did see her on television at the arraignment. I've tried calling her a couple of times, but she hasn't taken my calls.

Cal Morris is still nowhere to be found. I have an image of him on a Caribbean beach, drinking piña coladas and selling *Des Moines Register*s to the tourists. I have no hard feelings toward him, and I've managed to create new superstitions to take his place.

I've been busy, working on a bunch of cases at once. I'm trying to lure Kevin out of the Laundromat, but he's resisting. If he doesn't relent soon, I'm going to have to hire someone else to help keep up with the workload.

Laurie and I have settled into a nice rhythm, going slow and enjoying ourselves. She's as much friend as lover, and I don't want to do anything that might rock that boat. I made mistakes with Nicole, mistakes I'm wary of repeating.

I've never been accused of being an intellectual, and I get my philosophy wherever I can find it. In the movie *The Natural*, Glenn Close tells Robert Redford, "I believe we have two lives. The life we learn with, and the life we live with after that."

I want Laurie to be a leading player in my "life after that."